# The Fields of Memory

# The Fields of Memory

SHORT STORIES
*by*
CAROLYN OSBORN

Shearer Publishing / Bryan, Texas

ACKNOWLEDGMENTS

"Ancient History," *Riata.*
"Dreamer When Last Seen," *Thicket.*
"The New Castle," *Cimarron Review.*
"Man Dancing," *Antioch Review.*
"Stalking Strangers," *Antioch Review.*
"The Last Of It," *Twigs.*
"Other People's Mail," *New Orleans Review.*
"Reversals," *Vision.*
"House Of The Blue Woman," *Mid-American Review.*
"The Circuit Rider," *New Letters.*
"Running Around America," *Antioch Review.*

*First published in 1984 by*
Shearer Publishing
3208 Turtle Grove
Bryan, Texas 77801

Copyright © *1984* by Carolyn Osborn
Library of Congress Catalog Card Number 84-072581
ISBN 0-940672-23-5

*For two of my Tennessee aunts:*
Dorothy Culbert Lucas
*and*
Elnora Phillips Culbert

# Contents

"Great is the power of Memory, Lord; an astonishment, a deep and boundless manifold. . . . The fields, the caves, the dens of Memory cannot be counted; their fulness cannot be counted nor the kinds of things counted that fill them . . . . I force my way in amidst them, even as far as my power reaches, and nowhere find an end."

St. Augustine, *Confessions*

# Ancient History

 MISS AGNES DOYLE had two hats, a high beaver toque she wore in the winter and a patent leather sailor with a big rose on the front for summer. Her long black dresses were buttoned from elbow to wrist and from waist to hem with tiny black covered buttons. The long skirts and all the buttons closed her up against all the town and the people in it. When she came into Leon on Saturdays, she swept around the sidewalks with a brisk, commanding air. No one ever got in Miss Agnes's path. If they did, she would have marched right over them. She went to two places in town, the bank and the corner where her father's livery stable had been.

At the bank she asked for Camedan Lockly, who had started as a teller years ago and was now the first vice-president. That didn't matter to Miss Agnes. She'd stride in and ask for Camedan in her decided way and she'd get him. I don't know what she would have done if he hadn't been there, probably gone down to the drug-store where he usually drank coffee and yanked him up by the collar. I was always imagining Miss Agnes picking somebody up by the scruff of the neck the way people pick up kittens. We scuttled to a side street when we saw her sailing down Main. We were afraid Miss Agnes would turn her hard stare on us because we were wearing shorts, or had our hair in pincurls, or because we were hanging around town on Saturdays. All these things we did in spite of our mothers' admonitions, but the silent majesty of Miss Agnes meant more than any *don't* we ever heard. As far as we knew, she was Queen Victoria, the Baptist preacher's wife, and the Angel of Death all rolled into one.

It was hard to learn anything about Miss Agnes. She lived out of town on a two-thousand-acre ranch, which is plenty of room to hide in, even out here where two thousand acres isn't much. I knew about the number of acres because that's what everybody knew. What else Miss Agnes had nobody knew except maybe Camedan Lockly, and he wouldn't tell.

Once I asked, "Camedan, what does Miss Agnes do when she comes to the bank?"

"Oh, she passes the time of day and cashes a check." Then he turned to my father and asked him something about business.

When he was gone, my father said, "What makes you so nosey? You know Camedan can't go around telling about people's bank balances."

I didn't care about how much money Miss Agnes had. What I wanted to know was what she said, and what she thought, and why she still wore long dresses. Neither my father nor Camedan could have answered all that, though it seemed that they and all the rest of the men in town had some secret about her. You'd see them talking to her and laughing loudly on street corners, but they wouldn't repeat anything she said. There'd stand Miss Agnes in her black dress crowned with one of the two hats and with her hands stuck in her pockets. She never carried a purse. All around her men hawed, showed their teeth, and spit in the gutter. Sometimes Miss Agnes would spit, too. The first time I saw her do that was one Saturday when Ann Frances McConnell and I were downtown together. We had on bluejeans because we were going riding later, but at the moment, we were getting ready to duck into the ten-cent store to avoid Miss Agnes. We figured she wouldn't like long breeches on girls in town any more than short ones.

When Miss Agnes spit out of the side of her mouth as expertly as any tobacco-chewing courthouse loafer, Queen Victoria slid off her throne and the Baptist preacher's wife quit coming to church on Sunday! I poked Ann Frances in the ribs, so she saw it, too, but we went right on into the ten-cent store anyway.

"Well, I'll be darned!" That was the closest Ann Frances ever came to hard cussing.

The most curious habit Miss Agnes had was going down to the corner of Main and Ninth every time she was in town. One of my father's filling stations was there. He's the wholesale gasoline distributor for this area and has a ninety-nine-year lease on this particular station. Miss Agnes wasn't going down there to use the ladies', and certainly not to buy gas. She was the only person in Leon that still had a buggy and a trotting horse. She'd get in that rickety buggy, flap the reins lightly on the horse's back, and off they'd go like they were starting to meet the U.S. President on an incoming train. All in the world she was going to do was to drive three or four blocks to Main and Ninth to sit and stare at a gasoline station. I looked at that station many times trying to find out why it fascinated her so. True, her father's stable had been there, but there wasn't a board, not a fence post, not a piece of wire left. There was just an everyday Texaco service station with a registered restroom sign out front. Next to it was a lumberyard. Miss Agnes would sit in her buggy, sit there as silent as a public monument, and stare. Maybe she wasn't seeing what was there at all. Maybe she was seeing what had been there, Doyle's Livery Stable with hitching posts and watering troughs out front. I don't know. And the trotting horse, maybe he had memories, too. He stood so still, hardly twitching the flies off, struck dumb. I never saw a horse look so dumb. After this inspection they'd wheel around and go back to Miss Agnes's ranch.

The day we saw Miss Agnes spit, we followed her out there on horseback, not thinking we'd see anything more than we'd seen before. There was nothing to be seen from the road. We followed her because she had ceased to be the person we thought she was and had become a mystery, a rare thing in a town as small as Leon. We endowed her with every eccentricity we could think of. The ones she had were not enough, since we were used to them. We had to make her grander.

"I bet her house is full of old tin cans and eggshells," said Ann Frances.

"And she keeps a goat and saves string. I bet she's got old newspapers stacked to the ceiling."

We'd read newspaper stories of recluses who had been found dead with their beloved accumulations around them and hoards of money stashed away in mattresses. For some reason we imagined Miss Agnes's mattresses were covered with cheap blue and white striped cotton ticking; perhaps it was because our own, which we saw once a week when the beds were changed, were covered with some kind of shiny pink stuff and embossed with roses. Ours were mattresses that no one would dare rip, even for the purpose of hoarding. Ann Frances and I were quite determined about those mattresses.

We decided, too, that her house was filled with old, ornate furniture. "Louis Fourteenth," said Ann Frances. We hadn't the beginning of an idea about periods of furniture, but we did know that Louis Fourteenth represented something grand and old, older than Miss Agnes.

We rode down a dirt road on cow ponies, mine a paint, Ann Frances's a black. We went hatless in the glaring sun because we couldn't make hats stay on at a lope. Our shirts were white cowboy shirts with little fake pearl buttons and pointed pocket flaps, our bluejeans were faded to the respectable shade of soft blue that meant age and wear, and the decorated tops of our boots were hidden under the jeans. Only dudes showed their boot tops. We rode by the brushy pastures of central Texas past live oaks, cedar, and cottonwoods. We talked about the Palace of Versailles, the Sun King, and the wonder of Miss Agnes Doyle.

We hadn't really expected to see her. She started her drive out to the ranch long before we did. We were merely going to ride by her mailbox as people ride silently by a war memorial, passing their eyes over it, paying public attention. The mailbox was the only memorial Miss Agnes had, and it was generally crooked. High school boys had the habit of knocking it over just as they were in the habit of putting an outhouse in her gate every Halloween.

We came on her hammering her mailbox on a brand

new post. She had stopped to do it on the way in. It was a new mailbox, too—didn't even have her name on it yet. She was hammering inside the mailbox, so she couldn't hear us ride up for the clanging. It was like the "Anvil Chorus" of *Il Trovatore*, I told Ann Frances. The "Anvil Chorus" was my piece for the next piano recital. I played it every time I got mad. Miss Agnes's hammering didn't have any rhythm to it, though. It was just loud.

She pulled the hammer out of the box. "There. Let the sons of bitches knock that down!" Then she saw us. "Old telephone pole sawed off and set in concrete," she said. "Makes a pretty damn good mailbox stand, don't it?"

We nodded.

"And I hope some of those little bastards wreck their daddies' cars on it!"

Ann Frances turned pink.

"What's your name, girl?"

"McConnell, Ann Frances McConnell."

"And yours?"

"Celia Henderson."

"I know your daddy. He's got the lease on that Texaco—" She stopped and turned to throw the hammer in the back of the buggy. "Well, Miss Henderson and Miss McConnell, what can I do for you?"

"Nothing, Miss Agnes. We were just riding by," I said.

"Riding, where are you riding to?"

"Nowhere, just riding."

"For the hell of it?" She straightened the patent leather sailor so the rose was directly in front.

Ann Frances blushed again.

"What's the matter? Didn't you ever hear anybody cuss before?"

"Yes'm."

"Then why are you blushing?"

"I never heard a lady cuss." Ann Frances was beginning to get flustered.

Miss Agnes sighed and wiped off her hands on her long skirt. "It's my one failing. I can't help it. Been around men all my life, men and horses, enough to make anybody cuss." She grinned up at us, her old bone-white face lined into a fun-loving boy's smile. "Crazy isn't it? Crazy cussing old woman." She looked out past us and laughed. "Well," she turned to me, "are you a Henderson like the rest of them?"

I guessed she meant respectable, so I said no. I wasn't feeling respectable at the moment.

"Humph!" said Miss Agnes, and with that sound of contempt she put me on the defensive. I wasn't feeling respectable, but I couldn't see anything wrong with my parents' respectability.

"I guess you don't see nothing wrong with the world as it is?" She cocked her head to one side.

"It's kinda hot," Ann Frances ventured.

"That ain't—is not," she corrected herself, "—what I had in mind."

We sat there letting our reins slide so the horses could graze and waited for Miss Agnes Doyle to tell us what was wrong with the world as it is.

"The trouble is that all the world is off riding like you two, not knowing where it's going, and what is more, it don't even know where it's been. Of the two kinds of not

knowing, not knowing where you've been is the worst."
She paused and looked up at our stupefied faces. "You
don't know what I'm telling you, do you?"

"Well, we've been in town," I said.

"And, we're fixing to go back," said Ann Frances.

We congratulated each other with a mutual snigger.

"And before that?" the old woman persisted.

"Well, Miss Agnes, I was born in 1933 and I can't remember everything that happened between then and
now and I don't think I want to." Ann Frances got off to
tighten her saddle girth, leaving me to answer all the
questions.

"And before that?"

"You mean like history?"

"Yeah, history, ancient history." She drawled the "ancient" out, making it a long, important word.

"We study that in school, world history. We have it
next year I think. Ann Frances, don't we have it next
year?"

"Yeah, I think so." She emerged from behind the
horse, wiping the sweat off her face with one hand. "Listen, what time is it?"

"About four," she guessed.

"It's five till four."

"I'd better call Mother and tell her we'll be late coming in. You know how she worries."

Ann Frances's mother, as far as I knew, never worried
about anything much. Her children could ride all over
the county and drag in at midnight for all she cared. It
was my mother that was the worrier, but I went along

with Ann Frances because I knew what she was up to, what we were both up to, getting inside that house.

Miss Agnes was gathering up the reins lying on the ground. She patted the horse on the flanks and heaved herself into her buggy. For an instant the tops of her high black shoes showed beneath her skirts. When she got back in the buggy it seemed she was somewhere we could never reach her. Whatever it was she was trying to tell us was forgotten, snapped off the minute her head was under the protective hood of the buggy.

"Miss Agnes," I called to her. I felt like I was shouting into a cave. "Miss Agnes, have you got a telephone?"

"Hell, no. Hell, no, I don't have no telephone. You're not more than ten miles out. Poke those good for nothing ponies you're on right hard and you'll get home before sundown. You don't need no telephone, just a switch." With that she pulled at her reins and was off down the drive to her house.

"Snubbed!" Ann Frances kicked her horse. "Snubbed by Miss Agnes Doyle, crazy old Miss Agnes Doyle."

"Hell!"

"Celia Henderson, you better watch your language. You'll be as bad as Miss Agnes before you know it. I never heard such words fall from the lips of a woman!"

"Hell, watch your own, Miss Prissypants."

We rode home silently, dulled by the hot sun. I was thirsty and angry at Ann Frances and at Miss Agnes with her riddles. I knew where I was going. I was going to finish high school, and go to college, and get married, and have children, and do a lot of things Miss Agnes had never done so the hell with her. She was too old even to know what was going on in the world, and she didn't even have enough sense to have the convenience of a telephone. She should have had one, too, living out there alone like she did.

# Dreamer When Last Seen

 "UHLAN IS MY NAME, Leon is my station. I go to Leon Pig-Pen to get my education." In the late 1940's Victoria Uhlan chanted the same doggerel as the rest of us. The disdain was as affected as the dangling earrings and black ballet slippers everybody wore for six months. We did not truly believe Leon High School was a pig-pen, nor did we ever call each other by our last names. Though we were not insensitive to her preference for the rolling grandeur of Vic-tor-i-a, we called her Vicky to make her seem more like the rest of us. We all had short names: June, Fran, May, Sue, Sarah. Vicky and I were the only ones who could not be called in one explosive puff. Born at the tail-end of a depression; raised in an atmosphere of abbreviations, World War II slang, and acronyms— W.P.A. and ack-ack, radar and NATO whirled in the air we breathed—we settled on the quick and clipped. Understatement was nearer to truth, one supposition rigorously followed by another; waverers never win.

Vicky was our waverer. Why do I remember her so vividly now? There's a Vicky in every group; ours was not unusual. Her success is not unusual either. Ugly ducklings become swans daily. Vicky hasn't become a swan exactly, yet in discovering her again I realize the persistent strength of the dreamer. When we were in high school she was a fat girl, chubby fat the way babies are, and she had a baby's fine hair worn in limp curls about her neck. She would not sleep the punishing sleep of the righteous stylish ones who wore metal curlers to bed. This was as impossible for her as practicing handwriting. While everyone else was self-consciously imitating an English teacher's modified Spencerian script, slanting angular letters to the right—hoping we too could be adults with characters matching those well-formed letters—Vicky's handwriting remained round and open. Instead of dotting her i's, she drew tiny balloons over them, little circles of herself floating above the hard facts of a report copied from the school library's out-of-date encyclopedia. She paid so little attention to the facts about anything that, eventually, out of pity or shame for one of our group who was making such low grades, someone would try to help her with her homework. The helpful one soon despaired. "She can't get algebra through her head!" was a common complaint. We knew very well why; her head was stuffed with dreams, and all her dreams centered about one place, Hollywood. She had a sister, so much older that none of us could remember seeing her, living in California. That was her one touch with reality, the one actual person she knew out there. In the summers, Vicky went to see her sister and came back to Texas each fall murmuring the magic names. Brown Derby, Grauman's Chinese Theater, Clark Gable, Van Johnson, Rita Hayworth. She had seen them all, she said. We nodded our heads and smiled, so confident she was lying we didn't bother to tell her so. We had spent our early years trying to get our understanding wrapped around World War II. Compared to memories of victory gardens, sugar rationing, soldier fathers, and mushroom clouds of atomic bombs, Vicky's world was nothing but a pink cotton candy fantasy. As adolescents we had our own rich tribal life. Only that was real to us.

Our fathers were real estate men, retail merchants, gasoline wholesalers, doctors, but none of us were wealthy. Or, at least, we didn't think we were. We lived in modest houses with unused front porches—families sat in backyards—and large lawns. Vicky's father owned a drugstore where, it was rumored, he took his own drugs. He was a mild-mannered man with dark jaws. Mr. Uhlan's beard grew so fast he had a noon shadow instead of a five o'clock one. He gave ice-cream cones to his daughter's friends whenever we came to the drugstore with her. We took them, licking the cold mounds with scornful tongues. It wasn't generosity that drove Vicky to her father's drugstore, nor was it only a desire to please us with free ice cream. She believed the myth about movie stars being discovered in drugstores, so she went nearly every afternoon after school to feed her starving hope with all ten of Uhlan's flavors. She was the only one who tried them all; we stuck to vanilla, chocolate, and strawberry.

Once she invited us over to her house to try some caviar she'd brought back from California. Her mother, a thin, soft-voiced woman, was gone shopping. We dipped into the black glistening stuff, spread it on crackers, and gagged at the taste. Vicky ate hers with aplomb, and we knew again she was a fool. "Everyone in Hollywood eats it at all the parties," she said. We didn't deny that. We were equally certain Hollywood stars were fools also.

Glamour, we had been told, was false. Hollywood was

an illusion. We went to the movies, but we didn't believe in them. Stupid older girls might swoon at Sinatra's feet. We watched him sing "Old Man River" wearing a white suit, standing on top of a white column in the grand finale of a musical, and were all too aware he never lifted a bale of anything. The song should have been sung by a big black man wearing a sweat-stained blue shirt. Sinatra was all wrong for the part. We saw *Miracle on 34th Street* and hooted at Natalie Wood for believing in Santa Claus, and when Bing Crosby played the priest in *The Bells of St. Mary's*, we knew Hollywood was a mad place. We wished there was one boy in Leon who could dance as well as Gene Kelly, but in our little town in central Texas any boy who tap-danced would have been branded as queer. Anyway, it took years of practice to do what Gene Kelly did, and none of our boys had even begun. We looked with narrowed cynical eyes at the overstuffed rooms stars moved through and solaced our envy with comments like, "It's all papier-mache." And when Sinatra sang, "It's only a paper moon sailing over a cardboard sea, but it wouldn't be make-believe if you believed in me," we believed the part about the paper moon and the cardboard sea.

For all our skepticism we continued going to the movies, particularly the ones we weren't supposed to see. I saw *Duel in the Sun* late one Friday afternoon, came out blinking at the drugstore cowboys standing in front of the fly-spattered windows of the cafe across the street, and was more certain than ever that the blood lust exhibited by Joseph Cotten and Gregory Peck over a no-count girl did not exist. The drugstore cowboys chewed their everlasting toothpicks and spat on the forever dusty pavement. I went home refusing to waste time staring at the technicolor sunset at my back.

"Sarah, where have you been?" My mother insisted, as all the other girls' mothers did, on knowing where I was every minute I was out of her sight.

"At the movies." I would not lie about something so minor, but evasion was a useful tactic.

"*Duel in the Sun?*" She had a wonderful instinct and a memory refreshed daily by a drive past the only two picture shows in Leon. On her way to the house from the post office Mother waved at her friends while reading grocery store special signs and marquees above their heads.

"Yes." I sighed.

"It's a trashy film."

I agreed it was, but was sent to my room without supper anyway, the only time in my life I can remember being punished in that fashion. I was fifteen and I realized the penalty was ignominious, a child's punishment for a childish mistake.

Vicky, switching from a passion for Alan Ladd to undying love for Gregory Peck, saw *Duel in the Sun* twice. Her mother never found out, and if she had, she wouldn't have reacted as our mothers did. Though generally on their side as an adult opposing a teenage daughter, she was ineffectual. If we brought home B's on our report cards, our mothers were sure to ask why we had fallen to that disgustingly average plateau. Mountains and A's had the same shape, and through unwavering pursuit, tops could be reached. Loss of allowance, six weeks of dishwashing, and monitored study hours in straight chairs under bright lights without any background music— these were the threats we knew would be carried out. Worse than these was the constant warning, "You aren't living up to your potential." We were made to understand there were no boundaries to "potential." It was always lurking above to be lived up to. We asked Vicky what her mother said when she came home with her C- and D-covered cards.

"Oh, nothing much. She sighs." Vicky sighed like her mother. "Then she sits down in the nearest chair and signs them. Sometimes she says I ought to do better. I know I ought to, but I don't." By looking down at her shoes she deferred to us on our mountains.

"Well, you could make better grades if you wanted to," said May. The last one to give up on Vicky, she made straight A's with apparently effortless grace just as she rippled through popular songs on the piano, playing by ear, without having to read a note.

"I guess so, but I don't seem to want to. I hate studying!" She made the stupid face composed of lower teeth stuck out and crossed eyes. Her faces and poses usually made us laugh; this time we refused. It was 1949, we were juniors in high school, and we had already chosen our colleges, visited the campuses, and decided on which dormitories we would live in.

"Don't you want to go to college?" I asked.

"And study for four more years!" Vicky made her sheer terror face, opening her eyes wide and stretching her mouth to one side.

"But what will you do?" June's voice reflected her own

terror of an unplanned life. She wanted to stay in college at least two years, marry a rancher, have three children and a four-bedroom house.

"I'll go to Hollywood and get a job at Schwab's. I know all about drugstores. If I'm not discovered there I'll . . . I'll find Gregory Peck and throw myself at his feet." She lifted her arms to the sky—the total abandonment pose.

"If you don't lose thirty pounds he's going to step right over you." Sue weighed 105 and could eat anything.

"I've found a new diet—grapefruit."

Fran, the only one of us who liked home economics courses, said, "That's a lot of vitamin C, but no protein."

"There's more to it than just grapefruit."

"What?"

"I don't remember right now. I've got it written down at home." Vicky began looking through her purse for something. Anytime we put too much pressure on her, she changed the subject.

"Hey, look at my new lipstick. It's called Tangerine. You want to try it?"

The only lipsticks our parents approved of were called Rosebud, or Pearl, or Apple Blossom, sweet pale pinks which hardly showed at all. For the remaining twenty minutes of our lunch hour we dabbed on Vicky's lipstick. Tangerine lived up to its name, a satisfying neon orange that had to be wiped off before we went home that afternoon.

Our major form of rebellion was smoking, something Vicky didn't do. She didn't like cigarettes. Neither did I, but I learned to like them. As soon as we knew how to inhale, about the same time we got our driver's licenses, we headed for Tobacco Road, a highway east of Leon our fathers seldom used. We spent a great deal of time that summer organizing picnics in the country. I'd gather all the girls in the back of my father's old pickup and off we'd go in search of water and shade. We took Vicky. Our mothers all believed the Uhlans' child should be included and we didn't mind. She never told on us. We smoked all day long. Cigarettes were lit between sandwiches, while we played bridge, after swims. These were drought years in Texas and we had to look hard for water enough to hold us afloat. The summer of 1950, the last year before graduating, we were down to dry creek beds. Vicky didn't go to California that summer. She sat on tangled grapevines swinging like a large sun-baked pear and watched us, her eyes shifting focus from her movie magazine to us in the distance and back again to an interior world probably occupied by Ricardo Montalban and Esther Williams gliding through an endless supply of swimming pools.

We had almost ceased to regard Vicky at all until she started dating Eddie Daniels, a wild boy who drove a battered green convertible with the top crunched down no matter what the weather. He had little rain to worry about; still, when winter came the nights were cold. Even then Vicky wouldn't concede to reality. When we teased her about cold nights she smiled and sang, "I've got my love to keep me warm." We smiled back and told her in friendly tones the ominous warnings we'd heard at home.

"He'll get in some kind of trouble yet."

"Eddie's a terrible driver."

"He'll probably end up chopping cedar for a living."

"Why do you go with him?" I asked.

Vicky gave me her most glamorous stage look. "Sex," she said.

Determined virgins though we were, we understood her and gasped. How could she! Did she want a shotgun wedding? She shook her head and said, "You don't know how it is."

We dated according to a strict code; we were kissed, we were stroked in forbidden places, we kept our pants on, and we were frustrated. The boys we dated were frustrated. They tried in every way possible to break down our resistance, and they would have been disappointed if they had broken it. "Nice girls don't" was the order of the day. They knew the code. Their nearest release was a Mexican bordertown across from Del Rio a long way to the south, Boys' Town in Ciudad Acuña. With everything to lose, we stayed in Leon clinging to our half of the double standard.

Our urges were relentless. We sought release in talk, drawing analytical comparisons that would have shocked Kinsey, or we hoped they would have. Most of our revelations were made at slumber parties. Sue, during one of these, had just finished telling of one boy's technique of unbuttoning her blouse and we were telling her she ought not to have let him when Vicky entered my house, crawling in on all fours whispering, "Hide me! Eddie's after me!"

We were sitting on the living room floor. Vicky's freshly polished saddle oxfords left a trail on the dark blue rug, two long white streaks my mother was going to be upset about. We sent her to my room and threw a blanket over the streaks, and I went to the door when Eddie punched the bell. He was a rangy blond boy, already graduated from high school and filled out enough to look like a man.

"Tell Vicky I want to see her."

He didn't look or smell drunk, but he seemed dangerous. Anger sloughed off him. I would have called my father, but I didn't want to appear cowardly. I backed away ready to say, "She isn't here," and slam the door in his face. Behind me the other girls tried to keep talking as though nothing was happening. I could hear June describing a new dress, "Plaid with silver buttons." Before I could open my mouth, Eddie was shouting.

"Vicky, I know you're in there."

"She's not!" I said and heard the outside door to my room open. Vicky appeared at the other end of the porch, her face mysteriously radiant. The light from my bedroom shot out in a path before her.

"Eddie?" She was completely self-possessed, standing in the light in her bluejeans and best pink sweater, her saddle oxfords stained at the toes where she'd scraped across the rug.

"Shut up. I'm here." She walked in glory across the porch, took his hand, and left without saying another word. It was her scene. The girls crowded behind me and we watched them drive off in his convertible. Vicky's hair was flying in the wind. She didn't wave.

Immediately after we graduated Vicky ran off with Eddie Daniels and married him. Five months later she had a baby. We decided it was bound to happen. Our lives were to be different. The tribe was breaking up, going to various colleges where we were busy joining the right sororities and dating the right boys, fraternity boys provided by our sororities. We came home at Thanksgiving, Christmas, and Easter; slowly our ties began to dissolve. We had other friends, other loyalties. We were held together now by tenuous common memories and these began to change as we did. Sue remembered little things, all the words to "The Lovesick Blues" and the names of the boys who played football. The rest of us were in a hurry to forget how young and foolish we had been. When we ran out of reminiscences, there was Vicky to talk about. Her marriage to Eddie was brief. By Christmas we heard she was divorced and living at home with her baby. She had the green convertible now; the top was still down. She drove over to see me in it carrying the baby well wrapped up on the front seat beside her.

When she got in the house she held him on her lap after offering to let me hold him. I tried, but I didn't know what to do with a baby. I was eighteen years old; I knew how to memorize my way through a course and was beginning to learn how to write newspaper stories in the prescribed inverted pyramid form stacked with brick-hard facts. I had also learned the value of politeness to housemothers, absolute rulers of small domains. I'd been told it was all right to get drunk; however, the label of slob was automatically pasted on anyone who got sick-drunk in public. Finally, I had acquired the skill of organizing committees. Whether for alumni barbecues, foreign student aid, or blood drives for soldiers in Korea— the cause made no difference—the way things were accomplished at the University of Texas in the fifties was to organize a committee. Vicky changed the baby's diaper all by herself while I looked on with horror. She had lost fifteen pounds yet she was still too fat. Her hair had been dyed red brown—it was still limp. I thought she looked thirty and let her leave after a short visit without asking what she was going to do next. I had no advice to give her. I didn't ask about her sister living in fantasy anymore; she apparently had forgotten Hollywood existed.

The following Christmas when I came home I had to have a lot of dental work done. There, in Dr. Smithson's office, was Vicky, ten pounds lighter, her hair cut short. She had gone to Waco and learned to be a dental technician. She looked sleek and good-humored. The baby was with her mother. She set out Dr. Smithson's brilliant instruments, mixed various chemical potions, and when he'd done all the fillings, she vigorously cleaned my teeth. I closed my eyes as she came toward me with a whirling electric brush and wondered, "Oh, Vicky, where is Grauman's Chinese Theater now? Where is the Brown Derby? Who is going to discover you, beautiful as you've become, in a dentist's office in central Texas? Which of us is living in fantasy now, me on my protected campus with all bills paid by my parents, or you working with these cruel tools, a marriage behind you and a baby at home?"

Hollywood carried on with Debbie, Doris, and Tony. Betty Grable quit making movies. Marilyn Monroe flaunted briefly before us, and Clark Gable died. John Wayne came to Texas to shoot on new locations. Vicky, where were you then? Why weren't you down in a little town in South Texas? You could have brushed superstar teeth and been discovered.

I graduated from college, got a newspaper job, and quit going home to the dentist. Vicky wasn't in Leon anymore, though I didn't know she'd left. Now I was to know other realities. As an escape from woman's work on what was then called the newspaper's Society Section, filled with weddings, recipes, and occasional feature stories about ladies who did awesome amounts of volunteer service, I began to write foreign film reviews. Fellini, Bergman, and Antonioni trouped into one movie theatre in Austin—three wise, sad men who said we trap ourselves, love is bondage, look at the wasteland. And sometimes they said all human folly is both pathetic and comic; we will die dancing on the brow of a hill with death; in the meantime, we need our illusions for survival. Which one said what? They run together in my memory. Fellini's weary circus performers dance on Antonioni's deserted island holding hands with Bergman's magician.

Their visions, especially Fellini's in *La Dolce Vita*, stunned me. For the first time I saw naked people displaying a grossness of flesh, ridiculous hope, and sexual appetite which contradicted all of Hollywood's prettifying. These images overran my senses like the Chinese horde had overrun the American army in Korea. Fleeing the terror of too much, of too many ways of knowing, I married a gentle cynic, a news correspondent who believed about a third of what he wrote. After I married I turned an interest into a profession and became a news photographer, a female Diogenes with a set of inter-

changeable lenses and a strobe light, attempting to capture the evasive moment of actuality—the burning
building's flames at their height, the victim's terror, the
impact of the car crash, a candidate's professional grin as
it faded to weariness, an empty street crossed with ban-
ners welcoming President Kennedy, who was supposed to
arrive in Austin after Dallas, peace signs flashed by
marching protesters. Chasing after a whole set of half-
truths, I forgot about Vicky until my first child was born
in 1964. Vietnam, our longest-playing nightmare, was
showing in full horror on TV screens in every living
room. My husband and I were living in Saigon, both of
us covering the war for a year. Since I was seldom allowed at any front line—wherever those shifting points
happened to be—I took pictures of refugees, the
wounded, defoliated forests, bombed cities, orphaned
children. Soon I could not look at another child's face
without feeling accused. I began to be sick every
morning.

"It's this war," I said.

My husband looked at me closely. "Maybe it's the
water."

"I've been drinking it for six months. It would have
gotten to me before now."

He grinned. "Maybe you're pregnant."

When we found I was, he said, as men usually say to
their women in wartime, "Go home. Go back to Texas
to have the baby." He would not be reconciled to good
hospitals in Tokyo or even in Honolulu. Home I flew,
pressed hard by the irony of being a pregnant American
among the dying Vietnamese and by an inner desire

to return to the nest. I took an apartment in Austin. Mother came to stay and help with the baby the first weeks of his life.

One morning while we were busy bathing him, trying to hold onto his slippery body, fearful every second of drowning him, she said, in the way she generally interjects news in the midst of a crisis, "I guess you know June's had her second baby now."

I nodded and scooped my son up in a towel.

"And, Vicky Uhlan—I never can remember her married name—"

"Don't tell me she's married again," I mumbled through a mouthful of diaper pins.

"No, she moved to California a long time ago. She's living in Los Angeles."

"Mother!" I started so, the baby began crying. Quieting him, I nodded my head toward the living room, put him in his crib, and tiptoed back down the hall with Mother.

"Is Vicky Uhlan in the movies?"

"They call her Victoria now. No, she's not in the movies. She's in one of those TV soap operas."

"Have you seen her?"

"You know I don't watch that trash."

I didn't watch it either until Mother went home. Then I sat down with the baby, who still had to be fed every four hours, and watched every serial for a week. I became familiar with every theme song—yearning, sonorous lullabies for my son, who dozed as they played. The people in the serials agonized over decisions, and I agonized over their faces, trying to find Vicky. She ap-

peared early one afternoon in one of those stories showing the scandalous lives of everybody in small-town Anywhere, U.S.A. The druggist takes his drugs, a wild boy
seduces a lonely, unattractive girl who isn't accepted by
her peers, the mother wrings her hands and tries to help
in an ineffectual way.

There was Vicky Uhlan playing her mother, a little
smarter looking, but just as thin. She made anguished
faces, dabbed her eyes with a crumpled handkerchief,
sighed, and sat down in the nearest chair whenever fresh
news of failure was brought to her. I never saw Mrs.
Uhlan's reactions to Vicky's adventures, but Vicky had.
She played the part perfectly.

I've never found out how she was discovered and I'm
satisfied not to know. Perhaps it happened in a terribly
ordinary way; she could have been sent to a casting ses-
sion by her agent. I prefer to believe someone discovered
her in a California drugstore. Though I've made no effort
to learn if she's still playing in that serial or has found
another better role, I sometimes think I see her in crowd
scenes in movies.

My husband, son, and I have moved to D.C., a city as
full of pretenders as L.A. Loss of interest in the jour-
nalistic definition of news—repetitious disasters, recur-
rent campaigns, the dizzying rise and fall of movie stars,
music stars, and the stock market—led me to the private
interests of a freelance photographer. I take pictures of
sun slanting on wilderness trails, skiers' marks in new
snow, a whole series of inquisitive cats and dogs who in-
habit my neighborhood, children intent on their ritual
games, my family's and my friends' faces as they change

during the years, whatever pleases me. My field of vision has narrowed; I allow myself to think it has deepened. Part of every week is spent in my own darkroom, where I dabble with chemicals and adjust light, trying to order these black-and-white representations, attempting to capture a flicker of truth. Under the safelight's solitary red eye I play with shadows, tones of gray, emerging shapes. Here in this quiet place I weave through fluctuating times and spaces hypnotized by visual images, barely awake in a dream world. Is Vicky awake in hers? There is no way I could know even if I flew to California and found her at some studio where she might be making her way around the cameras' electric cable as she walked on set. If we talked for hours about our common past and did quick sketches of our last twenty years, as people do at high school reunions, I would still learn little about her private realities. Musing within these limitations and uncertainties, I am consoled by my craft as perhaps Victoria, the actress, is confirmed by hers.

# The New Castle

PAULO COULD NOT PAY attention to the ceremony. The room, filled with people, was much too warm, and the picture he faced above the mantelpiece distracted him. It was an early Matisse of a woman in a green and pink striped dress sitting in a blue chair. In the background stood the usual Matisse pot of flowers and an open window. The woman stared at him.

"I do," said Paulo. His English accent clipped the air. I do marry you, Barbara, regardless of every difference.

The woman in the picture accused him. "These continental marriages are disasters. She is buying you." Her voice was heavy with ageless European cynicism.

"Nonsense, Madame. I am rescuing her. You are only one form. There are thousands of ways to make a life. How could you know what the world has become since you were caught on that canvas sometime before the First World War?"

"I have watched everything that's happened in this room."

"Watch now and see something new."

Outside, it is snowing fitfully. Inside this hothouse, provided by great wealth, tropical plants cluster in small forests; bunches of white roses erupt from vases. Their odor pervades the room. Paulo traces an arabesque in

Barbara's grandmother's oriental rug. Birds and monkeys play on the floor. In his shiny patent leather shoes, chosen for the occasion, he could easily leap among them. Someone behind him tries to pour champagne in a silver punchbowl noiselessly. Barbara's blonde hair parts exactly in the middle. Longing to touch that precise line, so delicate yet so determined, he catches his fingers in his palms then loosens them. She glances at him but she too seems far away.

The J.P., who looks uncomfortable standing with his back to the cold hearth, steps aside. A priest dressed in a black cassock, white surplice, and gold and white stole sweeps in. Paulo and Barbara kneel before him. Raising his hands in the restless air, he blesses them both. They rise. Paulo kisses his bride slowly as though he's forgotten the crowd. They turn toward their guests.

"There. That's better. The priest's blessing makes you really married," Marian says. With her long dark hair curled under, she looks like a medieval pageboy to Paulo. She moves aside to explain to someone else that the civil ceremony was necessary to please Paulo's family in Turin. They are Communists. An old friend of Barbara's, Marian has been his invaluable ally. What she doesn't understand, however, is that the priest is also necessary to his family.

"We Italians . . . we use a little of everything," Paulo adds. While he does not mean exactly what he is saying, he believes every word. Church windows, sculpture, architecture interest him, but he is irreligious except in the most hidden part of himself, where he retains a childlike faith in prayer to an omnipotent yet negligent power.

"I'm not going to throw this bouquet," Barbara announces. Everyone laughs. Most of their friends are
married.

Robert, Marian's husband, shakes Paulo's hand. "Welcome to the state of legal matrimony." He uses orotund
phrases in a spirit of self-mockery. A tall man, wearing a
pin-striped suit with a vest, he is a comforting figure, a
lawyer who explains Texas to Paulo. For two years now
his explanations have not ceased.

Paulo puts his hand on Barbara's shoulder and lifts a
glass of champagne toward her, thinking, I will write
Mother about the notary and the priest. She will say,
"My dear, you did not have to have both." And I will
say, "Oh, but Barbara insisted." That will please her.
She's not like anyone here imagines her. She's not an ancient crone perpetually dressed in black. Ah no, my
mother wears the latest designs from Rome made of silk
woven in her factory.

Excellent champagne, but too dry. They all like their
drinks too dry in this country. Dry martinis, scotch on
the rocks, bourbon on the rocks. Robert has tried to explain why people wish to drink so much whiskey so fast.
"Sedation, numbness. That's what we want." Paulo refuses the idea. He understands the words, but numbness
at five o'clock every day remains incomprehensible. Dry
martinis and whiskey on ice he lumps together with businessmen who wear cowboy boots and rich ladies who
wear bluejeans in his secret category—Native North
American Rituals and Costumes. He began thinking in
these terms long before he arrived in America. At his
grandfather's hunting lodge, a small castle in the Valle

d'Aosta where his family fled to wait out the war, he read through the old man's vast collection of *National Geographics*. Every day he traveled to Zanzibar, to Lithuania, to the Belgian Congo. He hunted with Eskimos, dove with sponge divers in the Aegean, marveled at fire walkers in Ceylon. Before his older brother Marcus left to join the partisans, he taught Paulo all the math he knew. From his grandfather he took Latin lessons, from his mother, French, and from Eric, who arrived with the other soldiers to live in the castle, German. The cook—ah, Antonio, he could have been a Borgia—poisoned Eric and three others. Paulo helped Antonio bury them in the park surrounding the castle. They would have all been shot except the war was almost over and everything was so confused. It did not seem strange for an eight-year-old boy to bury soldiers; it was only necessary. His grandfather was too feeble to dig graves. A beloved wisp, he said prayers for the dead over the Germans, and as he had nothing else to give him, he offered Antonio his gold watch chain, which Antonio refused.

Paulo takes a tentative bite of wedding cake then smiles at Barbara. He eats, blinking while flashbulbs pop. He eats anything and always has. Antonio fed them on squirrels, wild birds, roots, berries, plants he found in the forest, and whatever he could barter for after the war. Once he traded a suit of armor for five kilos of flour.

"There goes Henri. We sell his armor so we may cover our bones." Grandfather, musing at the library window, looked at his great-grandfather's form respectably rolled in a white linen tablecloth and lying in a small cart Paulo had made. Antonio disappeared around a bend in the road, trundling the ghost to the village.

"Grandfather, who would want armor now?"

The old man, so frail that his smallest movement was like a candle flame wavering in the wind, turned toward him. "Someone will always buy the past once it's comfortably over. No one remembers which battles Henri wore that armor in. In time—you will live to see that time, I imagine—people will buy the relics of this war. They will pay for guns, swords, helmets, medals, whatever lasts and is portable. Each generation carries the remnants of preceding ones forward." He clasped his hands before him and bowed his head slightly, the gesture he made when a conversation was finished.

Bowing over Mrs. Garden's hand, Paulo's lips whisper across thin, blue veins. Her right hand, where she wears the rubies and diamonds her husband gave her, rests on her cane. Sitting erect, refusing to lean against the chair's carved back, dressed in mauve instead of her usual black, she could be an Italian contessa. Paulo has told her this. The comparison amuses her. Rich as she is, she is as accustomed to flattery as he is to poverty. Yet she is never bored. When she begins to be, she invites musicians to play for her. "My hired entertainment," she says because she gives thousands to the symphony and to promising young pianists. "Music is my last passion," she tells everyone. She has raised Barbara to fulfill it. Enormously proud of her granddaughter's talent, she was reluctant to see her marry Paulo even though they had lived together for almost a year. Marian Forster introduced them at one of Jenkins's interminable cocktail parties.

"What are you doing in this country?" Barbara asked. Later she told him he looked like a peacock lost in a group of chickens.

"I'm not sure." Every state was a new country to him then. "I came down from New York to see Jenkins two days ago. We were at Oxford together. We are supposed to talk about business when Jenkins gets through celebrating my arrival. I'm opening an antique shop. He's my partner. It is his idea that I should come to Texas. For some years I have had a shop in London."

"And you've been in his house for two days?"

"Well, yes, and at the same party it seems." He was only a little drunk, though he felt like he'd been drinking for weeks.

Jenkins began passing the marijuana around then. Paulo waved it aside. He didn't want to live in timelessness anymore. Jenkins was merry about his refusal. He was merry about everything, an English Puck, yet he had a kind heart. He did things for people, took them in, gave them drinks, loaned them money.

Barbara disagreed. "He dissipates himself, throws his interest in all directions. He's written one good book. I'm afraid he'll never write another."

Paulo nodded. She was precise without being mean. He liked her immediately. That night he went home with her. He could not remember exactly how he got there. Although he knew Barbara had given him directions, the way seemed like a magical journey over a dark twisting path which ended on a hill far above the city. A little further up he thought he saw castle walls rising.

"My grandfather's. He was, as Jenkins says, a bit dotty about architecture. He's dead. Grandmother still lives there. I have what used to be the carriage house."

Worn our, slightly dazed by whiskey, he did not perform well in bed. When he apologized she said never mind and went to sleep immediately. Everything would happen later if it happened at all, he reminded himself. He was profoundly grateful she'd gotten him out of Jenkins's house. Waking up that Sunday morning, the first thing he saw through her bedroom doorway was a grand piano.

"You didn't tell me you were a musician."

"But, Paulo, when did I have a chance to?"

"I talk too much. I'm sorry. I've been listening to Jenkins for two days."

"Now it's my turn. I give concerts."

Then she jumped out of bed and went directly to the piano to play the "Grand March" from *Aida*. Raising her hands high over the resounding chords, she laughed aloud.

He often thought of her like that: dressed in a short embroidered Mexican shirt, her bare feet pressing the brass pedals, the morning light filtering in through white curtains. For the first time since he'd arrived in America, something was familiar. The music, Barbara's high spirits, the orange and blue flowers on her shirt, but most of all the light, reminded him of spring mornings in the Valle d'Aosta where light poured off the glaciers surrounding Mont Blanc, Monte Rosa, the Gran Paradiso, and the Cervino.

She gave him breakfast. Together they plotted a way to get his suitcase from Jenkins's house. For a while he thought she simply lived in the world doing what she pleased, that she was an artist free to ignore social rules. He was letting himself be ignorant then, remaining a foreigner drifting on the surfaces of people's lives. Actually she lived within certain complex conventions. For a week he was allowed to stay with her. He found himself in such a state of greedy sexuality he told Barbara she had turned him into a satyr.

"What about me?" she said, "You hardly let me get dressed."

It was not a real complaint. They pleased each other too well. However, she insisted, it would be best for him to have a place of his own, so he moved to an apartment which Barbara helped him find. Where was she, the lady he'd rented that place from?

"Miss Tines." He bent over her hand.

"Paulo." A friend of the family's every bit as regal as Mrs. Garden, and of the same generation, she draws back to look at him.

"It's almost as wild out today as the first time I saw you. Do you know how we met?" She turns to Max Davis, who says by his smile, Paulo, we're in for it. Miss Tines is a talker.

"It was a stormy night, all lightning and thunder. He knocked on my front door. You know that brass dolphin knocker weighs a pound at least. Well, I couldn't distinguish between the clatter it made and the thunder. I have the same irrational fears as most savages have of storms. I couldn't force myself to answer the door, and I wasn't sure, you see, whether anyone was truly there. So I stepped out onto the balcony. Paulo waited on my terrace. The moment he saw me he bowed from the waist. I waited in my tattered robe looking like the madwoman in a gothic novel while lightning tore holes in the sky and Paulo inquired if he might rent my garage apartment. I always thought he had on a cloak that night, but he assures me he doesn't own one."

"'Course not," says Max, who is a large, blond man with a considerable paunch. A trust officer at the bank, he's in charge of Barbara's inheritance received from her parents.

"He's butter-colored, the color of riches, of gold," Paulo once told Barbara.

"Money is green in America, darling."

"Real money is gold anywhere."

"You have these ancient ideas about things, Paulo."

"If you had ever to flee one country for another, you'd have the same."

"Did you sew coins in linings?"

"No. We did not even have to flee. My father was— How do you say it? Yes, provident. He put most of our money in a Swiss bank just before the war began."

"Why didn't he put you in Switzerland too?"

He shrugged his shoulders. "How could anyone know that war was going to be so long?"

Miss Tines rattles on. She will, if given time, circle back to her original point.

"I saw so little of you once you'd moved in. How long were you with me?"

"Three months, about."

Max salutes him with a champagne glass. Paulo excuses himself. Someone else will relieve Max, or he'll pilot Miss Tines over to Mrs. Garden's chair.

For a moment he tries to remember what furniture was in that apartment. She had some fine Sheraton pieces in her house. Nothing comes to mind except one lumpy chair and a bed which was too soft. He was seldom home. Some nights he spent at the shop, especially the first month, when shipments arrived. They were English antiques, eighteenth-century mostly, and he was eager to see that they had gotten to Texas in good condition. After those early months Barbara allowed him to move back to her house. He could not understand why she wouldn't marry him immediately.

"Your grandmother— Doesn't she mind that I live here with you?"

"She does in a way. But she is more worldly than you imagine. My parents lived together a year before they married. Grandmother doesn't want me to marry at all. She says marriage ruins artists. So we have this fiction. She's aware you're here, yet ignores the fact."

"Ah. She thinks I will vanish eventually. I do not wish to be ignored."

"What are you doing in there, Paulo?" It is Peggy, Max's wife, peeking through the swinging door.

"They are so slow with the champagne. I came to see if I could—"

"No you didn't. You're hiding out in the kitchen. I know. I do it at my own parties." She laughs heartily at herself, at him. Her eyes are blue like Max's, but her hair is dark red, and she is so pale always, like a child who never gets enough attention. Why should that be? Barbara says Max is still in love with his wife. Is Peggy still in love with Max? How long does love last? With his parents—forever.

"I had to get away for a moment."

She will understand anything he tells her.

"Yes." Peggy holds her empty glass up to the window and watches the snow through it. "Barbara is in one of the bedrooms changing her dress."

"Again?"

"It's the custom. American brides don't go away in their wedding dresses . . . but I will go away now."

When Barbara first refused him, Robert said, "She isn't sure. Mrs. Garden hasn't invited you to the castle yet."

"I don't care whether she does or not. The doors are not locked. She hasn't cast a spell on them, has she? I will simply walk in."

"And then ask for Barbara's hand in marriage? I wouldn't do that. She has had other suitors, and one way or another, Mrs. Garden has dismissed them all."

"How?"

"I don't know her methods. She's a formidable old woman, and she exerts a great influence on Barbara. I don't know how she does that either. Perhaps it's because Barbara's parents died when she was so young. She's an unusual girl, Paulo. She grew up in that crazy castle. Her father disappeared when she was eight. He was in South America hunting emeralds. They never found him. And her mother, the family's first musician—she was an opera singer . . . always on tour—died two years later, some say of grief, some say of an overdose of pills. I don't know. So Barbara was left to raise as Mrs. Garden pleased, and Mrs. Garden has always kept her nearby. Most of her life has been given to music. Can you imagine a child practicing all those hours?"

"Yes. We have musicians in my own family."

She had told him she'd loved it, the octagonal tower, her own piano on the second floor above the trees, above the porch's tin roof. All the castle's paradoxes were plain to her; crenellated walls rising above stables converted to garages by her grandfather's decree, the porch tacked on later when he decided he must have it, a gazebo no one used.

"First he had to have style. Later he wanted comfort."

The place looked quite mad to Paulo. An austere Romanesque-looking building rose three stories; around the first story of the tower and two wings, an awkward porch spread like a wide skirt hastily discarded by a giant's wife.

"A combination dream plus Texas farmhouse," Barbara said. She led him from her carriage house to look at the front of the castle by moonlight. The heavy scent of an unknown flower lay on the air. Magnolia, she told him. Two magnolia trees flanked them.

"My grandfather was a farmer before oil was found in his fields. I don't think he ever forgot what he had been."

Paulo laughed, then seeing she was annoyed, he pulled her to him. "Try to understand. I believe he was . . . yes, a free man. Europeans are always being told they must forget. We carry the weight of too much time with us. Your grandfather . . . he must have liked all his times." He slid his fingers inside the band of her jeans.

"Here?"

"Why not?"

"Grandmother has insomnia."

"The trees are so low . . . like tents."

They crawled beneath a magnolia, laughing.

"The ground is hard. You stay on top of me."

"Really?" Even though she is twenty-eight, she has not slept with many men. Every time she went somewhere for a concert, her grandmother went with her. Was she peering malevolently out a tower window while the princess rode a poor man in the dirt beneath a green leather tent? Barbara forgot herself and cried out.

"It's all right. You sound like a nightbird." He held her to him. He must keep her. Of all the women he had known, he must have this one. He did not question why.

Robert was the one who questioned. "Did you come over here looking for a bride?"

"No, but I will have this one."

"Let me suggest a tactic. Go away awhile."

"All right. I will make a buying trip, only I will buy nothing."

He went to Houston, checked on a shipment at a warehouse near the docks, wandered the streets, priced furniture in other antique shops, visited galleries, saw the Rothko Chapel, looked up John Wortham, a friend of Jenkins's, went to a ballet performance, and was utterly heartsick. He longed for Barbara, her gaiety, her Mexican shirts, her music, her body. He had been in love before, but he'd never felt he wanted neither to sleep nor eat. Houston's towering office cubes, its traffic, exhilarating in the daytime, seemed hopelessly remote at night. The spaces between skyscrapers made him long for Torino's eighteenth-century piazzas. Columned, with roofs extending to the pavement's edge, every square provided shelter from winter's snow, summer's sun. There a man could order coffee, sit, and drink, and dream. Even in that mercantile northern city full of Fiat factories there was time to dream.

"Tell me some old place to go."

John Wortham said, "New Orleans, over in Louisiana."

"Too far. Some other place. Isn't there some old town in Texas?"

"Galveston."

He found decaying white wooden houses, some restored, most rotting. But there were masses of pink and white oleanders and tall palms lining the streets. Almost every building facing the seawall was new or looked to be. The long thoroughfare reminded him of the Boulevard Anglais in Nice, though Nice was far more cosmopolitan and the Mediterranean a clear bowl of blue compared to the gritty Gulf of Mexico with its six—or was it eight?—tides daily. No one seemed to care, though they warned him about jellyfish and stingrays. He lay on the sand murmuring to himself, "A savage sea," while watching a black woman in a red dress pull her skirt up to wade.

On the sand he wrote BARBARA; over that, PAULO. He had been by himself in many places. First, the known, the family's empty factory before Marcus returned. Every day he had gone to see if someone had broken in. The idle looms, row on row, some half-filled with cloth which would never be finished, waited like hungry jaws. He visited his grandfather's grave and vowed to find his father's but never did. ("He is with some others. Near Padua. It will be difficult to find the spot." One of the partisans had told him.) Then there were the unknown places.

Oxford. ("I promised your grandfather you would go. I have sold the castle. An education is more important than a building." His mother wrote. She did not tell him until he'd gone, or he would not have left Italy.) Oxford. A small, gray place; incessant rains fell. Finally the sun came out to turn the stones yellow. His courses in art history took him deeper into the world he'd discovered in the *National Geographic*. Everywhere man had ventured there had been artists. He made friends, found a job at an antique shop, opened his own shop in London. Then New York. Confusion, screeching, street vendors as in Italy, so many skyscrapers. Looking up at the sky made him dizzy. And the museums. Some days he almost hoped to be locked in the Metropolitan. He was far too busy in New York for real loneliness.

He pulled his long legs toward him, got up, and ran to the water. How far away was the deep? Slowly he waded out, swam along the shore, drifted in.

Brushing himself off with the motel's small white towel, he walked back and called Barbara. "Come down here, please."

"I can't. I have a concert in San Antonio tomorrow. Grandmother's driving down with me."

He felt like throwing himself off one of the piers, the longest, ugliest one. Instead he returned to Austin two days later. Familiar with Mrs. Garden's dislike of the telephone, he sent her a dozen white roses and a note saying, "With your permission, I will call on you at ten Monday morning. Paulo Moncalieri." He considered including one of his engraved cards which read Conte Paulo León d'Montois Moncalieri and decided against it.

In the New World no farmer's wife, not even one who financed orchestras, would be impressed. The title would only make her suspicious. After all, in Italy there were a laughable number of noblemen.

Mrs. Garden, almost as tall as he was, dressed in black—worn for her husband, then for Barbara's mother, her costume had become as habitual as an Italian peasant woman's—received him in the living room. It was sedately yet comfortably furnished with a mixture of modern couches and chairs, oriental tables and screens, a Steinway in one corner, and excellent pictures—a Matisse, a Kirchner, a Valasco, and two others, probably Latin American, that he didn't know.

He complimented her on her taste.

"I am told you have very good taste yourself."

Her tone was somewhat acerbic, but he took the opening. "Yes, I like your granddaughter. I want to marry her." Holding up one hand, he stopped her before she could reply. "I am aware of your feelings. But surely you must know I would never hinder Barbara's career. I may be able to help her."

"How?" Mrs. Garden clutched the arms of the chair as if she were holding onto life itself.

"I can speak Italian, French, and German. If she chooses to make another European tour, I am familiar with all the capitals. There are many musicians in my family. Barbara would have pianos available for practice before concerts, good pianos, all over Europe. My mother keeps a Bechstein in her apartment. My uncle plays with the Vienna Philharmonic. My cousin is a violinist with the London Symphony. Both of them have contacts everywhere in the musical world. My grandfather played a cello for a string quartet in Torino. My father did the same for a while. His career was finished by the war."

"And you?"

"I chose another field. So did my brother. Marcus runs my mother's business, a silk factory. There is room only for one boss. Like many younger sons before me, I came to America. I speak of the family in order to let you know your great-grandchildren will inherit musical genes."

She looked away from him for a moment. A Siamese cat which had been asleep on one of the sofas stood up, stretched, and stalked carefully out of the room.

"My great-grandchildren?"

"You'll agree that we must think of the future." Staring at her—she appeared younger than seventy-six—he saw that she had not wanted to consider great-grandchildren. Perhaps they seemed too remote. Perhaps she had simply clung to one person as those who have lost everybody else often do.

"Yes . . . one must, but if Barbara has children, she will no longer play." She sighed as if the idea of the future was difficult to bear.

"That is an archaic idea. She may play even better. There are many pianists, many opera singers, who have children. And people have nannies even here."

"How old are you?" Her voice gathered strength from rudeness.

"Forty-two. I have never been married, for I have never wished to be. I expect you know that Italians believe the family is most important. You will not have to search for me in South America. Because I am fourteen years older, my experience in the world is larger than Barbara's. Do you understand me?"

Mrs. Garden nodded. "Where would you live?" Again she clutched at the chair's arms.

"Where we are living now," Paulo smiled. "If that pleases you."

"Yes." Mrs. Garden picked up her cane. "That pleases me." She smiled cautiously for the first time. "You are a practical young man."

He did not think he was. Love had made him both foolish and cautious.

The following day he called Robert. "Barbara will marry me this winter . . . in January."

"When did she say yes?"

"Last night. Now I must get rich. I never wished to before, but I must now."

"Why?"

"She is rich from her father and will be from her grandmother. We will not be equal."

"Paulo, there's nothing wrong with marrying a rich girl."

"I know. For you there isn't. For me— I'm an impoverished Italian with a noble name and a lot of old furniture. That is not enough."

"But Mrs. Garden has oil wells."

"I know. She is stinking rich, a real capitalist."

"And you want to be one too?"

"No, not truly."

He gave up the idea. It was impossible. The shop did well; still, no one would become stinking rich selling antiques. He was no more interested in being rich than he was in being poor.

"What sort of Communist are you?" Barbara wanted to know.

"No sort. I don't belong to the party. Only my brother Marcus does, and he does it for the business."

"He has to be a Communist to stay in business?"

"Yes. I know it's a paradox, but that is how we live—by combining the absurdities. What am I doing here in Texas selling English antiques?"

"You . . . Paulo, you are an accident of history."

"So are you if you look back far enough. Your grandmother married a man who happened to come from somewhere and happened to buy land which happened to be covering an oil field."

"My father's people were French. They came here from Louisiana. I don't know why exactly."

"There, you see."

"Time for you two to leave now." Mrs. Garden leans toward him. She likes to tell people what to do.

Paulo smiles sleepily, a little stupidly as though bowing to her will. Then he shouts, "Musica!" and claps his hands. This is his part of the ceremony, a surprise for Barbara. Two violinists, an accordionist, and a tenor clutching a guitar file out of Mrs. Garden's kitchen singing "Funiculì, Funiculà." The buzz of conversations ceases altogether while the tenor, a stout young man, bellows "Torno a Sorrento." Behind him the string trio which has been playing during most of the reception waits as if frozen. Mrs. Garden's grand piano stands open, its mouth agape, while the indulgent songs of southern Italy fill the room.

Jenkins grins. "What marvelous vulgarity! What sentiment!"

"They are not vulgar songs," Paulo insists, "not in the way you mean. They are democratic, loved by everyone."

"Perhaps not by Mrs. Garden, Paulo."

"So? We play them only today."

Marian winks. She has helped arrange this. They selected only folk songs; operatic arias might sadden Barbara and her grandmother.

Robert runs his hand through his hair. Excesses embarrass him.

Barbara, laughing, kisses Paulo on one cheek. "Will they play 'Santa Lucia'?"

"Of course, if you desire."

In her castle, where vulgarity has been banished since the death of her husband, Mrs. Garden sits as though chained to her chair and whispers to Paulo as he passes, "I can't think where you found those performers."

"In the music department of your university here. They are all students except the tenor. He teaches."

"Well." She sinks back slightly and allows herself a small smile. "I suppose we must have something Italian at this wedding."

"Yes. Something of my country."

He moves away and glances toward the woman in the painting. "You have seen?"

"A charming fellow, a trickster."

"No, Madame, I have tricked no one. I have only used what is available as I learned to long ago."

He takes Barbara by the hand. They dance on the parquet bordering the carpet. All their guests follow. Out the door, down the wide front walk they whirl while the musicians serenade them from the porch. It has begun to snow again, but no one minds. Since it happens only every seven years or so in Austin, people are enchanted by the snowflakes. Even though he is in the middle of Texas, Paulo feels he is quite at home, in his own province, Piedmont, near the Alps.

# Man Dancing

 A TIE. Anyone could buy a tie. First he had to find a cab, though. He rifled through the directory. Cabinets, Cable Splicing . . . Cabs— See Taxicabs, Cafes—See Restaurants. He would never understand the mind behind the yellow pages. There it was, a two and a bunch of ones. A child could remember it. A seventy-year-old man could forget it.

Mr. Isaac called the cab to come pick him up at nine. He would go to one of the men's stores on Guadalupe Street across from the university. They catered mostly to students; however, the older shops he'd used in years past were downtown, further away, a more expensive trip to make. Bending down, he scratched the top of Homer's head. Kate had named him. She'd named everything including both children—Theo, the oldest, after him, but they called him Ted. And Kenneth, the youngest, after her uncle. He could see her standing in the kitchen doorway saying, "Theo, let's give our children family names. I like that tradition." Wearing a loose pink dress, her cheeks rosy in its reflected light, she wavered a moment more in his memory then was gone.

The cabbie honked just as he was knotting his old tie; he had no chance to inspect his clothes. Not until he was inside the store did Mr. Isaac catch a glimpse of himself in a mirror. The oil spots from the salad he'd spilled yesterday at Rose Davis's house gleamed wetly on the front of his trousers. Black as they were, they still showed stains. Black as a crow he looked and dingy! Umph! Shaking his head in disgust, he turned to a round table where ties were laid in an overlapping kaleidoscopic design and considered the wild flowered prints, silk stripes, polka dots. He'd not seen such a profusion of color and pattern since 1923 in London when he'd gone with Kate to Liberty's, where a clerk unrolled bolt after bolt for her to examine. He saw them again tumbling down the counter, the bolts thudding softly, richly until the bare surface was covered with shining rivers of silk. And he could afford just enough for one dress.

1923. Thirty-six then, an associate professor in the history department. His first grant, their only year abroad, all of it spent in England and most of that time he'd hidden in dimly lit libraries. Ah, no use to denigrate it now. He had loved those hours he gave to searching out British views of the American Revolution. When he came home, he wrote a book that other American historians had to read until yet another writer furnished a newer view, something he'd expected. Historians seldom had the last word. Who were they reading now in 1967? Somehow it didn't matter much. When he'd retired from teaching, he'd also retired from keeping up with the latest books in his field. There were a great number of others he'd been promising himself he'd read— Dr. Johnson's letters, Southwestern history, traveler's tales, and every once in a while, a glossy new novel, though he liked rereading the Victorian ones better.

This shop looked like something straight out of Dickens's novels. Everywhere he looked there was nineteenth-century golden oak and brass. Must be the fashion now, to make the new look old. Where was the clerk? Didn't they wait on people anymore?

"Can I help you, sir?"

Though he kept his gaze on the ties, he said, "I would like to see some suits. Summer suits."

"What size, sir?"

Mr. Isaac coughed discreetly and let his eyes run over what seemed to be almost a hundred suits catalogued behind size numbers. Then he looked at the clerk. The young man was wearing a veritable flower garden on his tie and a shirt marked with thin green stripes. He lifted his eyes and confessed, "I'm not sure. I haven't bought a suit in some time." Not since Kate's funeral, and he'd planned to be dressed in it when he died. Since yesterday though, since meeting Rose Davis again—she must have thought him a melancholy sight—he'd decided he needed some more clothes. Vanity? Yes. But when so much else was stripped away from a man—when vigor was gone, when so many of his friends were dead, when wrinkles clustered, why not indulge his vanity? He'd never done so. As a history professor he'd dressed like all the other birds in the flock, and except for an occasional red tie around Christmas time, they were a colorless bunch.

"You'd take a thirty-eight, I'd say," The clerk slid his hand between the racks, pushing away all the other sizes as if they were offensive to him.

Mr. Isaac bought three suits: a dark blue, a light gray, and a blue and white striped seersucker, he thought. Dacron and cotton, said the clerk, who was full of information about exotic blends. He also bought five shirts to go with his new suits. All of them mixtures of something or other. He was particular about the collars. "I like them soft, not floppy though." The clerk displayed them against the suit coats, slapping each folded shirt down authoritatively. One was blue. Mr. Isaac accepted it. He selected five ties, stripes and small paisley prints. "No blooms. I draw the line at flowers. You're young enough for them, but I'm not, decidedly not."

He paid his bill with a check, adamantly refusing to start a charge account. Since Kate's death he'd spent money only on groceries, household bills, occasional cabs, insurance, taxes, his yearly medical examinations, and a few things for his grandchildren. He had plenty of cash. Now he wondered at his carefulness. For years, especially when the boys were growing up, thrift was a necessity. Later it was a habit. Until today, frugality was one of the ways of accepting loneliness—he'd gone on as before, looked after himself, and asked nothing from anyone. Perhaps his self-sufficiency, a characteristic he might have admired too much, had added to his isolation.

He felt at least ten years younger when he left the store carrying a bulging sack. His only regret was he couldn't have the suits until the tailor was finished with trouser alterations on Wednesday. When he got outside in the sun he glanced up at the clock on the university's tower. It was almost noon. He started to a taxi stand on the corner. A screech from a transistor radio assaulted his ears, a primitive wail from an electric guitar. Would his grandchildren, growing up with such sounds, ever have to learn how to waltz? Could he teach them to? He stepped under the projecting awning of a women's shoe store with a window displaying rainbow-colored shoes.

What color were Rose's shoes Sunday? He hadn't noticed then. He would notice next time. Waiting at the taxi stand he traced a diminutive waltz step on the pavement, an old man fidgeting, someone might have thought. Light-headed, hungry, and precariously joyful, he knew he was dancing on a street corner at high noon.

The dog nosed at the sacks, then ran under the bed and stayed. He was too deaf to hear paper crackling. Perhaps he smelled the clothes, smelled something new and fled. Everything else in the house was old. Mr. Isaac coaxed him out, fixed himself some lunch, and deviating from his usual schedule for the second time that day, went to his study to write to his sons.

*Dear Ted,*

*I received your letter dated March 17, and am delighted to know your research is going well. As for the teaching, though it is, no doubt, a strain to lecture in another language, you are to be congratulated for attempting to do so. The year in Mexico City will also be good for the children. They have probably learned a lot of Spanish by now.*

*My situation here remains much the same except an old friend Rose Davis has moved back here from France. You may not remember her. She has a son Phillip about your age. He lives in Dallas, and his daughter is living with Rose until May when she graduates from college.*

Mr. Isaac stopped. Entangled in generations. Well, out with it!

*When Melrose, the granddaughter, leaves, I am going to live with Mrs. Davis. We are both old and both live in big, empty houses. Hers is emptier than mine because she brought no furniture back from France. I will take a few pieces from here. If you and Margaret want any of this furniture, let me know, and I will have it shipped to Tulsa. It can be stored till you return. I will make the same offer to Kenneth and Sally.*

*As I do not want to worry with renters, I will sell the house.*

*Let me hear from you as soon as time allows. My best to Margaret and the children.*

*Love,*
*Father*

He read it through, carefully tore the letter into neat squares, and began again, this time neglecting the amenities:

*Dear Ted,*

*This is to let you know I'm selling the house and moving to an apartment in June. Write to me if you want any of the furniture, and I will have it shipped to Tulsa and stored there until your return. This place is far too large for one person. I'm weary of rattling around in it and tired of taking care of the yard.*

*My love to you, Margaret, and the children.*
*Father*

He could be devious if he pleased, and after all, it was none of Ted's business who he lived with. Sociologist though he was, Ted was only forty-three; he would understand his moving in with Rose as an old man's folly. And Margaret might let her children call her by her first name, yet she was a wife.

He sent approximately the same letter to Kenneth and Sally in Palo Alto. Somehow it was easier to write Ted first; probably it was because he was the farthest away, the one least likely to interfere. He did not anticipate any repercussions. Both sons were university professors. Though both had their summers free, neither liked hauling their families back to Austin to simmer there in hundred-degree heat. He'd gone to Tulsa to spend last Thanksgiving with Margaret and Ted and to Palo Alto for a surreal Christmas with Kenneth's family. When his mind was ready to accept Santa Clauses in bathing suits and the scent of roses in bloom, he'd arrived to find instead dark gray rain blowing across dark green hills and the acrid sour smell of soggy eucalyptus trees. He sat in front of a fire most of the time telling his two grandsons all he knew about cowboys and Indians. The damp wind and the boys' war whoops drove him back to Texas. Perhaps he would return for a visit in the summer. He certainly had a traveling wardrobe now, not that he could actually see himself hand-washing his clothes. The drip-dry idea was ridiculous. The sound of anything dripping, faucet or suit, would keep him awake all night.

The week passed uneventfully as usual. Then he began to wonder if Rose's invitation was serious. Suppose she often said such things capriciously?

She'd asked him. He remembered the laughter in her voice when she said, "Why not stay with me? I'll put a sign on the wall saying OLD FOLKS' HOME, and we'll sit here and be cranky together."

He demurred. He told her she ought to decide if she really wanted an old man around.

"I don't want a gigolo, and I don't want just another old lady. That might be worse than any old man. I like my sex, but I prefer to live with the opposite one. We ought to get some young people too, have a *ménage à trois* or *à quatre*."

He sat there all locked up, knowing what he wanted and too scared to say so. It was easy to write to his sons, easy to decide what to do, almost impossible to voice his decision. His existence had narrowed so—the house, the grocery, his part-time job at the museum on Saturdays. It had been a great deal wider when he was twenty-five and Rose was eighteen, when he was her professor. Now she seemed to be his teacher. Her world was less cramped, less hedged about with custom. Even her house was larger.

By Wednesday, unable to stand his own silence anymore, he called Rose.

"If I'm still welcome, I'll move to your house when Melrose leaves."

"Of course you're welcome. I need someone here, Theo."

"I would like to share expenses, and you must charge me rent, too. That's only fair."

"Why should you pay rent? The house is already paid for. You'll be staying in what would only be an empty room otherwise."

"Rose, I insist. It's a matter of pride."

"All right. But it's not like you were moving to an institution."

It took him ten minutes to calm her. Still, that was easier than the conversation he had with Kenneth Thursday night.

"Dad, what's this about moving to an apartment all of a sudden? I thought you hated apartments."

"Yes . . . well." Though he could lie on paper, it was much more difficult on the phone.

"Well, why are you moving to one?"

"For all the reasons I told you and Ted." They had been conferring. He could almost hear the sound of Ted's voice coming through the wires from Mexico City to Palo Alto. "Did you get a strange letter from Dad about selling the house?" That's what he would have said.

"Dad, are you feeling all right?"

"Except for creeping senility, I'm fine." Kenneth was inclined to pry.

"I've always liked that house." He was inclined to hold onto things, too. Kate wanted to get rid of his rock collection when he went to college. None of them were identified or labeled. They were just rocks that Kenneth happened to like the looks of. He had insisted on putting them in boxes in the attic. They were still up there with his electric train, his old yearbooks, and all the letters he'd received from girls. Did Kenneth want him to remain as custodian? Was every old person required to run a private Smithsonian containing the relics of his children's past?

"I'll ship anything you want, but you'll have to take care of the charges." Mr. Isaac had a welcome vision of movers heaving out boxes of rocks.

"No, Dad. I may want something, yes. I only meant I liked the house."

"I'm tired of it. I intend to move."

"Have you picked out an apartment? Can we help you? Sally says she'll be glad to come to Austin and—"

"I appreciate the offer, Kenneth, but Sally has enough to do. I can find an apartment. I'm looking for one now, and I can move. I'm not feeble. I'm just a little slow." He laughed. He was almost beginning to enjoy himself.

"Well, we thought being uprooted might—"

"I'm not being uprooted. I'm transplanting myself, and in the same town I've lived in for most of my life." What he really needed to say to his son finally came to him. "Don't worry, Kenneth. Even old people need a change. I'm just providing myself with one."

Mr. Isaac put the receiver down, heard a gratifying final click, and said to the night, "Whoosh!" Whirling slowly around, he stopped the swivel chair, stood up, and moved across the carpet to the light switch while humming "Tea for Two" unconsciously. Then he heard himself, and for the second time that night he laughed aloud.

Saturday Mr. Isaac wore his new gray suit to the museum. Ever since Kate's death it had been the one place he was needed. He liked going to the Ney even though all he had to do was hand out pamphlets to a few visitors, make sure they signed the book, and answer the phone. Tim, the Negro caretaker, did all the real work, and no matter what he was doing, he wore a starched white jacket. Mr. Isaac never asked him why. He guessed the jacket made Tim feel less like a janitor, or maybe it was an old-fashioned museum uniform. Tim never mentioned it, so he didn't either. They talked of other things. Some days when the quiet was too heavy for both of them they shouted through the vast rooms to each other. Tim's rich baritone and his own reedy voice swirled up and down stairs, in and out doors. Though they had worked together for only two years, Tim knew more about Mr. Isaac than some of his best friends did. Sometimes Mr. Isaac suspected that the reverse was also true.

There was Ricardo waiting for him on the front portico. The boy followed him inside as soon as he opened the door. Mr. Isaac showed no surprise. Last Saturday Ricardo had happened into the Elisabet Ney by accident when playing in the surrounding park. Once he came in, he seemed fascinated by the work—plaster casts of various European and Texas dignitaries mostly. Shabby-looking lot on the whole, laughable to eyes accustomed to Epstein and Moore; still, a nineteenth-century sculptress couldn't be denied in a state as young as Texas. Ney deserved some notice. The museum had been her home; it had become her monument. Working there every Saturday, Mr. Isaac saw that she suffered more from neglect than from derision. Few people were interested in what she'd done. They had forgotten or never learned she'd turned the mighty into stone.

Ricardo looked up at him. "My father, he says I should come with him, but I don't this morning."

"Where was your father going?" Mr. Isaac turned on the lights in the north studio.

"He goes to cut grass for people. I help him some."

"Your father does yardwork?"

The boy tensed his hands into fists and hit them together. "You got a yard?"

"I've got a friend, a lady, who needs help with her garden. There are fountains and all sorts of flowers."

"Are fish in the fountains?"

"I doubt it."

"Goldfishes eat mosquitoes."

"Do they?" How many things he didn't know still, how much Ricardo already knew—Spanish as well as English, his way all over town on a bicycle, how to rid pools of mosquitoes.

"Every fountain must have goldfishes. Next Saturday I bring my father and the fishes. Okay?"

"All right." Mr. Isaac gave him Rose's address. "I can't be there, as I have to come to the museum, but you will like Mrs. Davis."

"I like the flowers. I don't like the grass."

"Well, you can't have all flowers." Mr. Isaac turned to go upstairs and check on the latest abominations that had arrived for the art show—the directors' most recent attempt to bring people to the museum. He was stopped by a shout from Tim in the back. Mr. Isaac couldn't hear exactly what he was saying, but it was a complaint of some kind. When he was working—dusting statues, sweeping, painting, watering the lawn—he would sel-dom allow Mr. Isaac to help him. "No," he'd say, "I'm hired to do this. Besides, I'm a lot younger than you." Then he'd laugh because he was sixty-five. But he did like an audience for his troubles.

He stood with his hands on his hips before a large crate. "Look here. I got this thing to undo, and it says 'Glass, Fragile' all over it— Say, you got a new suit." Tim laid his hammer on top of the box and came over to him. "That's sure a good-looking suit."

Mr. Isaac thanked him. Foolish how a little praise from Tim made him feel so good. One new suit or three didn't make him a new person, yet praise from a kind-hearted man gave him an almost childish pleasure.

"And a new tie too!"

Tim grinned, then began prying nails out of one side of the crate. Ricardo stepped around him to the opposite side.

"You hold it steady now, and we'll find out what's in here."

Mr. Isaac left to turn on the lights in the west studio. Overcast as it was that morning, the figures all took on a ghostly appearance, especially Lady Macbeth wringing her hands in mid-air. She and Prometheus were the only literary characters Ney had attempted. Miss Ney had frozen her in the "All the perfumes of Arabia will not sweeten this little hand" scene. It wasn't a bad idea to try, but under bright light her permanent anguish seemed overwrought. Friedrich Wöhler, prominently displayed on the mantelpiece, gazed indifferently toward the tortured lady. The green streak running down one side of his lean nose only served to increase his hauteur. A German chemist, he had been one of Ney's best-known works. How he had discovered her, or exactly how the Munich Polytechnic Institute had chosen her to sculpt his head, or how the cast had arrived in Texas, Mr. Isaac didn't know. He marveled at the ability of anyone to discover anyone else. The tenuous strands connecting one person to another, how insubstantial they were, yet how tough and elastic. He had known Rose's parents, had her briefly for a student, admired her beauty and her spirit, supposed she was gone forever, and found her again.

"Mr. Isaac, come see what we got!" Ricardo was calling. "It's a box, a glass box with a pink man dancing. You
got to come see."

He didn't think he wanted to, but Ricardo kept insist-
ing, so he went out to them.

Tim was laughing. "I don't know. I don't know why
he—"

Ricardo jumped up and down as excited as if it was a
gift he'd just opened.

A square glass box firmly attached to an iron stand and
on two sides pictures of a Negro man—pink. At right
angles on the other two sides the man was reflected in
bright green. Mr. Isaac didn't know what to think. He'd
never confronted anything like it.

"Whoo-ee!" Tim shook with laughter. "That fellow's
colorblind all right." He was sitting on part of the crate,
his head thrown back.

"I like the colors," Ricardo said.

"So do I, boy."

Mr. Isaac stopped frowning over the box and looked at
them, the Negro man in his white jacket, white on black,
the Mexican child, his yellow tee shirt against his light
brown skin, himself, a gray on white. Then he looked
again at the pink and green Negro dancing. It didn't
matter. Their color didn't. He had never believed it
would matter in the end, someday after all the suffering
was over, when the wars were fought, the marches
finished. Sometime . . . years after he was gone, a man's
color would no longer determine his life, but this artist
broke the barriers now, broke them laughing.

"He managed to get it here just in time. They will
judge the pictures this afternoon."

"Do you think he'll win?" Tim asked.

Mr. Isaac agreed that "Man Dancing" should win. He and Ricardo stayed past closing hours that afternoon waiting for the jury to decide. They promised to call Tim, though he said his phone was "on vacation," which meant he hadn't been able to pay his bill. The phone went on vacation often.

"You can call next door. Those people will get hold of me."

Mr. Isaac started to offer to pay Tim's bill then checked himself. He'd offered before, and Tim said he'd rather owe Bell Telephone than anyone else he knew.

The jury arrived at five and spent an hour and forty-five minutes making up their minds. There were three judges; a young man who was head of the art department of a nearby Catholic college, a woman painter of some distinction who lived in Austin, and a museum director from San Antonio. Mr. Isaac would have liked to have heard every word they said. The temptation to eavesdrop was so great he confined himself to Miss Ney's old kitchen in the basement, where he made himself a cup of tea. As soon as it was ready, he escaped into the adjoining dining room. Perhaps it was cheerful when a fire was burning. Now it was simply cold and empty. Stone walls with tiny barred windows at ground level might have made Miss Ney feel safe. He felt imprisoned and was glad Ricardo kept running down from his post at the bottom of the stairwell to repeat muddled phrases and impressions.

"Somebody, the San Antonio man, I think, says, 'Not much!' The lady she likes the picture of the old tire. The other man walks around and around."

Mr. Isaac sighed. He was as impatient as Ricardo. They met the jury at the bottom of the stairs. "Man Dancing" won first. The depressing picture of a flat tire was second, and a still life of some lemons was chosen third.

They dialed Tim's neighbor, who went to get him. When he came to the phone he spoke first to Ricardo, who reported, "He says he don't believe us. I told him 'Man Dancing' won, and he says, 'How could a pink nigger win?'"

"Ricardo's right, Tim," Mr. Isaac shouted, then took the receiver. "He's right." Tim was saying something to his neighbor.

"He thinks I'm crazy, Mr. I. He don't understand about that picture. I been trying to tell him—"

"It did win."

"How much does it cost? I wish I could remember. I never saw a picture I wanted to buy in my life, but I sure would like to buy that one."

"Three hundred and fifty dollars, I think."

"Humph! That's more than I owe Bell Telephone."

"Perhaps the museum will buy it. Sometimes galleries keep permanent collections of pictures just as we have Miss Ney's things."

"Well, it's her place. I don't see no pink black man getting in there for good." Tim's voice was mournful.

"You can never tell what they'll decide to do here next."

"That's true, Mr. I."

Before he left Mr. Isaac put an envelope containing a check for $350 and a note saying he wished to remain anonymous in the Voluntary Contributions box by the door. On front of the envelope he wrote: "For the Museum's Purchase of 'Man Dancing.'" He did it for himself as much as for Tim. It was peculiarly satisfying to be an anonymous benefactor. It would have been more practical to give Tim the money. He wouldn't have taken it as a gift, and if he had, his conscience and his wife wouldn't have allowed him to spend it on a picture. Three hundred and fifty dollars would have gone to the telephone company, to doctors, to department stores. He and Tim needed the picture more than any of those people needed their money. It was the first modern thing that either one of them had liked. He debated about telling Rose and decided against it. Better to remain completely anonymous, to have a private joy, much more rewarding than a private sorrow.

He would see her that evening. "My Fair Lady" was showing at one of the theaters near the university and within easy walking distance of her house. It was her idea, the first time she'd been to a movie since returning to the states. He couldn't remember the last time he'd been. He used to take Kate to musicals. She liked them. He didn't particularly because most of them seemed vapid. Since "My Fair Lady" was based on one of Shaw's plays it should contain enough of the original vitriol to be amusing.

He found he'd worried needlessly about amusing Rose. As a returned expatriate she found novelties everywhere. After years of walking about Paris, she could not make up her mind if she missed the surge of traffic or not.

"It's so calm," was her first reaction. Then, "Maybe it's too calm. I miss the feeling of achievement after crossing a street."

They cut through a small park near her house, and she wondered at the lack of chairs. Twilight drew in around them.

"It doesn't last long here. I'd forgotten. In Paris the spring and summer evenings are much longer. There's no gabble of conversation in the streets, only me complaining like the French do when they're in another country. Oh, I have become hard to please!"

Walking down Guadalupe she could not help but notice that houses had been replaced by cheap restaurants and small businesses. A giant figure of a man in a red shirt and blue trousers, his feet planted wide apart, glared at them from the roof of an open-walled shed. A sign stuck in the asphalt read, "Car Wash." The man, twice as large as the building he straddled, had a square-jawed smile more forbidding than beckoning.

"Even if I had a car I'd never drive it in there!" She tilted her head back and stared up. "He makes me feel like a pigmy! Isn't that the most terrible smile."

"Yes, but you should see some of the other figures around town. There's a monstrous termite that revolves twenty feet above the corner of Enfield and Lamar, and on Congress there's a grotesque steer, also turning. Every time I go past it I hope a small boy with a B-B gun will use it for a target." Ricardo might do it. No, it wasn't a thing to suggest to a child, destruction of property. English common law had made respect for private property a virtue, and Adam Smith had justified free enterprise by defining it. No point in taking up a B-B gun against all of that. He sighed quietly. Rose heard him anyway.

"Why, Theo, what's the matter?"

"I was plotting the overthrow of the government."

"What's the first thing you'd do?"

"Oh, I don't know. I was thinking I'd send out bands of young boys to shoot holes in things . . . a sort of old grouch's program."

"I don't know what I'd do myself. I lived through most of the fourth Republic and the return of de Gaulle. I couldn't help but think of him as a nation saver. Generally I'm in a muddle about politics. Thomas used to try to comfort me by saying no one made as great a muddle as the French. He was in England during most of World War II as a member of de Gaulle's army. Sometimes his point of view was rather English."

Thomas . . . so that was his name. When he saw her again for the first time he'd asked what she'd done all those years abroad. She'd answered in her direct way, "I lived with a man I loved. He's dead now, and I've come home." But why had she chosen to speak of Thomas now? Maybe it was because they had been talking about politics. No matter. She had to say something about him eventually. There was no canceling out those years. His familiarity with grief made him certain of hers. It took people at the strangest times, with no warning. You could be looking at a kitchen door or walking down a street. Memory keeps no hours.

Rose turned her head to stare at the passing cars, but she refused to cry. In a moment she looked over at him and said in her normal voice, "I'm sure I'm insufferable, complaining about America so. Some days I think I have too much to remember."

Mr. Isaac smiled. "Better too many memories than too few."

The entrance to the theater was flooded with light.

Posters advertising "My Fair Lady" promised song, dance, romance while intimating gaiety, renewal, forgetfulness. Mr. Isaac, collecting his change from the ticket seller, looked down at Rose's shoes beside his. They were pink, pink as the flowering peach blossoms in bloom now. Yes, of course, they matched her dress. What marvelous frivolity! Forgetting his timidity, he took her arm and guided her through the door to the lobby as if he were leading her into a grand ballroom.

# Stalking Strangers

1) THE RANCH

There's no one here but me, as I requested. Though my parents own the place, they stay in town and come out only on weekends. My mother inherited what was left of this ranch after her brother, Watson, drank most of it up. Uncle Watson celebrated his birthday any day he pleased; the older he got the more often he celebrated. His final two-week party ended at the Cadillac Bar in Nuevo Laredo, where, we were told, he was chasing tequila with tequila. My father says Watson never went on a cheap spree or a lonely one. At least forty-five guests joined him on the last. None of them made it to the funeral, an oversight that embittered Mother.

"I guess they would rather remember him like he was," Father volunteered and immediately wished he hadn't. Even though he is a judge, he tends to be conciliatory in family matters.

"Forever drunk!" Mother sputtered. He was her only brother and she loved him.

His house has become a sort of shrine, a place where my family's past is collected. Uncle Watson's gun and spurs hang over the living room mantel next to Grandpa's. My grandmother's best silk fan, spread open like a peacock's tail, is framed on one wall. We poke the fire with Uncle Watson's old branding iron and put our feet up on what used to be the parlor furniture, now cheerfully covered in a flamboyant print—Mother prefers tiger lilies to plum-colored plush.

Everyone in my family is a keeper. We discriminate, however. No one clings to an old toaster or saves empty coffee cans. Currently we're working our way through my brother Jack's matchbook collection, useful for lighting all three fires. Mother, as curator, gets to make most of the choices. I suspect she is still hiding my Shirley Temple doll in an attic somewhere. After seeing one of Sweetie Cutie's movies, she came home to tie up my straight hair in rags—knots at night, kinks in the morning. When Shirley T. was given to me on my sixth birthday, I cut off two of her sausage curls with the fingernail scissors before I was caught. My sister Cicily tried to throw away her tea set when she was thirteen. She said she'd outgrown tea parties. Mother rescued that also. Jack's daughter plays with it when she visits; hours go by while she stirs sugar water into blue willow patterned cups and we pretend to drink. My father can't part with his hats. He vows they become a part of him; after a year or so each one is an extension of his personality. They hang, like a group of premature ghosts, from the deer antlers lining the hallway. Anyone else is allowed to wear one as long as the hat's returned. Mother got rid of the doe's head Watson had stuffed. She despises stuffed animals. The doe used to hang on one side of the fireplace balanced by a buck's head on the other. When Uncle Watson was alive, Cicily and I threatened to give him a HIS and HERS sign to put under each head. I don't know what Mother did with the doe. The buck collects dust in Jack's garage. It's in a season of perpetual molt. Jack says he keeps it to remind him of Uncle Watson, a peculiar memorial I once thought, then changed my mind. How could I find Jack's choice peculiar when I've kept every postcard Henry ever sent me? And most of them show the same picture, an Indian woman selling beads on the porch of the governor's palace in Santa Fe. It's the same Indian, too.

## 2) PREOCCUPATIONS

Of course one ought not ever to let something like this happen. It is avoidable. You can cloister yourself in a library (keep your eyes on the books), in an office (there's always overwork), at home (don't answer the door or phone). The cloister isn't really necessary. As hard as it is to meet your heart's desire in this country of strangers (see the classifieds) it ought to be almost impossible for anyone over college age to fall in love. But it isn't. Uncle Watson, at sixty-three, fell for a sixty-two-year-old woman he met at a country dance. He waltzed all over Texas with Charlotte and married her when he was sixty-four. She divorced him the next year after discovering that he was too falling down drunk to two-step one Saturday night. The family has always referred to Charlotte as "the dancer." When she left, Uncle Watson had an excuse for alcoholism for the first time in his life.

He's not a good example, though our trouble is somewhat the same. Henry and I met on a ski slope when I was thirty-six, fresh from a disastrous marriage. Almost four years later I'm looking back at an equally disastrous love affair. Like Charlotte, I was the one who walked out. After a long, uncomfortable silence I left Henry standing in the doorway of his two-hundred-year-old adobe hacienda in Santa Fe, walked right out fully clothed and coated into the snowy night. Because he wouldn't say anything. Try a long silence with a tall, dark-headed, obsidian-eyed man. Intense? Yes. What's to be done when you've told him you love him and he won't answer in kind? What I did, what I'm doing. Go away. Forget.

What are the ways of forgetting?

A new scene. Provided.

Work. Unfortunately this is my vacation time, which I usually spend with Henry. I close my crafts shop every January. My customers, having exhausted themselves by December, disappear in clouds of glitter and trails of beads. I have projects, however. There's always something you can do no matter how much you don't want to do it. Uncle Watson shot at empty bottles he lined up on the porch railing for a month after Charlotte left. Ordinarily I wouldn't classify this as work, but it was difficult for Watson to balance a bottle on a rail, hard for him to hold a pistol, and harder for him to sight it. We are still picking up the shards.

Music. Keep it loud. Try not to play anything you like; you'll hate it later. I prefer classical. Right now my radio's dial is set on a country-western station, where I hear a continual howl about love lost. It suits me fine, although I'm hoping to weary of this theme any day.

Willpower. This is the most tiresome one, since it involves thinking about not thinking. Do-it-yourself brainwashing. I have to give up murmuring "Henry" to the dumb pillow every night, to the unfeeling sun every morning. Goodnight, moon. Hello, morning. Henry has got to be moved out of my head. He's taking up altogether too much room there. It's time to concentrate on someone else.

3) PINKY

Down by the east entrance gate, Pinky, the foreman, and his wife, Jane, live. As a child I invented reasons for his name; because he crooks his little finger when he drinks coffee, because he's been bald and pink-headed since he was thirty, because he sunburns easily. None of these is correct. My father, who takes true delight in other people's peculiarities, gave me the whole obscure explanation: Pinky, originally named Sam, would come by the house every morning to confer with Watson. Like most of my mother's people, Uncle Watson was bad-tempered early in the day. In an attempt to be civil, however, he always asked Sam how he felt. The unvarying reply was, "Oh, I'm in the pink . . . in the pink!" Watson remained stoic about his foreman's good humor and health until the morning after one of his birthday parties.

"In the pink! Never in the red! Never feeling green! Never blue!" He roared.

"Never!" Sam roared back.

"It's Pinky from now on then!"

And so it was.

In Uncle Watson's early days, when he had more land and cattle, Pinky was a real foreman. Since the place has shriveled to five hundred acres, it'll support only thirty cows. Pinky, grizzled and sagacious, says, "It's a toy ranch." We've never pretended otherwise, but he has memories of a more glorious past which annoy my parents. His good old days were the ones when Uncle Watson was drinking up three thousand acres. "He was a fine fellow, drunk or sober," says Pinky, sounding like a vassal to the last of the cattle barons. Though Jane is devoted to her husband, she never lets him get away with this. She insists, "Watson was finer when he was sober."

Our conversations are brief and as wide-spaced as the valleys around here are. I left Austin's hill country and drove northwest to the edge of central Texas, where mesas stretch out like immense flat fingers and valleys lie between. You can see a long way, further than some people want to. Most of the land has been cleared of cedar, leaving live oak trees in clumps. My companions are armadillos, jackrabbits, wild turkeys, hawks, buzzards, who like to ride the air currents over the canyons, and deer. Snakes, including rattlers, are all denned up waiting until a warmer day to crawl out and strike. Pinky has warned me to look out for poachers. It's still deer season, and we've already lost one cow to hunters.

"Couldn't they tell the difference?" I never have understood this kind of confusion.

"Some people can tell the difference between deer eyes and cow eyes in the dark, but poachers don't look too good. Now I got to call the rendering plant to come haul off this registered Hereford, a five-hundred-dollar animal worth exactly minus one dollar and fifty cents you'll have to pay to get her carted off."

"Pinky, why didn't they take the cow when they shot her?"

"Mar-gar-et!" He wants to ask why I don't know a damn thing, but he's soaked in the code of Western politeness and spares me. Later he'll go home and tell Jane, "Margaret don't know a damn thing about ranching."

"First of all, a dead cow weighs about a thousand pounds and ain't easy to carry. Second, she's got your Pa's brand on her. Those boys can gut a deer, but they don't know nothing about butchering a cow, and if they turn up at the meat locker with her wearing that brand they'll get put in jail for rustling."

"Do you know who they are?"

"Sure. Worthless sons—"

"Can't the sheriff—?"

"Him? He's not going to do a damn thing. You can't get the sheriff to come sit out in the pasture all night, nor the game warden neither. Not a one of them is worth the chairs they sit in all day long. What you got to do is catch poachers with the blood still on them. You tie them up and take them in to the sheriff, deliver them like a Christmas present. Your Uncle Watson did that once, took a feller in with a red bow tied around his neck."

Pinky stomps off, leaving me looking at one of the ridges, half expecting to see a white hat appear on the horizon, a glimpse of the figure of Uncle Watson drunk in the saddle, carrying a six-shooter in one hand, a spool of red ribbon in the other.

This apparition doesn't appear, so I begin to be extra conscious of sounds. Toward the end of the week I struggle out of a deep sleep before sun-up, listening to a rhythmic grinding. Gears? Someone can't get a car started? Triggers catching on rifles? I glare out the window at three cows chomping grass just on the other side of the fence. Poachers would have to be riding cows before I could catch them.

### 4) WHAT I DO ALL DAY

I pick up stuff—rusty license plates, square-headed nails, scraps of leather, bird feathers, fossils, bottoms of broken bottles, stones, dried pods, doorknobs, cracked saucers, bleached animal skulls, lids of pots, marbles, hinges, old painted metal boxes, buttons, parts from old cars, worn-out frying pans, faded photographs, warped records. The photos and records I find in the ranch house attic; the rest comes from the gullies where people have been dumping trash for generations—all are objects that nature hasn't assimilated and man has forgotten. I pound, glue, shape everything on weathered wood or in recessed panels of wind-stained doors. Decorators buy them, call them "ensembles," and sell them for twice the price. People see them at my crafts shop.

"What is this?"

"Rescued junk."

They pay me two and three hundred dollars a panel. I'd make them whether anyone paid or not. Once I took a small piece to Santa Fe to show Henry. (These references to Henry are unavoidable. Though I am in the process of exorcising him from my memory, traces still remain.) "Found art," he said. Like every artist he'd known, Henry assured me, I was a striver after perfection who detested loss.

"I like to pound and glue."

"I'd like to have a show for you at the gallery."

I declined on the grounds that (1) my shipping bill would be prohibitive, (2) someone has to make a distinction between art and craft, and (3) if no one else will, I will. Mine is craft.

I also read, listen to music, ride horseback, and look at the country. Sometimes I think about Henry; most of the time I try not to. Trying not to think about Henry has become a discipline like trying not to drink too much or remembering to brush your teeth after lunch. Isn't it dull in the country? Oh no! When your life has been too crowded with your own disasters, a few weeks of solitude are a luxury. My parents know this and don't interrupt. My friends don't know where I am; Pinky and Jane have a history of keeping to themselves. I run into Pinky at the tack room by the barn sometimes. There's only one thing I do that irritates him to the talking point: I ride English-style. Mother sent me to a posh girls' camp in Virginia two summers—she gave it up because she couldn't live with the accent I affected when I got home. My *a*'s were flattened out and I liked to say "crick" a lot. Pinky, knowing nothing about girls' camps anywhere, scorns them as places that teach you how to be even more effete. An English saddle, to him, is nothing but a postage stamp, an utterly worthless piece of equipment. If I say I'm not going to round up cows or rope calves and have no need of a saddle horn, Pinky gives mournful warning, "You'll fall off that thing and bust your head."

"If I do fall, I won't be dragged to death. Look, the stirrup is designed to come off with the rider."

"Who wants a saddle without stirrups? Might as well go bareback."

"It's a lot more comfortable than a western saddle, Pinky. You have to sit up straight, so your back doesn't get tired. And you can post."

"Not me. I'm not going 'round shoving daylight between my legs, bouncing up and down like a jackrabbit."

"You don't bounce. You rise."

"You do it. Not me."

"Pinky, I bet you couldn't stay on an English saddle."

"I'm too old and too smart to try that."

It's a quarrel we have two or three times a year. The lines remain the same; so do the reasons. For me a horse is to be used for pleasure, while for Pinky they're work animals; anybody who gets on one just to ride is a time-waster and probably a sinner. He doesn't say so, but beneath my khaki-colored jodhpurs and plaid shirt, I'm wearing, he believes, black silk stockings with my high black boots. Pinky is stuck with the old cowhand's view of women. They're either ladies or whores. Ladies, like Jane, stay home with their aprons on. While I, though he's known me from childhood, have grown up to be a dance-hall girl. Oh, he wouldn't say so, would barely think it, but his categories were set up so many years ago, there's no way of wiping them out.

Old West is stamped on him. He still remembers roundups, trail drives, the arrival of the railroad, and his first automobile ride. And he still does things the way they used to be done. When it's branding time he uses two fires and two irons. Irons heated in beds of coals make clearer brands than those heated over a portable butane stove. He skins then carefully tans the hide of any animal he kills. Jane's dining table is surrounded by chairs with rawhide seats. He knows many curious facts about animal life. If you'd care to know, Pinky can tell you all the reasons why a cow will abort. Copperhead snakes are generally found under piles of metal, even in the summer. They like the heat. During a norther, sheep will huddle together for warmth until they suffocate themselves. Pinky doesn't think much of sheep. He has a keen eye for wildlife. "Saw two bobcats in the west pasture this morning," he reports, then adds, just in case you aren't sure he knows what he's talking about, "You know a feral cat and a bobcat runs different. A feral cat slinks off and a bobcat humps his rump when he runs." Other times he'll comment more laconically, "Wild turkey tracks down by the tank."

All his days are spent outside, where, according to his view of life, everything's happening.

## 5) TEA TIME

I have no doubts about the reason why the English take tea at 4 P.M. and 5 P.M. is the American cocktail hour. It's the lonesome time of day when light fades into darkness. Even with a good fire going and a hot toddy in hand—there's something about being in the country in winter that brings on a desire for hot whiskey drinks—I begin to wonder if I'm too completely removed from the rest of the world. Here I've isolated myself in the middle of a pasture while somewhere over the next two or three mesas people are singing, dancing, going to concerts, popping out to the movies, dressing for the theatre.

I summon Pop Sigh, my old companion who floats about in the atmosphere wearing a pin-striped suit,

pointy-toed European shoes, and white socks. He's pre-
dictable enough to be comfortable, outrageous enough to
be entertaining.

"Ah hah! You haf der boots on again. So much horse
riding is an expression of sexual unhappiness. You know
zis?"

"My riding is only riding. If you don't quit that sil-
liness I'm going to send you over to Pinky's. Now there's
a man you'd be interested in."

"Maybe. Now ve speak of you. Vat happens to bring
you to zis vilderness? Ze last time you vas in Austin. Before zat, Santa Fe. You vas splitting from Henry mit suitcase in hand. A cold night it vas too. Snow! Vow!"

He can't help himself. He has an excessive apprecia-
tion of "American expressions."

"I thought I wanted to get away from everything
awhile. Where have you been lately?"

"Everywhere. I spoke to your sister in London last
week. She has a small crisis. She vants to become an English person. She says a Texas woman in London is a resi-
dent anomaly. Everybody tries to speak to her about Indians. I told her she should enjoy zis."

"Cicily doesn't know anything about Indians. Neither
do I. They'd all been shuffled off to Oklahoma by the
time we arrived. You have to go to libraries and do research if you want to find out about Indians."

"You sound like her. A great complainer."

"You gave her bad advice, Pop. Cicily went to school
at Wellesley, married, and left. She hasn't really lived in
Texas since she was seventeen."

"Her formative years—"

"Never mind about that! You probably told her to send home for her cowboy boots. She never had any."

"You think she should pass as an English?"

"Why not? If she wants a disguise, let her have it. Other people choose their masks—Creoles become Mexicans, Mexicans become Anglos, Anglos pass as Indians, Indians pass as Creoles. Catholics become Protestants, Protestants become Jews, and vice versa in each case. Why shouldn't a Texan become English? That's minor compared to changing race or religion."

"Zat is a valid rationalization. One must get at ze root of ze problem."

"Why bother? It'll take years, and once you have the truth in hand, Cicily may still want to be another nationality. It's a harmless preoccupation, a small crisis, as you say."

Pop crosses his leg over his knee, pulls up one white sock, and sips the toddy I've fixed him. "You are irrational."

"Don't be rude."

"But zat is ze truth."

"No. It is your truth, not the truth. One more statement like that and you'll find yourself on the lone prairie in the midst of this howling wind."

"I vanted to ask if you vere afflicted vith ghosts."

He calls me crazy, yet he has this muddle-headed belief in ghosts. "No, it's only the wind whistling through the front porch."

"I vill see."

He steps outside, bangs the door, and walks the length of the porch. The wind's tone has changed to a scream. I run out to close the shutters, which are already beginning to rattle against the house. Across the front yard I see Pop veering toward the water tank. Before I can shout a warning, he's picked up and whirled away by a small tornado, which has already mangled the windmill. I shouldn't have asked him out here. A Texas ranch is the home of pragmatists; the weather is too violent for theorists.

6) Dead of Night

Is another tornado beating down the front door? I get out of bed to see. Pop Sigh, that figment of the collective imagination, can survive a high wind easily, but I would be unraveled. Throwing on a robe, I head out the back door to the storm cellar. A voice whips around the house corner calling my name. Awake now, I go through the hall and open the front door. At the same time, the back door slams to with a loud cr-ack.

"What is it, Pinky?"

"Poacher in the west pasture. I been by and spotted him. Get your clothes on. Hurry!" One minute I'm a dance-hall girl, the next I'm a stand-in for a righteous landowner soberly protecting property. Pinky doesn't mind switching my roles. I pull on a pair of jeans, a dark sweater, and wonder if I'm going to have to wear a cowboy hat too.

"He may get another one of them Herefords. Come on now. We got to go. Get a gun."

"I don't have a gun."

"Get Watson's." He lifts Uncle Watson's dusty rifle from its rack over the fireplace.

"I'm not going to shoot anybody."

"You don't even have to load it, Margaret. Just carry it. There's got to be two of us even if I get the drop on him. The more there is of us, the quicker he'll give up."

All of this is explained in a pickup jolting up a road over the mesa and down a gulch to the west pasture. Pinky repeats everything. It's about 3 A.M., the hour of the wolf in Comanche time, the hour of the true loony on my personal clock. You have to be obsessed to get up and do anything at three in the morning.

"We're going to park her here now and sneak up on him. I got this big flashlight." Pinky props Uncle Watson's rifle under my arm. I can feel the cool barrel through my jeans. I don't move from the truck.

"What if he shoots us?"

"He ain't going to know we're here."

"But, Pinky, if he's shooting at deer and hitting cows, what's to keep him from hitting us?"

"We're going to get the drop on him. I told you."

"I don't believe I want to. What if there're two of them?"

"There ain't but one. I seen him. He left his car by the gate. Dern fool. Didn't even hide his car. Comes on somebody's place to shoot it up and don't have snake sense."

I look out the pickup window at what seems to be the blackest night in the world—when it's dark in the country, it's truly dark—wondering why Pinky didn't get Jane to come on this loony hunt with him. In a minute I know why. She wouldn't. Jane has an old-fashioned belief in the necessity of sleep, one I share. Pinky doesn't know I have any of the old-fashioned beliefs. To him, I'm the younger generation, one capable of all sorts of aberrations. This idea makes me even more stubborn.

"Come on, Margaret. What are you setting there for?"

"I'm not going to carry this gun."

"All right. You can carry the flashlight then. I never seen anybody so balky."

We leave the pickup at the bottom of the gulch and play Indian, tiptoeing through a grove of walnut trees. Just at the edge Pinky holds up his hand.

"Over there in that old goat shed. That's where he's staked out."

That shed has been abandoned so long it's roofless. One rock wall is down and the other three are crumbling; high grass grows inside. It's not much of a deer blind though, because you can see out only one side. I don't mention this to Pinky because he's already creeping around toward the lowest wall. I'm to count to fifty, then join forces with the flashlight. The moon, which was out when I went to bed, has moved over the hills. I'm glad for the dark now. If I can't see too well, neither can the poacher. I hope he's given up and gone home, but doubt it, as hunters like to wait till deer begin browsing at first light. I run up behind Pinky, who's holding his gun on something, a shape I can't make out. Both of us are leaning over the jagged edge of the broken back wall. I flick on the light. It's a man curled up asleep in a dark blue mummy bag. The top is pulled around his head. He may be dumb enough to leave his car in plain sight, but he's not so foolish as to waste an entire night hunting.

Pinky shakes his head in disgust.

The man rolls over, flings open the sleeping bag, and, in one motion, draws out a pistol.

"By God!" says Pinky. "We have got the drop on you."

I slump against the wall laughing. "Henry, what are you doing sleeping out here in our pasture? Pinky, put your gun down."

"Does he have permission to hunt here?"

"I'm not hunting anybody but Margaret, and if she wasn't so damn hard to find, I wouldn't be here." Henry yawns, stretches, and lays his pistol on the grass.

Pinky hasn't lowered his rifle yet. I'm tempted to let him haul Henry into town to the sheriff. A night in jail would partially repay me for his hard-heartedness. No man ought to let the woman who loves him march out in the middle of a snowy night carrying her suitcase even if she has decided she ought to leave. I ought either to let Henry lie out here on the wet grass with his cold pistol or let Pinky have the pleasure of waking up the sheriff. But I'm not as mean as I ought to be. I insist Henry and I will drive to the house in his car.

"You mean he is a friend of yours?"

"Yes, Pinky." I nod when I should be shaking my head. Though he's been my lover for four years, I wonder if I know Henry at all. When people part after one of those it's-too-painful-to-stick-around-anymore quarrels, they become strangers. For the past two weeks Henry has been slowly becoming a figure—the man who wouldn't love me—framed in a doorway. Now he's jumped out of that frame. Has he driven down from Santa Fe? Why is he here? He looks at me as though he has every right to be here.

"Well, how come he's sleeping out here in the pasture?" Pinky echoes my own questions.

Henry says, "I got directions from Mrs. Stafford, but I got—"

"Never mind. I already know you got lost trying to follow any directions Clara Stafford gave. She should've sent you to the east gate and sent you west instead. A grown woman and still she don't know east from west. Don't know left from right half the time till she gets out of the car and throws a rock. I don't know what she does when she's in a city. Next time just ask Margaret's daddy for instructions. Go downtown, ask for the judge. Everybody knows him." With this, Pinky tucks his rifle under one arm and starts toward his pickup.

"Holler if you need me, Margaret. I can't say I'll hear you, but you can holler."

"All right."

"And tell your friend pastures round here ain't safe for sleeping." He slouches off, irascible as ever, the morning star shining above his weather-stained old hat. Out of the ground mist, it seems to me, the shade of Uncle Watson rises and lurches beside him, one arm thrown around Pinky's shoulder.

I turn to Henry. "Howdy, stranger."

# The Last Of It

 IF SHE MOVED to town it was going to cause a lot of talk. Let them talk, Maggie Ingram thought savagely. Let them say what they please. I'm an old woman and I have a right— age gives anyone the right to do what they want to do. There was no one else who knew the truth except Clara Stewart maybe. She had never known exactly how much Clara knew. After Felix shot James Stewart and tied him on his saddle, the horse carried him home; past that she didn't know what had happened. James was dead then and Felix died when he was seventy, so there was no one alive now who knew the whole story but herself, and she didn't know the last of it. She didn't know how Clara took it or what had happened to the children or even where James was buried.

She was too old to worry about talk. She wasn't going to worry about that any more than she was going to worry about the gate sagging or the windmill leaking. She'd gotten worn out looking at television alone; all those faces flickering on the screen were no more real to her than people she saw in her dreams. She wanted a sidewalk again and real people passing by. She'd stayed out at the ranch long enough, exiled—done it herself, but exiled nevertheless—for forty-five years to a garden, a clothesline, and the land surrounding her, allowed to go to town once every two weeks, another self-imposed restraint. Every second Saturday she drove to Leon and got lost in the crowd of country people, though she was not country, had not been. The only child of Waldron and Sally English, she had been raised in Leon.

The day after she was seventy Maggie Ingram got in her car and drove to Leon, sixteen miles from the ranch, nothing to it in a car, but a ways for a man to ride on horseback, sixteen miles out and sixteen miles back— a ways.

When she got to the top of the last hill where the road went swooping down to the middle of town she could see most of Leon before her. There was the courthouse— always looked like a wedding cake to her—tier on tier for three stories with the dome and figure of Justice on top. Around the courthouse were stores, then houses spread till they were bound by the river on three sides. The road she was on ran straight through town north to the nearest city, Waco, forty miles away. Maggie proved to herself she could still drive around the square without hitting anybody, and while she was doing it she had a minute to look up at the statue of Justice. Wind had jarred the scales out of balance not long after the blind silver-gilded woman with the silver sword at her side had been hoisted to the dome. The scales swung round and round in Justice's right hand like a weather cock, dipping and turning with the breeze. From the dip and tilt of the scales at that moment, Mrs. Ingram judged the wind was coming from the south.

She drove on down Main Street till the town dribbled out at the edges. Giving a left signal smartly with her arm—she never did trust those little blinking lights simply because she never did remember to watch for them herself—she turned into Aaron Smith's Used Cars.

Aaron came out of his tin shack head-first, his neck bent in a hang-dog droop from his shoulders. He was the only Jew in Leon and he'd tried to hide it by changing his last name, thinking, probably, Smith was a better name for the used car trade than Stein. He could have named himself Washington for all the difference it made. The slant of his neck repeated the crook in his nose. Every time she saw him Mrs. Ingram had to check herself from saying, "Aaron, hold your head up." He should have been proud to be the only one.

"Aaron, I'm too old to drive anymore. What'll you give me for this car driven by a sweet old widow woman back and forth to Leon for the past three years?"

"What model is it?" Aaron bent his neck further as if he were looking for the date the car was made under the front bumper.

"I just told you. It's three years old and I've never driven it anywhere but to town and back to the ranch."

"Pretty far," said Aaron.

"Thirty-two miles every two weeks and the road is a sight better than it used to be."

Aaron jerked his neck up. "You moving to town, Mrs. Ingram?"

"You in the used car business or the real estate business?"

"Cars, Mrs. Ingram."

"Well, take this one off my hands."

Aaron took the car and while he was writing her a check, Mrs. Ingram called Kinard's Cabs. Jerry Kinard, the oldest of the three boys, arrived in their newest cab. Old man Kinard was so lazy he'd had every one of his boys driving by the time they were fourteen. Jerry was forty-some-odd now, and he still had a mop of greasy black hair piled on his head and sideburns running down his face, a drugstore cowboy riding a Yellow Cab. He'd never amount to anything.

"Where you want to go, Mrs. Ingram, back out to the ranch?"

"What are you up to, Jerry, mind reading or taxi driving?"

"Taxi driving," sighed Jerry and gave Aaron a wink.

"Just drive on downtown and I'll tell you where to stop."

Jerry let her out at the bank, where she deposited Aaron's check and got a key from her safety deposit box. While she was still hidden in the bank vault, she pulled an old sunbonnet out of her purse and put it on. After she'd tied the strings under her chin, she took out a pair of sunglasses like celebrities wore on TV. Lord, it was dark! Scrambling through her purse once more, she found her compact. There, she thought, when all she could see was her nose and mouth in the mirror, Clara Stewart herself wouldn't know it was me! What was it down at the bottom of the right lens getting in her way? She removed the glasses and saw the price tag, $5.49, still glued on front. By wetting her finger with the tip of her tongue, then wetting the price tag with her finger, she finally scratched it off. Settling the glasses over her nose, she started out through the bank's side door. From this point on she would walk.

"Morning, Mrs. Ingram," said somebody to her departing back, one of the tellers maybe. It didn't matter, she assured herself, they knew her at the bank and at some of the stores, but most people wouldn't recognize her at all. Many she'd known were gone, dead or moved off; strangers moved in to take their places and there were generations of new children around. How would they identify her? Probably they couldn't, but they might have heard the tale about her and James Stewart and how one day his horse brought him home dead. Felix never stood trial for it because the law in Texas said he had the right to kill a man in bed with his wife. Never mind! Let them tell the children. Some of them might not marry to spite as she had done. She'd known it at the time, had known it on her wedding day and done it anyway—walked down the aisle smiling a sure, composed smile at Felix waiting at the altar, wishing all the time James was there to see her. Felix was about the same height as James, but dark everywhere James was light; dark-headed, brown-eyed, heavy on his feet. James danced up the steps when he came to see her. Felix put his feet down so slowly all the boards creaked with his weight. At first she was a little afraid of him—he took up so much room every place he entered seemed diminished by his presence, or was it only his darkness outlining him so definitely? He courted her for almost two years. Her mother said she was lucky to have another man turn up so soon after James left, especially Felix Ingram. He was five years older than Maggie and a steady man, held to one place by the ranch he owned. All he knew about James was he'd courted her and left. Apparently, this was all he cared to know. Ah, she stopped herself, she'd gone over her memories too often, mulled over them till they were frayed at the edges, picked and fondled them as a child does her favorite doll. Ah, who cares now anyway? Nobody but me and Clara.

She stopped and untied the sunbonnet, the wrong hat to wear on Main Street. The only place she'd ever worn it was out in her vegetable garden. Even if she had lived in the country since she was twenty-five, she knew what the fashions were in town. She had an eye for those things. On her trips into Leon she'd notice what the other women wore, how they'd shortened their skirts and went without hats, without gloves too. She went home to hem up all the skirts on all the dresses she'd made—couldn't afford the luxury of store-bought clothes when Felix was alive, didn't intend to start dressing fancy after he was dead.

Mrs. Ingram stuffed the bonnet in her purse, and without glancing around to see who was watching, she pulled off her sunglasses and threw them in the gutter. There weren't many people walking; most of them seemed to be in cars. She passed three little girls, all of them giggling and chewing gum with their mouths open, and there was a woman about her age pushing a two-wheeled wire cart with sacks of groceries on it. Mrs. Ingram studied her from across the street. No, it wasn't Clara. The cart was handy for carrying groceries, though. She might get one herself. She continued on down the street to the Baptist Church where she was married, turned east, walked two blocks, and turned again onto Pecos Street, the widest street in town. It was divided by a strip of green called the Park—not a real park, just grass and trees and a drainage ditch running through the middle of it. Her house faced the Park, her house with a No Trespassers

sign tacked on the pecan tree in front and the yard looking ragged even though she'd paid a boy to come over
and mow it. He hadn't trimmed it once. The yard was
small. Momentarily distracted by her thankfulness for its
smallness, she stood in the middle of the walk staring.
For so many years she'd been surrounded by land. On the
ranch all she could see from the front windows of the
house was the road running past the gate, a mailbox, and
a light pole, the only things that broke the horizon and
said people were there. Out there it seemed insolent of
man to scratch out his gardens and fields and to build his
little stick houses. The God she knew wanted his land
unmarked, his rules kept, and his people gathered together in towns near rivers. She had scratched the land,
broken the rules, and left the town, and she had been
driven to all this by necessities of her own. Now she was
back, according to her own necessities again.

Her town house was small also, sitting near the sidewalk on the corner. Across the Park on the opposite
corner was Clara and James Stewart's house, but Mrs.
Ingram did not turn to stare at it. She could do that
when she got inside and could look out her own windows
again.

She waited, making the time pass by working as she'd
always done. The house was the first one she and Felix
owned. She came to it as a bride of twenty, married to
spite James Stewart after a quarrel. What had they quarreled about? She hadn't forgotten. People said you forgot
old quarrels, but she didn't forget that one. She had too
little else to remember.

She and James fell out over a horse, a chestnut-colored thoroughbred. He had to have that horse, a fast, nervy, high-bred mare, worthless to a cowhand. All he needed was the paint quarterhorse he already had, all he needed and all he could afford. He said he'd have to have two horses, the quarterhorse for roping and this mare: To ride to town to see you, Maggie. Not to see me, she said, to let people gawk at you riding down Main Street, riding proud on a beautiful horse you could do without. What do you want it for, James? You want it to suit the length of your legs? He was tall. He danced well. He was proud of his height, his dancing, his roping. I can't do without, Maggie. I'm riding by to see you on that horse next Saturday. You'll not, she said.

"Maggie," her mother called to her, "here comes James Stewart riding like the King of the World down the street on his new horse. Come see him. It's a lovely horse—matches the color of his hair."

"I won't look at James Stewart or his horse," she shouted from her room.

"Well, it's a fine sight. I wonder where he bought it? He's got a new saddle too. You ought to see him."

"I'm not going to see him. When he comes to the door, tell him I'm out!"

"What have you got against the horse, Maggie?"

"He doesn't need it."

"Needing a horse has nothing to do with buying one. You didn't need that new dress I bought you yesterday. What are you doing with it on when you aren't going to see him?"

Her mother's voice ran before her through the house. She came pattering after to Maggie's room.

"I would see him if he hadn't bought the horse."

"Can't he do one thing you've forbidden? You're about as stubborn as sin, Maggie, as stubborn as James, anyway. You'd better take him and the horse. He's the only man I know who's as willful as you."

"James hasn't the money to spend on—"

"He must have had enough to buy. Men don't trade horses for eggs."

"He'll be a cowhand forever if he buys every horse he likes."

"Oh, so you're already saving his money for him, are you? If it's gone that far, you'd better come on and see him. I hear him prancing back and forth on the porch."

"I won't."

"Well, I won't lie for you. You'll have to go somewhere quick."

"You won't have to lie, Mother. I'll go to town, go anywhere, I won't set eyes on James all tricked out on his new horse. If he wants to know where I am, tell him you don't know. It won't be a lie."

She ran out the back door to the shed where her father kept his buggy. Climbing into it, she crouched down sideways in the seat. Right in front of her head a slit of daylight showed through the wall, so she saw James Stewart and his chestnut mare all the same, saw him leading her through the yard all around the house, both of them walking like two peacocks on the lawn with her mother popping her head out windows to shout, "Watch out for my flower beds, James Stewart! Maggie isn't here. I told you. I don't know where she is. She said she was going out. Watch where your horse puts her feet down, James!"

When he got to the back corner of the house, he

jumped up in the saddle and rode away. He was gone for three years and nobody knew where, Maggie least of all. People asked her, "Where's James Stewart? You know where he's gone?"

"No," she would say. "How would I know? He was riding a fast horse the last time I saw him."

A year after she married Felix he was back, already married to Clara and living in the house across the Park—to spite her, she thought; to be near her, James said.

When he told her this, she knew she was in danger. "Go away, James, and let me be."

"No, I left you once." He shifted his body until he was pressed against her side, his leg half hidden by a fold in her skirt, both of them hidden by the lattice covering the side of the porch and a tall crepe myrtle bush growing in front. Felix and Clara came around the side of the house then, Felix holding a fern he'd dug up for Clara and calling, "Maggie, where are your flower pots?"

"On the back porch." She could see them through the screen of vines on the lattice, Felix holding the delicate plant in both hands, Clara standing beside him. Plump from the beginning. Clara was overflowing her corset when she was only three months gone. Like a lot of fat women, she had a small waist—smaller than Maggie's though Maggie was stringbean skinny. Usually Clara wore skirts and blouses belted so tightly she seemed to be about to pop in two. Now she had on an expanding maternity dress, one which she moved the hook over to the next eye every time she added an inch. Now her hourglass figure was lost, and instead of being divided in the middle, she was as lumpy as an old pillow. She acted as if she had feathers in her head too—never minding where James was gone, and he was gone often, nights as well as days. Sometimes he had to stay out at the ranch where he worked. Other times, Maggie suspected, he was off drinking or dicing. Clara evidently didn't suspect anything. Either she was too feather-brained or too innocent herself to have any imagination for evil. Looking through the curtain of green vines at Clara and Felix standing quietly and peacefully side by side. Maggie envied them their innocence.

"I'll run get you a flower pot," she said, wanting to do any kind of favor she could do for him.

"Never mind," said Felix, "I'll find one." He didn't expect her to wait on him as other men would have. She had to make him sit down at the table and let her bring him food. The eldest of the four Ingram children, he was used to helping. After his mother died, he'd helped raise his two sisters and brother. He and Clara went around to the back of the house, Clara following docilely, rocking forward a little as she walked.

The first baby was a boy. Seven months after James died, she had another boy. The first one was named after James; the second they called Kenneth. Maggie saw the first boy, but the second one she'd never seen.

The night after she and James had been sitting on the porch together, Maggie told Felix, "I want to move out to the ranch." The only thing that was going to cure her of James Stewart was distance.

"I thought you were bent on living in town, Maggie."

"We could keep the house and come in now and then."

"I'm afraid you'll be lonesome."

"We'll have children. That's the only company I

need—you and our children. Anyway, it's better than you riding back and forth all the time."

"We might get one of those new cars," he teased.

They couldn't have afforded one if he had been serious, and he wasn't. Felix loved horses almost as much as James did. When they moved to the ranch he bought a buggy to take her to town in, though she could have ridden horseback herself. She wouldn't because she wanted sons of her own and her mother had cautioned her against riding. "Jolts a woman up too much, Maggie. You're so thin you need to protect yourself. I think sometimes I might have had more babies if I hadn't been trotting around the country so."

Maggie said she was taking care. Out at the ranch she felt safe. James and Clara were sixteen miles away, and she didn't have to see him every day. Only he came riding out there on the fast chestnut mare and he picked his times well. At first he came when Felix was home. Then one day, and she remembered exactly what day, August 12, 1915, not long after she'd turned twenty-five, and five years since she'd walked down the aisle to marry Felix wishing James was there to see her, James stopped by.

Felix said, "Help me talk Maggie into going back to town while I'm in Abilene. We kept the house just so she could stay there once in a while. I never can get her to use it."

"She's turned into a country girl, Felix," James laughed heartily, full of himself. "You know you can't talk her into anything. I never knew anybody who could. Maggie, why are you so stubborn?" He tilted the straight chair he was sitting in back, balancing himself in front with the heels of his boots, and laughed again.

She was so angry she would have run across the room and pushed the chair over if they'd been alone together, but she held her temper. "Maybe I'll go to Abilene too," she said gaily.

She didn't though. By that time she thought the only thing that would cure her of James was James himself. Let him come and let it be over with. She didn't go with Felix to Abilene. She made her excuses and stayed home thinking James would come; she would have him and she would be over her longing, finished with the burning sickness that kept her awake every night following his visits. Felix could not cure her, no matter how much joy she gave him, no matter how much he loved her. If she could have James, she could be saved from hating Felix.

He came to her the night of August 12, a little drunk. They did not speak of what they were doing, or the right or wrong of it. He kissed her, swung her up in his arms, and carried her to the bedroom, and she, thinking all the time, Not here, not in the bed I share with Felix, not here, anywhere else, outside in the grass even, but she said nothing. He made love to her, not as Felix did, not with care and tenderness, but impatiently jabbing into her as if only her body existed and she, Maggie, was not there. When he was through, she lay thinking. It's Felix who knows me. Now I am free.

James said, "We shouldn't have slept together."

She laughed at him saying, "It's best we did. Now it's finished," wanting him to be free also.

The wind was up that night. They didn't hear Felix's

horse, nor did they hear his footsteps. For once he walked as light as a cat until he was in the doorway to the bedroom. James raised himself up on one arm, his right hand stretched out in front of him. Felix shot him before he could say a word. He fell sideways out of bed dragging the sheet with him, leaving her naked, shouting, "Shoot me, you fool! It was my doing! I allowed it to happen."

Felix stood with his back against the wall and she knew he was thinking, "Why?" though he wasn't saying anything. She didn't know whether he meant why he should shoot her, or why she had to sleep with James, or why James had to have a horse he could have done without, or why she had to have James Stewart when she could have done without, or why she had her new dress on when she wasn't going to see him if he bought the chestnut mare, and while all this was reeling through her head she could see James Stewart parading around her parents' lawn leading the mare, and her mother popping her head out windows like a jack-in-the-box, telling him, "Watch where your horse puts her feet down!"

Felix picked up James's body and dressed him completely, even putting on his underwear while she waited clutching at a corner of the sheet, frozen to it. Wrapping the sheet around her, she went to the window to watch him tie James to the skittish mare. He laid him over the saddle, not as a man rides, but as a thing is carried, arms on one side, legs hanging over the other. When he hit the horse on the rump to get her started, Maggie ran out the back door, tripping over the sheet still coiled around her, thinking that since he hadn't shot her, he must have something more terrible in mind. A dress she'd forgotten to bring in with the rest of the wash flapped on the line.

If it hadn't been for the dress, if she hadn't forgotten and left it there, sun-dried, wrinkled, the buttons winking in the moonlight, if it had not been for that she would have kept on running, to the barn maybe, to a horse to ride into town to her parents' house. They would have told her she'd done evil, but they would have protected her. She thought of herself riding into Leon, taking the back road by the river with nothing on but the sheet, riding like some pagan demon, a ghost, they would have said, and she remembered this idea forty-five years later and grinned her close-lipped grin to herself, for what else did she have to smile about but that foolish memory—a thought she had drifting in her head the night Felix killed James? Except there was the dress, its little printed sprigs of flowers billowing on the line, waiting for her. She put it on, leaving the sheet lying on the ground, the worn-out skin of an animal, a husk to blow. Walking back to the house on the flat stones embedded in the path going from the kitchen door to the barnyard, she felt like she was walking on tombstones all the way.

In the door Felix waited. He'd taken his gun off.

"Go get your gun, Felix. Go get it and kill me now. You won't have to dress me. Look, I've got my clothes on." She taunted him bitterly, standing in the path while he leaned in the door looking past her.

Maggie touched the white hair framing her face. Her hair had been blowing loose that night. Felix said, "Put your hair up."

"No, I won't." It would have made no difference what he'd told her, whether he'd said to put on shoes, change the sheets, go to bed. It didn't matter. Whatever his first command was, she would have disobeyed him. She would not say, Yes, Felix, to him, not then, not for a long time, for he'd killed arrogantly. He had warped their lives for the sake of proving she was his wife, and there was nothing to prove.

The house was clean from floor to ceiling, windows and curtains washed, the yard mowed and trimmed. She stood over the boy while he did it and made sure he trimmed all the flower beds. She would grow only flowers now: iris, sweetpeas, larkspur, zinnias. For forty-five years she'd been growing squash, tomatoes, onions, greenbeans, peas, and okra, and she would open cans the rest of her life before she'd weed another vegetable garden. After the boy had gone, she got a hoe and started cleaning up the flower bed, but she let the withering vines on the porch lattice be. It was August. They would die back soon enough.

"You work too hard, Mrs. Ingram."

That was Martha Gibson next door, a young mother with two little boys, Billy and Chris. Billy, the younger of the two, scratched on her screen every afternoon and called, "Cookie Lady! Cookie Lady!" She brought him cookies and they sat side by side eating, both of them brushing chocolate crumbs off their mouths.

"Cookie Lady, what are you doing?"

"Playing in the dirt, Billy. Don't you like to play in the dirt?" She was on her knees spading, dividing the iris where they'd gotten too crowded—too bad she'd not been there to see which ones bloomed.

"I don't know how you do it," said Martha. "I'm worn out by noon."

"You've got the young'uns to chase," said Maggie. She didn't know what to say. It seemed she'd forgotten the rote of exchange of pleasantries between women, forgotten how to take on over children even though she loved them. Sometimes she thought the only woman she would know how to talk to would be someone her own age, and the only woman she knew who was almost the same age was Clara. There was no use waiting much longer, either. Clara wasn't going to come across the Park to her. She'd never really expected her to. All along, she'd known she'd have to go to Clara, though it would have been so much easier to meet her accidentally somewhere, walking in the Park or coming back from church.

Maggie didn't go to church, but she sat out on her porch dressed in her best clothes and watched people walking on Sunday mornings. It was, she'd found, about the only time anybody in Leon walked anymore. One old man passing by would tip his hat to her, and she nodded in his direction even though she didn't know who he was. The Gibson children stopped by on their way back from Sunday school to show her their lessons, the same folded page she used to get with the bright picture on front, a picture of Jesus suffering the little children to come unto him, or the boy Joseph in his many-colored coat or David with his slingshot. None of the children in the pictures looked like real children. Their hair was too curly, their faces were too sweet, their arms and legs were too fat, and they had on biblical costumes, droopy pieces of cloth tied around the waist. All of them looked as if they'd been painted by an artist who didn't know how they looked. She believed in their

Christianity, but she didn't believe any children anywhere were ever so curly-headed, so sweet, or so uni-
formly fat.

When the lessons were read, Martha Gibson would
call Billy and Chris to come in and stay with their father
while she went to church. She'd invite Maggie to go
with her. Maggie answered, thank you, no. She had exiled herself from town; as far as she knew, she was exiled
from heaven also. She had confessed: "God forgive me
for committing adultery," she prayed every night without
feeling at all sure she was forgiven. "Forgive Felix for
killing James Stewart. There wasn't any reason for any of
it. In the name of Jesus Christ, Amen." Her prayer was
the same every night; so were the questions she asked
herself afterward. "Thou shalt not kill" came before
"Thou shalt not commit adultery." Shouldn't she ask
forgiveness for Felix first, since his was the greater sin?
But she was the cause, wasn't she—or was she? Was she
wholly responsible? She was punished. God left her bar-
ren. Anything else would come later when the sheep and
the goats were picked. She refused to think about hell,
turning her mind instead to Judgment Day. Felix and she
and James Stewart would probably be lined up with the
goats, all of them waving to Clara on the sheep side.
Would Clara wave back? Probably not. If she wouldn't
take a walk in the Park so anybody could approach her,
she certainly wouldn't waste her time waving to sinners
on Judgment Day.

The last Sunday in August, Maggie kept her best dress
on instead of changing after lunch as usual. Taking the
bridge over the drainage ditch, she went straight through

the Park to Clara's house. Before she got up the second step, she saw something through the screen that nearly turned her back; a large, tinted photograph of James Stewart sitting on the chestnut mare. The frame was intricately carved in dark crisscrosses, like the white porch lattice at her house, and it was mounted on a high stand so James appeared to be looking down at her. As she climbed the steps, she saw the color of his hair and the color of his horse matched just as her mother had said they did. Closer to the screen, the picture became clearer. It was James precisely as she remembered him, an old picture, yet a surer copy of an actual man than the flickering make-up people she'd seen on TV. Somebody had taken a snapshot, and he'd had it blown up and tinted to give to Clara. He was that vain, and young, so young. Were any of them ever so young?

"Clara it's me, Maggie," she announced.

"Come in, Maggie. You'll have to open the door yourself."

Maggie caught the screen before it slammed behind her as she entered the living room, dark as a cave. Her hand quivered toward the bridge of her nose—she didn't have on those fool sunglasses, did she? No.

Across from her sat Clara in a wheelchair, fat as she used to be, but she'd been pregnant every time Maggie saw her, always swollen, rocking when she walked, her mind locked in her body, lost in a dreamy cow trance. Now she looked like a big balloon somebody had stuck a pin to. Her flesh descended in folds around her, hung on her like the Sunday children's clothes hung on them. In one hand she held a plastic gadget for turning on her TV, and in the other was a fly swatter. A pink cotton coverlet, the kind babies were wrapped in, was draped over her knees and legs.

"The woman who stays with me has Sunday afternoons off, and I can't get to the door without running into something," she explained.

"What's the matter with you?"

"Same thing's the matter with you: old age."

"But the wheelchair—"

"Broke my hip. You'd better watch out. Skinny as you are, you'd break into a million little pieces if you fell. Why don't you sit down."

It wasn't a question. Maggie sat and looked at Clara, not the plump, docile girl she'd known, but Clara, an old lady sagging in a wheelchair, an old lady with a mind of her own.

"How are the boys?" Maggie asked.

"Gone."

"Where?"

"What does it matter, they're gone. And they don't get back to Leon often, either. I'm here with a car I can't drive and a woman to look after me, sitting here high and dry, getting crankier every day. Of course, I have this," she grimaced in the direction of the blind TV screen, "but it seems like all we get here on Sundays is preachers. I go to sleep watching them at home worse than I ever did in church. The most exciting thing I do on Sundays is swat flies. I used to wonder why God made them, but I know now. God made flies to keep old people from being bored to death!" She waved the swatter like a big baby all wrapped up in a blanket waving a rattle.

"Well, where are they . . . the boys?"

Clara flicked one finger in the fold of the coverlet. "James is in Houston working for an oil company and Kenneth is in Dallas working. He's a stockbroker for some other company. I forget the name. You could have come to see me before this. I never got to thank Felix to his face for sending them through college."

"Felix died five years ago. He's buried at the City Cemetery."

"I know," said Clara quietly and Maggie understood her. She was saying she knew everything, had always known. Felix had put money for the boys' education in Clara's account, but he'd done it anonymously. "I don't want her to think," he'd said, "that I'm trying to pay for James's life. I don't want Clara to know where the money's coming from. I can't pay for a life."

James glared down at her from his frame. "Where is he?" she nodded toward the picture.

"Same place as Felix. Didn't anybody ever tell you?"

"I never asked. There was nobody to ask. My mother wouldn't see me after . . . for awhile, and when she and Papa came out to the ranch, we never mentioned—"

Clara let the plastic box drop to her lap and wheeled her chair closer. "You mean to tell me you stayed out there all these years and never talked to nobody?"

"Nobody but Felix."

"It's a wonder you didn't go crazy."

"I could have," she said, wondering if she wasn't a little bit crazy.

"How did you keep from it?"

"I worked," said Maggie dryly. I planted gardens. I dug

in the ground. I played with dirt. I cleaned house. I watched the sun come up and the sun go down. I lived with Felix Ingram."

"Maggie," Clara's voice was hesitant and she looked as if she was pondering something. She lifted her chin out of a jowl and spoke, "There were others."

"Other what?"

"Women." She nodded toward the picture. "He was always chasing women. It's a wonder he didn't get shot before." She seemed to be speaking of a well-loved but troublesome child. Her chin merged complacently with her jowl once more.

"Did you know he was all the time?"

"Yes, but what could I do about it? I was always pregnant."

Maggie waited silently, her arms lying slack against her sides. She felt she had broken into a million little pieces and wasn't going to come together again.

# Other People's Mail

 HE SITS DOWN on the park bench at a discreet distance from her. She continues writing a postcard without looking up. Tired, a little dazed by wandering about Paris on her own, she's searched out a quiet part of the Luxembourg Gardens off to one side of a quiet part of the palace away from the Medici Fountain with its plume of spray always surrounded by a rim of people whose eyes constantly shift from the fountain to the faces of strangers. Public Paris makes her uncomfortable at times. The flickers of interest, the unasked, unanswered questions—Who are you? What are you?—the delicate probing glances, humans waving their antennae like butterflies, create a peculiar exhaustion. Too many eyes have swept over her body, made contact with her own, and flitted off. Another fountain—she never learned the name of it— covered with moss is in front of her. She lifts her head, wondering what gods are those all entwined and green?

"Vous êtes Américaine?"

The voice is brusque, stating more than questioning. She looks at the man. His opening line is familiar, but he is older than the students who usually try to pick her up. Also, he is more formally dressed: suit, vest, a striped tie, Windsor knot, buttonless collar tabs, heavily starched collar. His face is angry, as though he's barely concealing impatience with his own misery. At first she imagines he might be a well-dressed gangster.

"Non, je suis Armenian." She lies pleasantly. The brush-up lessons in conversational French help on the commonplace level. At this point she hasn't had an opportunity to go beyond simplistic questions and answers. She can order meals, though she has eaten more omelets than she really wanted, find the ladies room, go straight ahead, to the left, or right, and buy a round-trip train ticket.

"What are you doing?" Again he insists on the obvious.

"Writing a postcard."

"To a friend?"

She nods, another lie. She is writing to her husband, Roger, who is in Yugoslavia because he detests Paris, but there is no need to explain this to anyone. Wanting to get up and walk away, she stays for fear of him following her. Twice already she's been hounded all the way to her hotel: once by an Algerian boy a head shorter than she who kept telling her she should come with him, and once by a young art student who commented on her anatomy as though she were his nude model. Both incidents had been embarrassing. She is thirty-three, has lines around her eyes to prove it, and still walks down the sidewalks of the city saying no-no to children.

"You need a friend in Paris." He makes the statement quietly yet emphatically, rather like Roger saying, "You need to take an aspirin."

She puts her pen and postcard in her purse, snaps it shut, and faces him. "J'ai des amis en Paris. I have a husband, two children, and a lover in Paris."

The man threw his arm on the back of the bench. "Vous êtes complète!"

"Oui, je suis . . . complète." She took the word he gave her, and the moment she'd spoken she knew it could be the final word between them. In its most literal sense it is too grand a lie. Accustomed to denying everything, she refuses at last to deny herself. Who could boast of completeness? Certainly she couldn't.

"No, that's not true. I am writing my husband in Yugoslavia. My children are in the United States. I do not have a lover. I do not know anyone in Paris . . . and I can't speak French very well." It was the longest speech she'd made in French in two weeks.

He withdraws the arm he'd thrown on the back of the bench and offers his hand saying, "Louis Delman."

He's lying now, she thought as she shook his hand and said, "Catherine Sanders." When he told her he was a professor of literature at the Sorbonne, she did not know whether to believe him or not. How long had it been before he told her his real name? All the time he was watching her write, those irretrievable minutes before they spoke to each other, what had she been saying to Roger? The question flashed through the dim green light penetrating the trees surrounding her meeting with Louis, a scene she replayed often in teasing slow-motion. She could not recover from the experience, removed from it as she was. Her memory is avid, grasping for details, the look in his eyes, the blunt ends of his fingers, the sound of her stocking swishing as she crossed her legs, the precise second of her interest in him. From all these sensory details, she has no detachment. To her the scene is immutable and, therefore, always novel. What if? What if I'd been sitting on a different park bench five minutes later? What if I'd never answered? What if I'd left it at "Je suis complète?" What if and what's the use of asking what if? She is back in her own living room in Austin, Texas, sitting on her own yellow velvet sofa where she sits every morning after Roger goes to work, waiting for the postman to bring a letter from Louis. Though she's been home for five days, nothing has come from him yet. Once again she reminds herself sometimes it takes six days for an airmail letter from Europe to arrive.

Rising slowly, she drifts to Roger's study to look for her card. He keeps everything, especially letters, security blankets of some kind. She finds her card to him under a stack of unpaid bills. Roger's mental file works according to his zany personal chronological order. Bills were there when he got home, but he's received his European mail before. All of it had been sent to various hotel addresses in Yugoslavia. At first she'd written letters, then postcards, big ones which became progressively smaller as the weeks passed. There it was, the one with the picture of an old man feeding birds in front of Notre Dame.

*Dear Roger, I spent all morning at the Louvre, where I got lost in the Egyptians. I know there are many other things to see, but I always end up with the mummies. I'm resting on a quiet bench in the Lux. Gardens trying to pay no attention to a mad Frenchman who's staring at me. Help! I'm being kidnapped for the white slave trade. When last seen I was wearing my navy suit, the one with brass buttons.*

*Love, C.*

The last sentence is scrawled so wildly she has trouble reading it. Studying the forgotten loops and whirls, her state of mind at the time she was writing returns. Yes, that was when I was still trying to make him jealous, the last time. After that I had to try to keep him from being jealous. Then, when I was writing this card, making up an obvious lie, I was being most truthful. Now, all I do is lie. She leaned against the desk, a tall, fair-headed woman, holding onto the corner of the card, flipping it back and forth, angry at her husband for letting her stay in Paris alone, angry at herself for blaming him. Roger did not like the French; he resented the fact that his medical convention chose to meet in Geneva, that most conspicuously French part of Switzerland. The main reason Catherine was sure he would not go with her to France was she adored it, romanticized it, as Roger complained. She knew his exact words, for he repeated them often.

"Their food is marvelous, but they are chauvinists. They're greedy and rude while they advertise themselves as the world's most civilized people."

"If you only spoke the language."

"But I don't. You do."

That was the other reason he would not travel in France with her. She'd studied French, and even though she spoke it haltingly, Roger could not bear for her to be the one who was constantly speaking. He disliked giving up command, letting a woman give directions to a bell-boy or a waiter. Male vanity. Catherine sighed, sat down in Roger's desk chair, and wished her husband had a more heroic flaw. Though he gave orders to his nurses and his wife, who passed them on to patients, children, yardmen, and plumbers, he could not give orders to be passed on in a foreign language.

Catherine told him he was inconsistent. Finally, she asked, "Can't you trust me?"

"Yes, but I do not trust the French."

Rather than slog through that particular argument again, she decided to go to France while Roger went to Yugoslavia. She'd been to Paris before, but this was her first chance to discover the city alone. It changed all the time, yet no matter how, even when traffic overflowed to take up parts of the quais, even when a superhighway careened by one side of the Louvre or steel-boned skyscrapers rose like threatening skeletons above old roofs, she walked through Paris fascinated by ordinary life. She bought fruit from street vendors at the first price asked; while absentmindedly wiping cherry juice trickling down one corner of her mouth, she moved aside to watch other women haggle. She went into pastry shops just to see what people would order and poked through a pharmacy just to see what was there. Sitting behind a *Herald Tribune*, she strained to understand what two men were arguing about at the next table. Above the quais at bookstalls, she opened books written in many languages and stared greedily at unknown words. What appealed to her most were all these bits of mundane life, including her own regular morning trips to museums, existed within a splendid setting. Her joy in the city was indiscriminate. The Seine, its ornate bridges, Notre Dame, Montmartre, the Arc de Triomphe, the skittering, pacing crowds on the grand boulevards, the students lounging along the Boul' Mich, the Eiffel Tower—these readily accessible spectacles made her happy. Yet she could never know Paris completely. Its continuing mystery was the greatest attraction.

She spent a morning at the Musée Carnavalet looking at tiny replicas of Paris in earlier states. Dazed by the richness of a past her mind could not encompass, she carefully committed dates to memory and forgot them a few yards outside the museum. She remembered a few famous people, a few wars, then distractions of the present took over. Where was the music coming from? Three blocks from the Carnavalet she found two young men playing a lute in a sidewalk cafe where they were the only customers. She stayed and listened, watching them laugh heartily at what must have been ancient obscenities in songs she'd never heard before. Leaving to go to lunch, she swung out on the sidewalk again, swaying slightly from cognac she'd poured in her coffee, swinging like a luscious peach, ready, inevitably ready to fall into some man's lap. She hadn't been aware of her readiness, for her world seemed pure sensation—swaying through it, she acted and reacted, her senses all keyed to elation. Awareness of where this excitement might lead came only after Louis had so scornfully announced, "Vous êtes complète."

How cold it had been that day, unusually cold for June. How delicious to walk about in summertime wearing a coat. In the same district she found a restaurant, one a friend had recommended for its steak *au poivre*— too *au poivre* for her; the peppercorns nearly burned her mouth—but she was so hungry she didn't care. That was where she'd been the morning before she met Louis, not at the Louvre as she'd written Roger. She'd made up the tour among the mummies because the Louvre was comfortably familiar to him. He would have preferred for her to stay in the middle-class hotel he remembered from his one trip to Paris, and as far as he knew, that was where she was. She'd spent one night, taken all the free stationery in her room, and moved into a small hotel on the Left Bank, playing at intrigue before she had one. Life is full of contrivances. Hadn't everything happened because she was so fully prepared for it? Of course there was the accidental quality of her meeting with Louis, yet it was exactly the sort of accident needed. Right after they shook hands he took her to a café for an innocuous cup of coffee and asked her to lunch the next day. Unaware of the Parisian custom of a hearty dinner followed by lovemaking, she accepted quickly, especially as she was tired of eating every meal alone.

Sitting across the table from a strange man, I ate whatever it was he'd ordered for me. It was a relief not to be intimidated by a menu. In my purse that day was a postcard showing only a dull stretch of coast and a bossy message:

> Tired of skin-diving. Will fly to N.Y. from Zagreb Sunday. Get your ticket changed and meet me at The Plaza. Roger.

Not even "Love, Roger." Messages of affection on postcards embarrassed him. She was supposed to know he loved her because he said she should meet him in New York, supposed to be tired of her vacation because he was, supposed to be and do a lot of things. All of his presumptions came at a moment when she felt herself out of bounds of his demands for the first time in twelve years, she realized while gazing at an attractive Frenchman. If it was true, and it wasn't necessarily, that a woman went from man to man, she was walking into a well-planned accident.

"I told you a false name yesterday. My real name is Louis Mandel."

Her mouth is full. After she swallows, which gives her time to think out her response, she says, "I think you are married also?"

He nods. "Twice. To the same woman."

That was more than necessary, but she is kind enough not to say so. He too had been contrived against; that was what she wanted to tell him. She began looking in her purse for her *Larousse's Dictionary*. By the time she got it out, conversation had moved on and she forgot what she wanted to look up. He was trying to tell her about his work. All she could understand was he was not a professor, he was a journalist.

"What are you writing about now?"

"Trade fairs. I have just come from one. Very dull. How long are you in Paris?"

"Three more days."

He put his hand over hers. "So little time. Can't you stay longer?"

In her mind flicked a scene, her navy suit folded on the back of a chair, the brass buttons twinkling, her underwear neatly folded on the chair seat and her sensible walking shoes stuck under. Next to her clothes were Louis's suit, his pants carefully creased and hanging on the back—he would do this, as he seemed to wear the same suit every day—the vest, coat, tie, and slightly wrinkled shirt draped in layers over the pants, his underwear in a pile next to her, his shoes, slightly dusty, under the chair with hers.

"No, it's impossible."

"Anything is possible."

"Not for me. I have to go home." She shows him the postcard. He glances at it and places it picture side up between them on the glistening white tablecloth. "I thought American women were independent."

"Some are." She is glad he does not accuse her of being repressed, for she is particularly tired of that approach. Every time she was accused of being repressed, she readily agreed.

"Do you love him?"

Catherine hesitates for a moment. "I suppose so. I am married to him."

"I do not love my wife. I married her again because of the children. They are mine."

"I've got some of my own."

"Yes, I know. Two. You have told me."

He pays the bill, gets up, and leads her out of the restaurant, one she never saw again, a place lined with mirrors reflecting old-fashioned chandeliers and scratchy, red, plush-covered chairs, an Edwardian seduction setting filled with the heavy air of opulent intimacy. She thought he would give up, deposit her at her hotel much as any Frenchman would discard an unlucky lottery ticket; instead he drove to the Bois de Boulogne, to a forested part she had not been in before.

"Come, let's walk." A path stretches out through the woods by the car. He bends down and takes her hand. They walk along without speaking, in step like two dancers about to glide onstage. He moved his hand to the back of her neck and turned her face toward him. At the instant she was earnestly thinking of all the reasons she should not be walking through a park with a strange man, she met him in the middle of the path. They kissed until Catherine thought they would both fall down with the sun's broad spotlight on them.

Slip, slam. Why does Mr. Kieger always throw the mail down just inside the door? Other postmen used the box outside, but Mr. K. insisted on using the tile-covered foyer, probably the real reason why all those wine goblets from Switzerland arrived so nearly snapped off at the stem. Catherine ran to get the mail. There was the usual junk, which she dropped in a wastebasket by the door, a card from Mike at camp, a letter to Roger from his mother, and underneath everything, as if Mr. K. had deliberately concealed what she most wanted, a thin envelope with a French stamp addressed to Mrs. Catherine Sanders. On her way back to the yellow sofa, she turned over Mike's card and read:

*Dear Mother and Dad, I am Having a good time at camp We have 7 activaties in all. One of them is nature. We need some gallon jars to keep snakes in Them (There dead) do you Think you could send some? Mike S.*

She shook her head over the idea of mailing gallon jars, then sat down to read Louis's letter. Her hands are trembling. She'd sent him a postcard from Orly Field just before leaving and included her address, an incredibly stupid thing to do, but she could not ask any of her friends to let her use their addresses, and she was usually the only one at home when the mail came. Her eyes, filled with tears, skittered crazily over Louis's letter. His handwriting is awkward and she can comprehend only a few phrases. He began by thanking her for her card and apologizing for not accompanying her to the airport, explaining he had to see his mother as he did every Sunday morning. Had he forgotten he'd told her that? The address she was writing to was his cousin's in Paris. There were bits about embraces, your body, misery, and love, all in second person familiar, a tense she'd never known well. What French she had was for public consumption, not for private. With the help of her old textbook and a dictionary, she slowly worked through the letter, skipping over phrases she could not fully understand. Why hadn't some intelligent person compiled a textbook filled with exercises involving love letter translation? It was almost twelve. She must do something before the day slid out from under her, must do something about deciphering the letter, and Oh God, there was the luncheon at 12:30. She had a symphony board meeting at three and Roger expected to have supper at home, since they had eaten out last night. Why must everything fall in a heap? Why couldn't she arrange events better, space them out more? Unzipping her robe, she dressed and got ready to meet the chaos of the day. The letter—I must hide it somewhere. Where? Roger is not a snoop; still, there's no reason to leave it about for him to come across. Unable to think where she could safely tuck it away, she put it in the back pocket of her purse where she kept the wire he'd sent her at the airport: "Goodby My Love. Write Me Soon. Louis." She went out feeling she was carrying a red neon sign blinking ADULTERY in one hand.

Between the luncheon and board meeting, she called her French teacher and said she had to have some help with a translation.

"So, now you have returned from France and you are reading. Good. What have you chosen?" The elderly voice was patient.

"Baudelaire." His was the only name that came immediately to mind. Catherine imagines Madame Escalier frowning at the telephone, which she distrusts as she distrusts all machines. Somewhere in her late seventies, Madame had been retired from university teaching for years, yet she continues to teach, not because she needs the money; she simply must have contact with students— anyone in trouble in regular classes, businessmen and housewives going abroad, anyone. The older she gets, the more enthusiastic she seems to become. Roger calls her the French Disciple.

"*Bien.* I cannot work out the rhyme on the telephone. One needs more time for that. I can help with the sense of it perhaps."

She pulled the letter out and read the troublesome sentences to Madame.

"Oh, yes. That is, 'I dream of your beautiful body and long to cover it with a thousand kisses' . . . sensuous isn't it? And, 'My misery fills every black moment of the endless day.' It sounds better in French, of course. I do not know the poem. What is it called?

"'*Le . . . Le Rêve*' . . . 'The Dream,' Isn't it?" With Madame Escalier she is a student once more, uncertain, appalled by her own ignorance.

"I know the classics better than the moderns, but if you need help again, call me."

Catherine assures Madame Escalier she will, thanks her, and goes off to her meeting, where she is forced to conceal hysterical laughter. Once released from the board room, she is caught up in five o'clock traffic snarling toward the suburbs. Her whole rattling day merges into a calculated frenzy of one way streets, lights, and signs: YIELD, STOP, LEFT TURN ONLY. Catherine pushes toward the grocery store thankful that Roger won't come home till seven. Driving slowly, the car's air-conditioning sloshing waves of cold air toward her, she quickly forgets her surroundings. There is nothing nearby she wants to see.

Louis drives her from the Bois to her hotel, both of them absolutely silent, absolutely determined. She had always believed Frenchmen became maniacs once behind a steering wheel, yet here she sits beside one, smoking her cigarette, tense as a cat, not giving a damn how he drives or how wildly other cars swoop around them. It is as if there really are no other cars, only Louis's Citroen moving toward the hotel unimpeded. Miraculously he finds a parking place nearby and holds onto her hand while they walk to her room. There, the little scene of the chair filled with neatly folded clothes, which she'd already previewed, plays itself out, though in their hurry they neglect to fold anything. Clothes fall all over the floor when they undress each other. Louis's trousers do land on the chair's back. It is no good the first time. They are both too nervous and in too much of a hurry.

Louis worries about his performance. "I am acting like an eighteen-year-old."

She reassures him. "We wanted each other too much."

They lie in bed naming over the parts of the body, he in French, she in English, laughing.

"I have never loved an American."

"Do you collect nationalities?"

"No, but I think about it. I have always wanted to go to the United States."

"Why haven't you?"

"It costs too much. My paper sends me to other countries, to Algeria, to Germany, never to the States."

She can't imagine why he'd want to leave France, and he tells her she sounds like the French themselves. Many people, even Parisians, are true provincials. "They will not go to countries where French is not spoken. Most prefer to stay in France. Even I . . . I take my family to the coast of Brittany in August. But, I want to go to America . . . to see the skyscrapers—"

"You have those here."

"Not as many. I want to see your West."

"It's bleak. There isn't a good restaurant in a four-hundred-mile radius of any town in West Texas."

"I will bring a picnic."

"If you plan to drive, you'd better bring a three-week supply of *foie gras*."

"I will take my children to see the Indians."

"Most of them are hidden in the desert."

"Have you seen one?"

"Once. In Taos in a dust storm. He was wrapped up in a pink and white cotton blanket and was sitting in the plaza. He looked miserable."

"You do not want me to come?" He looks rather miserable himself at that moment.

"Yes, I do. I don't want you to expect too much." She sees, just in time, he is fond of his illusions.

"Someday I will."

He cannot stay with her that night, nor any night. His wife would become suspicious. "She is jealous and, as you know, I do not lie well."

Half-dressed to go, he kisses her and pulls his clothes off again. It is much better the second time, slower, quieter. Catherine sat waiting for a left-turn light thinking of their bodies twisting in bed. Horns honk behind her. She'd not noticed the arrow flashing. In her anxiety to make the turn she mashed the gas pedal too hard and killed the engine. The noise of squawking horns followed her around the corner. When she got to the grocery she couldn't think what she was stopping for. All she saw were rows of shelves stuffed with food she had no interest in. At the bakery section she chose a dozen dry-looking fruit bars to mail to Susan at camp, then remembering she needed something for supper, she zig-zagged across the store to the opposite wall and picked up a carton of eggs.

She went home wondering if she was the only Francophile to fall in bed with an Americaphile. If she romanticized France, Louis was more than romantic about America. He wore his hair clipped short because the American businessmen he'd met had close-cropped heads; it was no use to try to talk to him about the newest French films because he preferred American movies; he had an old-fashioned admiration for *le jazz*, and, most disconcerting of all, he preferred water to wine. Catherine, pouring herself a glass of her favorite Chablis to drink while she fixed supper, smiled at her memory of a waiter saying, "And, the wine, monsieur?" Louis asked for bottled mineral water instead and explained to her wine was not good for the liver, a particularly satisfactory reason, since she already knew about that French preoccupation. In fact she found all of his inherent paradoxes delightful. So, why had she come home? Who or what had forced her to return? She was still questioning herself when Roger came in the back door.

"Hello, my dear." As he bent to kiss her cheek she smelled disinfectant. Taller and paler than she was, Roger looked like a TV producer's idea of the young doctor, although middle age lines were beginning to show on his forehead. His face was so open it seemed impossible to discern a mood, but she read weariness and a kind of contempt there, a distance he kept between himself and death. He didn't talk much about the shortness of life or the delicacy of human lungs; she knew, however, he was often discreetly morose. To brood openly about futility was an admission of hopelessness he could not allow himself. Roger was forever caught between professional competence and candor, between doing his best while silently acknowledging his best would not always do.

"You've been in surgery this late in the day?"

"Had to. Something came up. A bad car accident. I was called in."

Somebody must have been terribly hurt. Roger fell back on clipped sentences after hours spent in the operating room. She wanted to know if the patient lived, yet she knew better than to inquire. Roger came home to shelter; he did not come to broadcast news of life or death. Later he would, if he needed to, tell her who the victim was and what had been done for him. When they were both younger, he would burst in at all hours overflowing with details of an operation. After the children were born, they'd had a tacit understanding; no operations before supper.

Mixing himself a drink, he retreated with it into his study only to return to the kitchen holding the letter from his mother, who wrote sporadically and irrationally; her mind, cluttered with non sequiturs, was a grab bag of odd, useless information.

"Listen to this—"

"Roger, I'm frying bacon." She had to shout over the ventilating fan's roar.

He pushed the fan button off.

"Bacon grease fumes are bad for you."

"Who's the doctor around here? Never mind about the fumes. Listen."

Moving the pan of sputtering fat off the stove, she picked up her wine glass and assumed what she hoped was a patient expression. She did not want to hear her mother-in-law's letter, particularly not at the moment. Emotional crises had already consumed her day, and she was certain any letter from his mother would lead Roger to fulminate for the next hour.

He read quickly without stopping to comment:

*Dear Roger and Catherine,*

*How are you two doing with the children away now that you are back? Mike has written to me saying he hopes you will not throw everything in his room out while he's gone. I do hope Susan isn't too much for her camp. Have you ever thought of giving her tranquilizers? They have improved your father's outlook a lot. I know some doctors don't approve.*

*I have been playing bridge as usual. I went to a dessert bridge party in the afternoon Monday, played that night at Marge's house, and was out at Cynthia's for a game by ten the next morning. Three games in 24 hours is my limit. Next week I have the two table duplicate group on Friday and my Saturday foursome meets on Saturday, of course.*

*The big clock in the dining room has just struck twelve. The other night when it did I counted up to ten and then went on to jack, queen, king. I can't remember whether I was just sleepy or had a little sherry.*

*If you don't like the idea of tranquilizers for Susan, you might try an ounce or so of sherry. Put it in orange juice to hide the taste. Maybe soda pop would hide it better. Root beer will hide anything.*

*We both send love,*
*Mother*
*P.S. Maybe the sherry isn't a good idea. We don't want to create an alcoholic.*

"She is, of course, crazy!" Roger growled. "I have been practicing medicine for fifteen years and she's still diagnosing and prescribing. Do you know what she's decided about our daughter?" He didn't wait for Catherine's answer. "She's been reading ladies' magazines or a medical column in the newspaper and she's decided Susan is hyperactive."

"No, it's not that. The last time we were up there Susan rode the pony all morning. We went swimming that afternoon and she and Mike played hide-and-seek with the neighbor's children till ten that night. Your mother forgets Susan's not five years old any longer. She kept suggesting a nap."

"She's only got two grandchildren. Why can't she remember their ages? And why does she have this mania for bridge?

"Be glad she has a mania for something. It gets her out of the house and away from your father. Look, Roger, if we're going to eat tonight, you'd better put your mother down."

*Dear Louis,*

Catherine sits on the yellow sofa writing and wondering if he'll understand the words. He studies English at home in the evenings but has told her his progress is slow.

*I received your letter. I miss you terribly. It's strange*

No. the contraction might confuse him. She crossed it out and began again on another sheet.

*Dear Louis,*
   *I received your letter. I miss you terribly. It is strange to be back at home and not feel at home. I drive through the streets thinking about the streets of Paris and of you.*

*My children are still away at camp, but they will be back at the end of the week. Maybe I will know I am home then.*

*I do understand why you could not come to the airport. It is such a long way to Orly and I know about family obligations because I have many also. You were dear to send the wire. I carry it with me all the time. I do not know why since I have memorized it.*

*The flight back was all right. New York was terrible— hot, crowded, dirty. One does not feel safe on the streets.*

How glad I was to have Roger there. I felt safe with him. New York is really his town. He loves the wild pace—grabbing cabs and rushing off to a concert in the afternoon, a play the same night. For him the city means vitality; it's like him, aggressive, brisk. If I point to garbage spilling over curbs or possible muggers lurking anywhere, he lifts his chin and says, "Stick with me. You'll be all right." And I do. I go forth with Roger the Dauntless. For me New York is overpowering. I know Paris better. Nothing extraordinary about that. I've never been to New York without Roger. What would it be like to meet Louis there? We'd both be lost all the time.

*I did get to see several plays right before they folded.*

Too idiomatic. She crossed out *folded* and wrote *closed.* He did not even know she liked the theatre. All they had done was eat and sleep together every afternoon for three days—creatures of appetite. That was all we wanted to do. We had no time to be lovers walking hand in hand through the streets. The only day we had like that was the first one. He was haggard by the end. So was I. Our hours together ran away from us. When he left, I fell asleep, then woke to loneliness. I was not unhappy, though.

*Now, back here, I am trying to understand why I am here. Life presses in toward me. I try to keep it away. I have to go to meetings, luncheons, the supermarket.*

*Super-marché?* Wasn't it the same in France? Not quite, but she couldn't explain an American grocery store in a letter.

*My parents call. I have to write my in-laws.*

What was the French for that? Beaux-parents. She found it in the *Larousse*.

*I have to write to my children. Everything is supposed to go on as usual. It does on the surface, but just beneath is a whole secret life with you.*

But, it was not whole—those days in a hotel room with Louis. Let it be. I can't say everything in one letter.

*I try to see you in my mind, but it's hard.*

It is impossible. I see bits. His collar, the top of his head where his hair has been cut too short. His voice, what does it sound like? And, the music? The tape recorder he brought in his briefcase. What was the music he played? I thought I'd never forget it. Oh damn! The doorbell.

It was the yardman, Mr. Lovelace. Roger called him Mr. Lovelorn and made up extravagant stories about him running after nubile young girls. He'd gotten divorced six months ago, an action that produced doleful talks about property division and 3:00 A.M. telephone calls from his ex-wife. As sad as he seemed to be when relating these stories to Catherine, she felt Mr. Lovelace rather enjoyed being harassed. Quiet and cautious, dressed in dark green work clothes, he was in danger of blending into the landscape unless someone paid him attention. Apparently he was aware of how quickly he faded from other people's minds, for he usually called for some sort of notice whenever he was doing the yard.

"We're going to need more fertilizer for them bushes, Mrs. Sanders."

"All right. I'll get you some."

"Today?"

"Yes. Today. As soon as I finish a letter."

*Louis, I love you.*

                                        *Catherine*

He never asked me to stay. I never offered to.

She mailed the letter in a post office across town from her own. Ten days later another one came from him containing his picture. Catherine stared at the unflattering shiny black and white photograph for a long time. His hair stood straight up—the picture must have been taken when he needed a haircut. His expression was the same as it had been the day she met him. I never asked him what was so intolerable in his life, what gave him that bitter look. Was it his job? Was journalism repetitious and ephemeral to him? Was it his marriage? We never spoke of that. I didn't talk about Roger, and he did not tell me his wife's name. It was as if we agreed to pretend they didn't exist. We talked about our children though, showed each other pictures of them, even worried about the four of them reading too many comic books. What do I know about this man? I don't know the name of the newspaper he worked for. Did he tell me? Yes . . . and I forgot. I kept meaning to look for it, to read what he wrote, yet I didn't. Why not? Why did I lose all natural curiosity? I went about looking at things and people in the mornings, and in the afternoons, there was Louis. I know his body well, but so little of him. And what does he know of me? She slid the letter out of the envelope.

*Catherine, ma chère,*
 *Je vais en Bretagne avec ma famille.*

Going to Britanny with his family as he usually does. Doesn't he ever take them anywhere else? "For the month of August." Yes, as all Paris went away for the month of August. "I do not know if I can write to you there, as one has little privacy." My God, does his wife follow him to the post office? "Continue to write to me at my cousin's address. I have gone by your hotel and felt—" Where was the *Larousse?*

Catherine got up from the chair in her husband's study hoping to find the dictionary in a bookcase across the room. The children are home now, and she's had to lock the door in order to be by herself. Mike had already knocked twice to complain about Susan not helping him skim leaves off the swimming pool. As the house is built around the pool, she can hear them arguing. Damn the dictionary! It's not there. Must have left it in the bedroom. I could call Madame Escalier. No. I can't stand that act again.

Catherine shoved the letter down the front of her

dress and started through her house to her room as though she were a spy making her way carefully in alien country. Mike caught her in the dining room.

"Mother, has the mail come?"

"It's there in your father's study. Were you expecting something?" She looked closely at her son. The first years of his life he resembled her; now he is beginning to look more like her father and a bit like Roger. He has the same green-brown eyes, the same cast to his chin, not yet firmly molded, but the dominant genes are present working out their code.

"I got used to getting mail at camp."

"You have to write letters to get them." Mail is a form of magic to him, like playing Go Fish at birthday parties. You put your hand in the box and can never guess what you'll pull out. Ever since he got back from camp he's been going through the junk mail in the wastebasket and carrying half of it up to his room.

"I know," he says and leaves her.

Catherine finds the *Larousse* beside the paperback collection of French poetry she's been reading. Trying to learn the intricacies of the language, she covers the prose translations on each facing page and works out the poem herself before looking. It is a useless exercise, she believes, for poetic language is the hardest of all, and her translations stumble into nonsense. Reading the editor's translation, she is amazed every time to see how much she's missed. Still, she continues to work on the poems. They are a link to Louis.

What is it he felt when passing her hotel? Here, yes, "as if I were passing a beautiful ghost." She looks up every unfamiliar word in the last part of his letter only to discover he complains of holiday traffic he's sure to meet on the roads and wishes every day she was there waiting for him. The banality of his daily life is oddly soothing, for it matches her own. "I remember your tears of pleasure," she reads with a faint shock of wonder, rereads and negates utterly. They were not tears of pleasure; she had cried in real grief from a combined sense of guilt and despair over what loneliness had driven her to. Every time they finished making love she'd wet his chest with tears, crying easily and steadily every afternoon for three days after Roger's card came. Then she got on a plane and flew to New York. "We had no luck. Everything happened too quickly. My love, will you ever return?"

Catherine puts the letter in her zippered purse pocket along with the wire and his first letter and goes to the kitchen to make sandwiches for her children's lunch. Louis admires America, but what would he think of peanut butter? He says nothing about coming here. How long will it be before I go back? A long time, probably years. Roger has to have some extraordinary, tax-deductible excuse like a medical convention before he'll consider a European vacation. And if I went on my own? I don't enjoy traveling alone that much. How could Louis get away from his jealous wife in order to go anywhere with me? He could say his newspaper was sending him somewhere for two weeks . . . if only he were a good liar. Catherine shuts her eyes and imagines she is running down a beach in Normandy to meet Louis. Something is wrong though. He isn't moving. Behind him are vague shapes, a woman and two little girls. Opening her eyes, she considers his letter again. He has said nothing, has not reacted to the strangeness of her existence. He could not see it, could not even imagine it.

Right after lunch she locks herself in the study and writes to him, giving a detailed description of her house, including the view from the window.

> There are low hills. Some of them are topped with TV broadcasting towers and all are covered with houses. I see mainly roofs, electric lines, and telephone cables through the trees. Between my house and the hills there is a lake, but I cannot see it from here. I look down on a swimming pool and out to the hills. In the winter more of the houses show. I wish they were not there. The supermarket I drive to is in a shopping center. I do not think you have anything quite like it in France unless the idea has been copied. What a terrible thought! You must tell me if the landscape of your suburb is the same as mine. Our shopping center is a rectangular collection of stores with one long end of the rectangle used as a parking lot.

She draws a rectangle and fills in the types of stores. Looking back over what she's written, she decides the description of her house sounds like a classified advertisement in the real-estate column, four bedrooms, two-and-a-half baths, a bookcase-lined study and a vaulted dining-room, family-room combination. All she need add is a phrase like "contemporary, all-electric kitchen."

She riffles through a drawer looking for a picture to send him and finds snapshots Roger had taken of her on their boat. In them she looks everything she is not, relaxed, joyful, carefree. Discarding these as false masks, she picks up a copy of her passport photograph, which shows her smiling broadly in anticipation of the trip, another mask, yet a truer one. One eyebrow is slightly shorter than the other; she's forgotten to hold her lip over her crooked lower teeth. Yes, it will do.

Her life assumes its usual pattern. Roger goes to work, the children have to be taken to the pediatrician for pre-school checkups, to swimming meets and birthday parties. The house and pool are full of neighbors' children. Brother, their tomcat, gets his eye scratched in a fight, and when it's well he stalks off for four days angry because Susan has thrown him in the pool to drown his fleas. Catherine agrees to collect donations in her block for leukemia victims, gives two dinner parties, worries about raising money for the symphony, has the couch covers cleaned, and quarrels with Roger.

"Going back to the university is ridiculous at your age. You'll be in class with nineteen-year-olds. We can easily afford to have Madame Escalier come here."

They are sitting in his study long after the children are safely in bed. He has the desk chair, which he swivels from side to side. She is in an armchair, her legs tucked under, the chair's back a protective shell curving around her.

"Madame is a marvelous old lady, but I don't learn enough from her. I want to go back to school. I don't care if everyone else in the class is thirteen."

"But—wouldn't you feel a little silly?"

"No. You're the one who might feel silly. Quit thinking I'm you, and quit telling me I'm too old to learn anything."

"I didn't say—You can't know what I'm thinking."

"I'm going to take an advanced reading course in French this September."

"Even if I don't think you should?"

"What difference does it make to you?"

"You're my wife." He frowns and as he does, Catherine sees his abruptness is much like Louis's.

"Roger." She shifts her legs to the floor and stands. "We have been married for twelve years, and as far as you're concerned, I'm a shadow that follows you around."

"Oh, God! You've been reading those magazine articles again!"

"Maybe . . . while I'm waiting for the children in the orthodontist's office. Reading his six-months-old magazines. Or pushing a cart at the grocery store, stopping to sneak a quickie at the rack. Why don't you look under the bed? That's where I've hidden all my contraband books. Germaine Greer and Kate Millet and Simone de Beauvoir are all under the bed." She gets so carried away with the vision of so many feminists neatly lying flat under a bed muttering to each other she laughs.

Roger stares at her and asks quite seriously, "Have you been going to some kind of meetings?"

"Yeah. In the parking lot of the shopping center at high noon. We get in a big circle, and stomp around, and raise our fists and shout, 'Right On, Sisters!' Then I come home and walk around the house wearing your pants. They're a little big in the waist, but I manage. Sometimes I call your mother long distance and ask her what she's been reading lately, but it's cards as usual."

"What has my mother got to do with this?"

Catherine sinks back down in her chair. "I don't know. . . . It's just that I don't want to be an old lady like your mother, having to take up bridge as an excuse to flee the house."

"She likes playing bridge."

"It's all right with me if she does. I don't."

"Why don't you take up golf?"

"That's your game. I want something for my mind. It's filled with lists of errands to run. I'd rather be thinking of verb conjugations."

"Other women are happy—"

"What do you know about other women and their happiness? I'm going to take that course, Roger. I may even take two. I may even get an advanced degree." She hears herself say this with some surprise, as she hadn't thought of another degree until that moment.

"What about the children?"

"Susan is almost nine and Mike will be ten in November. They aren't going to suffer if their mother is less bored."

Catherine arranged to take her course in the morning so she could be home when the children returned from school. Accustomed to planning ahead, she gave some thought to the risk she would be taking. Louis's letters would be lying there in a pile right inside the front door until she got home around noon. If Roger should . . . but he never does, never has to come home for anything before five at the earliest. What if he does? He can't read French. I'll tell him it's an advertisement for gloves from a shop I went to in Paris. Louis doesn't put his name on the outside of the envelope. Or it could be—? Catherine ran through the possibilities of other correspondents and decided that letters about crystal she'd ordered which never arrived would be more believable. All one morning she went about the house making up beds and making up letters.

*Dear Madame Sanders,*
    *We are sorry to inform you the pattern you ordered will take a very long time to arrive. Our firm is an old one, as you know, and our glass makers are almost as fragile as our product. Several of the workers have been ill lately with—*

What should they have? TB. Chest problems would interest Roger. She constructed an elaborate letter of regret from an imaginary shop on the Rue des Trois Portes, the street where Louis's cousin lived, and for a while was so entertained with the idea of the fragile glass-makers that she almost forgot why she'd invented them.

When she first went back to school, she thought Roger might have been right; she did feel slightly ridiculous. The whole physical layout of the university had changed so much, she had a hard time finding her way around. Where there had been spaces there were now buildings and clusters of buildings, aggregate monsters combining dorms, classrooms, theatres, and cafeterias. What had been called the parking problem in her undergraduate years had grown to such catastrophic proportions that most students were simply riding over it in shuttle buses and bicycles. She had to rent a space for her car. Well aware that no one wore bobby sox any longer, she was still amazed that no one seemed to care what they wore unless it was something especially outrageous. The boy who sat on her right in a junior-level reading course came to class in a leather top hat one day. It was much admired. She surveyed her classmates much as an anthropologist might look over a strange new tribe and was reminded of Tacky Day, a high school ritual which allowed everyone to come to school in costume one day of the year. Tacky Day was apparently unending now. After the beginning week of the semester she let her first reactions slide. They might not care what they wore, but all of them spoke French better than she did. Three pages into *Carmen* she knew she had to do something about her accent immediately. Doing something led her to the language laboratory, where she listened to tapes and repeated the words for an hour every day. Sitting there speaking into a microphone with her head clamped between red plastic earphones she heard perfect French spoken by an unknown, disembodied Voice. Like Madame Escalier, she had always distrusted machines; now, hooked up to one, she could not help being pleased by mechanical ingenuity.

Coming back to the house one afternoon, she picked up the mail, found nothing from Louis, then checked the calendar. He had to be back from Brittany. Why hasn't he written? Perhaps I've faded out of his mind as he is fading from mine. What did we have in common after all? Loneliness, responsibilities, ties. He will never divorce his wife a second time, and even if he did, would I marry him? No. I never thought to marry him. It is not necessarily true that a woman goes from man to man. Even if it were, I wouldn't go to Louis. We had those days. . . . I cannot imagine being married to him. He lives somewhere in a crowded suburb, one I've never seen, and comes into Paris only to work. I've been lost in nostalgia long enough. I'll write to him and tell him he should not write again. As she began to mentally compose her letter, the phone rang.

"Madame Sanders?"

"Yes?" She wondered if Madame Escalier had heard she was studying French at the University and was angry over being deprived of a pupil.

"Madame, I do not read other people's mail."

"But, Madame Escalier, I never—"

"Your husband. . . ." Her voice sank to a hissing whisper. "I thought you should be told. This morning your husband has come to me with a letter, one meant for you."

"What did you—"

"Nothing. I did nothing. I told him I would not translate it for him."

"What did he do with it?"

"I do not know. He took it with him."

"Oh."

"I thought you should know."

"I'm grateful you called."

She put the receiver down and stood with one hand clutching it still. Somewhere, very far away, in the imaginary shop on the Rue des Trois Portes, she heard the sound of crystal glasses crashing, falling into thousands of glittering splinters. Why, of all the people in the world, am I the one who has to get caught? There must be thousands of women who fall into foreign beds and go home quietly keeping their secrets. Mixed with her anger at her carelessness, her sorrow over hurting Roger, is the certainty he'll get the letter translated somehow.

Thorough Dr. Sanders will pursue the truth even when he discovers he doesn't want to know it. He'll come home proud of his detective work and furious with me. Names will be called. The air will be poisoned with shouts of Unfaithful, Deceitful. . . . Slut. Should I pack myself and the children? My God, it would take their camp trunks to hold everything. I'd have to ask Roger to help carry them to the car.

She brushed the top of the receiver with her hand, wondering if she should call or write her mother from the nearest motel.

*Dearest Mother,*
   *I've run away from Roger. . . .*

No, that wouldn't do. She had some names to call him. Unimaginative, Unforgiving. . . . Dolt. Can't you see?

Outrage pounding through her head, she allowed him one line.

"What else is there to see?"

"I wanted you to stop me." Yes, that was the answer. How idiotic. How strange. I could have rented a post office box for those letters. I could have at least burned them after they were read, but no, I had to carry them around practically screaming, "Look at me! Pay proper attention to me. If you don't, I may not be here. I may be sitting on a park bench in Paris meeting another man."

Oh, must Roger and I act like competing volcanoes because my ex-lover is news to him? For me it's already past, not worth a night's explosion. But for him— Yes, he'll need the fireworks, the waterworks, the proper expressions of the fierceness of love.

# Reversals

*Tutankhamun returning from battle in his chariot, preceded by two captives. . . . The scene is symbolic of the king's dominion over foreign lands, for Tutankhamun himself is not known to have taken part in any military exploit.* [Metropolitan Museum description of a gold buckle]

 My FATHER, A FIELD ARTILLERY officer during World War II, was the man who stayed behind. He trained soldiers, but he never went to battle, a source of lifelong guilt. He reaped the rewards—promotion, salary, good assignments—yet proving himself under fire was impossible. After the war he went civilian, gathered his family, and settled near his last post in Texas, the most foreign place he'd ever lived. In mind he held the most stereotypical and, therefore, the most satisfying vision of peace—a house surrounded by a white picket fence with hollyhocks nodding over the top. My mother convinced him that hollyhocks would not grow in our soil and a white fence would need repainting every year. So he built an eight-foot cinderblock wall where ivy and honeysuckle crawled and choked each other prettily. The wall enclosed only the house's back side, containing a patio and a small yard. The front remained vulnerable to any passing stranger.

More than the realization of this fantasy, he wanted evidence that some of the men he'd trained had survived, especially when Korea began. He read the lists provided by old army friends at Fort Hood. There were too many names to remember; he went by battalion numbers. If someone was missing, he mourned privately.

His public reaction was to collect eccentrics; the lost, the forlorn, even the resolute who were so marked by their experiences they were hopelessly displaced from conventional paths. During Korea, God's measure of these people found their way to our door. There was a colonel, an ex-prisoner of a Japanese concentration camp who'd escaped, returned to his ranch in South Texas, and built a tall barbed-wire fence around his house, where he assigned himself guard duty on his front porch. All day he shot a 30-30 at nothing. A major showed up who'd survived Guam then drank himself into alcoholism and retired to a forgotten mountain in Arkansas. This one decided to move to Leon to be nearer to my father as well as to a veteran's hospital forty miles away. Father also magnetized a wealthy father's wizened son who'd retired from the service too early and lived in what his harsh-voiced wife called "the dog house," a little room tacked onto their garage. An old doctor who had done time in the air force came to visit. This one would not wear his false teeth and would not buy another set. He was incoherent most days.

Though he had other friends—people who sold real estate, ran cotton gins, were presidents of local banks— he saw more of the disturbed ones. He listened to them, drank with them. Gradually there were minor changes.

The major who'd lived on a mountaintop found himself a remote collection of hilly pastures and began raising goats. For six months my father had driven him to the VA hospital every Friday. The rifleman returned to his ranch, put his gun away, rolled up the barbed-wire fence which barricaded his house, and used it plus hundreds of reels more for a deer fence around his land. The colonel went to see him for a two-week hunt in November.

Mother, after patiently serving cases of liquor to my father and his friends, said, "The atmosphere is healthier. He's always tried to cure everybody. He's helped some."

She'd say things like that even when the man who lived in "the dog house" was still dropping by every Saturday and the toothless doctor still wouldn't wear his newest set of teeth. But Korea was over; my father was no longer a list reader.

Feeling optimistic, she went to Galveston to see her sister, leaving me home to do the cooking. I had been away in college for a year and was going to summer school in mid-July. It was my turn.

"Everything will be okay," Mother said.

"Of course." I reassured her though I knew I could never be as efficient as she was, nor would I know what to do if my father expanded his pack of loonies.

"It really will be."

I nodded and waved, remembering the time she went to Dallas on a shopping trip. The sink stopped up, my bed fell in, and my brother got expelled from school. At least I was older now, and only my father and I were home.

We were by ourselves three days before the twins appeared. Cousins, they called themselves, sons of my father's first cousin's son, hardly kin, even by Southern standards. The last time I'd seen them, they were two little boys in droopy drawers chasing each other around the house with bullwhips. The years hadn't improved them. Warren and Wallie zoomed up on matching Harley-Davidsons the Fourth of July. They were outfitted in filthy Levis, black leather vests, and the obligatory scuffed leather boots. Warren had a mermaid tattoo on his left arm; Wallie had one on his right. The mermaids' tails wriggled when the boys revved their motors.

"You know who we are?" Two narrow, clever-looking faces stared at a spot somewhere above my eyes.

"Yes."

They lounged on their cycles, letting them rumble.

"Which is which?"

"You're both the same except for the mermaids. Kenyon told me." I stood in the side door leading to the driveway. In my right hand I held a cooking fork, no use at all against Warren and Wallie, but holding it made me feel better.

"Where's your brother?"

"Jumping out of airplanes."

"Aww."

"It's the truth. He joined the paratroopers. Things have been a lot quieter since he left." Which was also true, since my brother had been in nearly every kind of trouble. Without anyone's permission, he'd ridden bulls in rodeos. Then he got involved in a one-man war against the entire football team—he stood on the roof of the stadium with a bucket of horse-apples and shied them at the team below when they finished afternoon practice. He also printed DEATH IS $ in three-foot letters on the pavement leading to the funeral home, and he went AWOL from the military school my parents finally sent him to. Sometimes I think my father collected loonies partially because he missed Kenyon so much.

"Is your daddy at home?"

"The colonel is taking a nap. I wouldn't disturb him if I were you."

Who could sleep with two Harley-Davidsons sputtering outside, two male voices rasping questions, and me shouting against them all?

My father hollered out his door, "Turn those damn things off, boys."

He commanded as usual, and the twins obeyed because, I suppose, they needed someone to obey.

"Who in the hell are they?"

I recited our long line of weak relationship like an amateur genealogist who's wandered too far out on a branch of a family tree. My father's loyalty to his kin prevailed. The twins swaggered through the back gate.

It was a long, hot afternoon, full of the noise of cicadas buzzing and glasses clinking on top of metal patio tables. Beer was all my father would give them; they drank all we had. Inside, out of sight, I overheard bits of their stumbling confessions:

"Never did get back to school."

"Yeah. We both got married too young."

"Naw. I don't think. . . . Was yours, Wallie?"

"I don't know. She never said she was pregnant."

"Mama didn't like. . . ."

"Daddy gone since we was three."

"Rode over here."

Warren said "over here" like it was the next town. They lived in Arizona.

After I fixed all of them supper, a steak and beans miracle, dinner for one stretched over one man and two wolves, I went to a family fish-fry with Royal Jimson.

We'd known each other since we were in high school and provided each other company when we were in Leon, a place we were equally ready to leave. He had to work on his father's farm that summer; I had to work in my father's kitchen.

The colonel called out after us, "Celia, I told the boys they could stay out in the empty apartment." Behind the cinder-block wall he'd built a duplex which faced the next street.

"All right." What else was there to say? I was thankful one of the apartments was empty. He could have asked them to move into Kenyon's room.

Warren and Wallie ripped out of the drive and flashed down the block before we reached the corner.

"Those are my out-law cousins," I told Royal. "I believe they think they're going downtown to buy more beer."

We both laughed. Leon is the county seat of a dry county.

Fauntleroy's Crossing is a big bend in the Leon River. Almost an island, it's still connected to somebody's corn-field by a road and to an opposite bank by the Fauntleroys' rotting wooden footbridge. The Fauntleroys themselves are long gone, leaving only their name and a picnic and parking spot.

We had to speak first to Grandpa Jimson, who was sitting, as he sat every year, in a slat-backed chair under a pecan tree. When somebody wasn't there paying respects, he told stories to children, sent messages to the men who were frying fish, or talked to the women who were unpacking bowls of coleslaw, slicing homemade bread, cutting up red onions, and showing off this year's pickles. They were all perfectly occupied, and I was perfectly happy to watch them. Other families' rituals are always impressive.

Grandpa Jimson was the nearest to Abraham I've ever seen, and like Abraham, he was interested in expansion. He asked, as he did every July Fourth, "Well, Royal, what's wrong with marrying this one?"

Royal had his answer ready. "I would, but she's too pretty." ("Too rich" or "too smart" were other acceptable variations.)

Grandpa Jimson laughed, showing a mouthful of his own teeth, and sent us off to the beer keg.

Sitting at a picnic table, surrounded by Jimsons, all of them eating fresh fried fish and drinking beer, I let Warren and Wallie sink slowly out of mind. My father might entertain every species of wildman who walked, my brother might be one, and my mother, who'd endured them all, might stay in Galveston all summer. For a while I was in a nest of peaceful folk who wouldn't even shoot firecrackers on the Fourth.

"Too dry." They said.

"Might start a grass fire."

"We can always ride over to Fort Hood and watch the army display."

That was where my father was going. He hated war, yet he loved guns, hunting, and fireworks.

After supper Royal had arranged a lazy boat ride on the river. The Leon is nothing much to look at. It's small, twisty, and full of sandbars, wicked currents, and water moccasins. On a hot July evening in the long twilight, it's a pleasant place to be in a small rowboat.

Royal and I were talking about places we planned to be later in the summer. I was going south to Cuernavaca to learn Spanish, which had swirled about me in a mystifying way ever since we moved to Texas. He was headed north to an uncle's wheat farm in Canada. Both of us were trying to imagine Canada—so immense, so far away, so cool, so full of European influences.

"Not that I'll ever get to see anything. I'm going to be tied to a combine until late August."

"Run away to Quebec," I suggested.

"I can't do that. I wish I could. I've never run away in my life. Have you?"

"No."

We were both silent; there was so much we hadn't done. Drifting under the Fauntleroys' footbridge, I looked up to see the Harley-Davidsons sitting on it, and not far downstream, slithering naked in the water, were those two overgrown toads, my cousins.

"Get out of the river you idiots. It's full of snakes and quicksand."

"Aww." Warren held onto one side of the boat. Wallie clung to the other. Both their mermaids were gleaming.

"Haven't seen one yet." Warren rocked us over to his side.

Royal knelt on the bottom of the boat to keep us from tipping.

"Don't do that!" I shouted. "Don't turn this boat over. You may need us." Self-preservation was the only angle I could think of that might appeal to the twins.

They did it anyway.

With only a halter, shorts, and tennis shoes on, I

made it to shore downriver pretty fast. Royal took longer.
He was wearing jeans. And he wouldn't pull off his almost new handmade boots in the Leon. The boat, up-
right and empty, caught by the current running round
the bend, slid past us near the opposite shore.

"Maybe it'll catch on the bank. Why did they want to
do that?" Royal stood in the mud beside me offering his
hand.

"Because I told them not to. I'm sorry."

"Do they always do what you tell them not to?"

"I don't know how they work." I smelled like a corner
of a dank closet. Dusk was drawing in; mosquitoes at-
tacked. I felt low, mean, vicious. Slapping bugs and
kicking vines aside, we crawled out. In the distance I
could hear two motorcycles creaking over the footbridge.
I hoped it would break, but it didn't. Their fools' luck
held.

Once we reached higher ground, Royal poured water
out of his boots. He bit the edge of his lower lip as he
pulled off the second one.

"Jealous bastards! They saw us having a good time."

I leaned over and kissed him. I don't know why. Maybe
it was because I'd never seen him so frustrated before, or
was it the way river water curled his hair around his
forehead?

We sat on top of an old picnic table kissing sweetly
and tentatively while blindly aiming at mosquitoes in
the dusk until Royal said, "The boat! I've got to get it
before dark."

He and three or four of his younger cousins went back
to the river. The hard-core beer drinkers were at the keg

finishing it off. I stood with them, paper cup in hand. Someone said, "Howdy!" in a foreign accent. It was Warren wearing a straw cowboy hat.

"Yes sir, I be-lieve I'll jes' have some of that."

Wallie was at the keg pumping up two beers. His disguise was a green baseball cap with John Deere printed on the back strap.

Both the hats were Kenyon's. He had a collection hanging off the antlers of a buck he'd shot.

"Get out of here," I hissed.

"A man can get mighty dry in this here part of Texas," Warren drawled.

"Now, don't we look like all those other thirsty men?"

It was so dark now it was hard to distinguish Warren and Wallie. I kept my mouth shut and let them infiltrate. The Jimsons' company never hurt anybody. When Royal appeared again, he caught me by one hand and led me to the pickup.

Just as we parked in front of my house and Royal raised one half-dry arm to pull me toward him, and just as I was about to complain about my own sogginess, we heard two motorcycles.

"Are they going to follow us everywhere?"

"I guess they don't have anything else to do."

A fist rapped on the rear window.

Warren poked his head in my side of the cab. "Y'all seem to have carried off the rest of the beer."

"Stingy!" Wallie sang from the back.

Royal looked around. "Now they've stolen the damn beer! It was supposed to go in Grandpa's truck." He stepped out to negotiate with the twins. The keg belonged to a distributor twenty miles away in McGregor, the nearest town in a wet county.

I ran inside, grabbed two big pitchers, and carried them back to the pickup. Royal was leaning on the tail-gate looking unconcerned. The twins were both leaning against the beer keg looking equally unconcerned.

"Here." I shoved a pitcher toward each one. "Fill them up and let Royal return that keg."

They gave me two half-drunk, arrogant winks.

"If you don't, you're going to be out of bed, out of board, and out of town by tomorrow."

They drew off the beer, then stumbled down the drive, wheeling their cycles and carrying a pitcher apiece.

Royal was embarrassed. "You didn't have to do that."

"What could you have done? There were two of them."

"I wouldn't have minded getting beat up if I could have just hit both of them at least once."

"Well, I would have minded. My father would have minded, and all the Jimsons would have too."

"We get in fights sometimes."

"This one wasn't worth getting into."

"You should have let me decide that."

"They are my depraved cousins. We're in front of my house."

He stared straight through the windshield.

"Goodnight, Royal." I opened my door and stepped out. If that was all the thanks I got for getting rid of the twins, he could go home and hug his hurt pride. Walking across the front porch, I stepped on a June bug on purpose.

Royal sat in his truck for about five minutes before he started the motor.

Early July fifth, the twins were still asleep, both on their sides curved toward each other. Under Mother's clean white sheets they looked like choir boys until I noticed the mermaids wriggling against the percale.

After gathering their clothes off the floor, I dropped them each a pair of my brother's old jeans and a shirt. On the way out I banged the front door, where I'd already tacked a note: NO EATS SERVED TO THE UNWASHED.

The colonel was up making coffee when I came in to start the washing machine.

"You're in a huffy mood this morning."

Why didn't I tell him they'd dumped Royal and me in the Leon, made us their stupid confederates in a beer heist, and followed us all over the county? Partially because he'd suffered through so many of Kenyon's pranks, partially because I needed his help.

"Can you get them jobs?"

"Sure, but they won't like them."

"Why not?"

"Celia, those boys don't like work . . . not the kind they'll have to do around here."

"Let's try anyway."

They wanted to ride their motorcycles. The colonel insisted on driving them to a service station, where they pumped gas, washed cars, and tinkered with other people's engines happily for five days. On the sixth day they tore down the engine of a Chevy belonging to the postmaster. They said they could have put it together again, but their boss wasn't interested in what the twins might do next.

"Why did you have to take that engine completely apart?"

Warren grinned. "We never saw one so old in such

good condition. We thought if we could find out what made it run so good, we'd—"

"We'd know something," Wallie added. They had the irritating habit of finishing each other's sentences.

The colonel said, "They can work on a fencing crew. Those boys will be safer out in the country."

When I brought up natural dangers, he assured me, "Warren and Wallie will know what to do with a rattlesnake."

From Monday till Friday their clothes were full of dust and grassburs instead of oil and grease. They demanded salami sandwiches, pickles, and a quart of iced tea apiece for lunch. When he gave me the order, Warren rolled his eyes like an aborigine who's just arrived at a salt lick. "Hot out there. We sweat all day long."

Of course I added hard-boiled eggs, cherry tomatoes, celery in Mason jars with ice like Mother packed it for family picnics, salt twisted in waxed paper, and brownies or cake. I baked three times a week now.

The second Friday when they got home, Wallie wanted to know if it would be all right to stretch a rattlesnake skin in the garage. When I said sure, he reached in his lunch sack and handed me the rattle. I'd lived in Texas eight years, and no one had ever offered me such a gift, nor had I been sitting around crying for one. Appalled at first, I stared at Wallie's expectant face. He was giving away a trophy. I counted the buttons.

"Eleven. Must have been a big snake."

"Yep." Wallie looked up at me. Both of them had light, light blue eyes, the sort that make a person appear a little crazy.

"Well . . . thank you."

"Welcome."

Then Warren, who'd been standing slightly behind him in the shadowy dusk, leaned into the light and placed a small obsidian arrowhead in my hand.

"How beautiful. Where did you find it?"

"Out there—" Warren gestured toward the west with his bulging lunch sack. As he swung it, a lot of little metal pieces dribbled all over the ground.

"What's that, Warren?"

"The post-hole digger. The foreman says we can come back to work when we put it back together again."

I sat down on the doorstep. The twins hunkered in the grass. At that moment I hoped the redbugs were chewing on them both, then I remembered that was impossible because I'd dosed them with flowers of sulphur every morning of the week.

"How long are you-all going to play this Humpty-Dumpty game? First it was a car, now a post-hole digger. If my father gets you a job where you have to ride horseback, are you going to take the saddles apart?"

"We don't know how to ride horses, Cousin."

"Your daddy . . . he's got these ideas about what we're supposed to do—"

"If the colonel's ideas don't suit you, find you own jobs."

"We will."

"Yeah . . . only, Cousin Celia, don't tell him about this old post-hole digger, please."

"All right." How many people have been bribed with a rattlesnake rattle and an arrowhead? "But he's going to find out anyway."

"We know. We just don't want to hurt his feelings.

Maybe it'll take a few days. And maybe we'll find something else by then."

I agreed to keep quiet. As long as they were doing
something, my father would be content, and so would I.
For a week I saw the twins only at supper. They were morose, sunburned, and usually dusty. I assumed they were
riding around the county looking for other jobs.

I was wrong. That summer I almost got used to being
wrong. Royal came by the house one night before going
to Canada. I hadn't seen him since July Fourth. After
our one attempt, neither of us had made a move. We
were too much alike in some ways, too different in others, and both of us were more interested in leaving than
in sorting anything out. I was glad he came to say good-
bye, though.

"There's something I ought to tell you. Do you know
what those two idiots are doing now?"

Royal leaned toward me. We were sitting next to each
other on the front porch steps, and this was as close as he
got all evening. "They're bootlegging beer. They've got
carryalls on those motorcycles. Two or three times a day
they go over to McGregor and haul it back."

"How do you know?" It was a ridiculous question. We
were both experts on how small-town gossip travels, yet
I asked, hoping it wasn't true.

"Haven't you noticed how the traffic's picked up back
there at night? Everybody calls it the Pleasant Street
Bar. You know the sheriff will be out to check on them
pretty soon."

Royal and I shook hands. The minute he drove off, I
ran down the drive toward the apartments. Two Harley-

Davidsons were neatly tucked into the carport. In front, five cars loitered. Some others were circling the block. I threw the front door open so fast I could have been a member of a raiding party. Warren was holding onto the open refrigerator door handle. Behind him cans of Lone Star, Pearl, and Bud solidly covered the shelves. Wallie sat on three cases of something. I didn't know what. I was too mad to read anymore. Altogether there were seven men in the room, more men than I'd seen in a kitchen all summer.

"Would you like—?" Warren stretched out his hand toward the beer.

Wallie shook his head sadly.

"I would like the premises cleared."

Five men shuffled out muttering, "Later." "Okay, Lady." "Haw!" "I done paid already."

When they were gone, I locked the front door and told the boys, "Your business is closed."

"What are we going to do with all this beer?" Wallie wailed. He didn't waste a minute looking contrite.

"We are going to take it back where it came from." I couldn't wait till the twins made twenty more trips to and from McGregor on their motorcycles. I couldn't trust them to get to the liquor store with the goods. They would be selling it to assorted customers all up and down the highway, roaring into farmhouse drives peddling beer door-to-door, spilling it in bowls belonging to miscellaneous puppydogs, baptizing startled armadillos by moonlight. They had no discretion and all the time in the world. My own time was running short. Mother was returning the next day. Father and I might be captivated by any number of loonies, but my mother was not going to like these two. She was patient. She would oversee and overlook the colonel's counseling sessions. But he was dealing with grown men who were war ruins, and they took themselves home or to a motel every night. Warren and Wallie had moved into our tent. All this came to mind when I went back to the house to tell my father I needed to use his pickup. He didn't ask what for, so I didn't tell him.

I drove both ways with the twins sitting next to me. On the way home, a can of beer in both shirt pockets, two in hand, and his blue eyes going almost yellow in the approaching headlights, Warren said, "Cousin Celia, what are we going to do now?" I suggested they learn horse-shoeing or some other nonmechanical trade that would sop up their energies. Then Wallie began talking about weighted shoes, dope, and other crooked methods of fixing horse races. I was sorry I'd mentioned it.

Wallie offered to drive.

"I'd be lucky to scrape myself off a hackberry tree if either of you were driving. I've seen you riding those motorcycles—weaving around like two Comanches on a war party. I'm leaving town in two days, and I plan on going with all bones intact."

It was 6:30 when we rolled into Leon. I hadn't had time to cook. On the outskirts of town I stopped and got half a dozen hamburgers to go. My father was pleased with the beer the twins provided. He told me after supper he thought they might even be learning a little about the conventions of hospitality.

"At least they're sharing."

So I had to tell him the six packs were the last of many cases they had sold at our back door.

"Celia, why have you been trying so hard with those boys?"

"Somebody's got to."

"Lots of people have. I called their mother right after they came. She couldn't deal with them any longer They've been in reform schools, in jail, in everything but the army, and the army wouldn't have them now. They stole over five hundred dollars' worth of guitars from a pawn shop. That's a felony. They pawned their own guitars, honey, then stole them. They pawned some of their mother's silver, too. She had to redeem that."

"Well, why do you try to help hopeless people?"

"Most of them aren't so hopeless. They're only confused by what has happened to them—by wars, bad marriages, bad health, reversals of various kinds."

"So are the twins—no father, too much freedom."

"And an inclination to daredevilment. They make their own disasters. My friends are only suffering from natural disorders."

There was no sense in going on though I could have. An inclination toward trouble seemed as natural to me as my father's list of his friends' turmoils. He was a strict line drawer, though, and if he made one, all you could do was either step over it and go or stay within his boundaries.

The twins were gone before breakfast the next morning. They left a note on the door saying, "Thanx. Warren and Wallie." And they left the dried snakeskin on the garage wall.

Mother drove in that afternoon just in time to unpack and advise me about what to pack, which she couldn't help doing although I'd been packing my own suitcase since I was ten. She looked rested, tanned, unworried. I was glad to have her back. There had been too many men around, too many of them needing attention. Mother attended to me and to the colonel for the rest of the day. We told her about the twins.

She laughed. "I'm sorry I didn't get to see them, but it's probably best they moved on."

"Yes," my father said.

The next afternoon, flying over the green valley of Central Mexico, I looked down at all the roads left by various civilizations—the Aztecs, the Spaniards, the Mexicans—and wondered if Wallie and Warren might one day weave over those curves on their motorcycles. What would happen to them? Anything could, for the world is full of dangers, and Warren and Wallie often went out to meet them. I hoped their luck would hold.

Except for a postcard from Zihuatanejo, an isolated Mexican town on the west coast and a collecting point for beach bums, dope lovers, and other escapists, I never heard from the twins again. The card was a familiar one, a palm-thatched roof on a pole, beneath the pole, a hammock, and behind these a calm sea meeting a blue sky. On the back were three lines: "Dear Cossin Celia, We are not workin. Yrs. Warren and Wallie." I kept the card.

# House Of The Blue Woman

 LIGHT FALLS EVERYWHERE about the land, shimmers on live oaks' leathery green leaves tough enough to endure southwestern sun, warms the gray rimrocks bordering the mesas, turns dark within the house.

"It will be simple," Celia says. "All we have to do is choose what we want."

Her husband does not reply, and she understands his silence. Nothing that is part of the past is simple, though she sometimes tries to pretend it is, tries to keep from wandering in the fields of memory. She throws away letters, yet will keep a postcard from a friend for years; she cleans out closets, but cannot bring herself to give away a single book or one of the children's old drawings. All of her mother's twenties party clothes were donated to a local theatre except a long-fringed Spanish shawl which no one will ever wear. Contradictory urges, to banish and to memorialize, pull at her.

Rain-sodden, wind-torn, the couch on the screened-in back porch is a good nest lining for field mice now. It used to be in the back room of her parents' house in Leon. Does some furniture always get shoved to the back? Mother had it moved here for Kenyon when he began ranching. What a hard-bitten life he lived out here in the country alone. Sometimes he had a wetback for company, but how much company is a man you can't talk to? Kenyon knew only ranch Spanish.

"Hoy rodeamos las vacas."

"What are you saying?" How strange a foreign language sounds when spoken by a brother. "Today we round up cattle. I don't know why I bother to tell him. He already knows. He knew when he saw me opening the corral gates."

Why had she been at the ranch that morning? Had she just stopped by on the way from Leon to San Antonio? And why can't she recall anything else Kenyon said? Her memory seems to operate like a defective tape recorder, one compelled to start and stop by the vaguest whim. Doesn't matter, she tells herself, knowing everything, every scrap and rag-tag bit she can remember matters too much.

Edward pushes the door open. There's nothing to hold it shut, not even a stick poked through the metal hasp. Why lock? It's a small, shabby house in a pasture two miles off the highway. Who's to break in and steal? To step inside is to enter a cave where people have been storing throwaways from all the houses they have ever lived in.

Oh, that wretched rug! Yellowish brown, bluish red, fuzzily stamped to look like an oriental. The Saturday mornings she spent vacuuming it . . . all those lost mornings. Too much of a woman's daily life is spent in repetition. Mother hung heavy wet clothes on their crooked wire lines. They might as well have hung there till next Saturday. Kenyon? Where was he? Riding his bicycle backward around the square? Up in the attic of the courthouse chasing bats out and being chased by the county clerk? At home seldom and in trouble there when he was. Her father? Gone downtown. He had his own work to do and despised being in the house while women were cleaning. If she was not finished by the time he returned, he'd tell her, "Turn off that infernal machine." She took her mother's attitude; it was easier to humor him than to fight. In the end, she got her way. She left . . . to school . . . to marry . . . to clean her own house.

Edward points to the dirt daubers' nests on the ceiling.

Celia nods. This is the one house she'll never have to clean. It will be moved, trucked away to clear the view from the new ranch house she and Edward are building. Obliterated, a hollow, bitter-sounding word. Once she'd overheard Kenyon saying something to one of the wetbacks about building.

"Hoy construimos un pedazo de cerca nueva." He read aloud from a manual.

"I've forgotten all the Spanish I ever studied."

"I'm giving Juan the word. 'Today we will build a new piece of fence.' He isn't going to like it. He'd rather chase goats."

"Do you mind fencing?"

"No. Why should I? It's part of the deal. I don't pay lease money, but I've got to keep the fence repaired and the windmills running. I've built fence for other people. I might as well do it on our own ranch."

Then he was out, in the saddle, and gone. Kenyon never stayed in any house long.

The walls, once white, are gray with dust. There's a broken rattan armchair, a twin bed tilting on three legs, a table painted red. Two kerosene lamps sit on top of a chest. Edward picks one up.

"Look, there's still kerosene in it." He seems as pleased as an archeologist who has unearthed an amphora with traces of oil inside.

"Trim the wick. Don't let it smoke." Her father's warning. She hears his voice more distinctly at the ranch than she does in Leon, and she sees him more clearly. He wears his old khaki-colored hunting clothes—he likes his old clothes best. Soft yellow lamplight glows on Mother's and Father's faces, on Edward's and the children's. They sit around the red kitchen table, the one with the legs in the wrong places, the table Mother got rid of after the last move. Celia helped cook supper in Kenyon's crazy kitchen. There's only one water faucet, which is attached to a pipe running underground from the windmill. Outside the house wall the pipe juts up and bends over a windowsill to the sink like a vine working its way in. He has a butane stove, a refrigerator full of pots of dried-out beans, and a skillet stuck with pieces of fried venison.

"William, he's been shooting deer out of season."

"Maybe one of the Mexicans did it."

"If he did, Kenyon let him."

"He's trying to make it on his own, Kate. Let him live off the land if he wants to."

Father's gun and Edward's lean together, barrels up, in a corner. Mid-October. Dove season. Both of them have been crouched in the dry weeds behind the high rim of a pond shooting birds as they swoop down to water at sunset.

Where's Kenyon?

Gone. Though he still runs steers and goats here, he leases another ranch also, one with a better house on it. Juan and Luis are with him though sometimes one of them stays at this ranch. Whenever they are parted Kenyon gets his two wetbacks together on Saturday nights. "So they can speak Spanish and get drunk. Hiding out all the time, they need it. Once a month they cut each other's hair." One of Kenyon's rare explanations. He's thirty years old. Now he pays his parents lease money. He has a hard time accepting favors; however, he still calls her every December twenty-third.

"Could you get Mother something for me?"

She is so sure of this yearly request that she automatically buys his gifts for him before he asks. Her mother does the same. Early every December she asks Celia what she should get the children from Kenyon.

"Don't you think we ought to tell him he's old enough to do his own Christmas shopping?"

"Celia, even if we did, he'd never get around to it. He's too busy."

"That's just an excuse, Mother."

"I know it."

She liked catering to men. After Father died there was no one left to look after but Kenyon. He began sleeping at home more; Juan and Luis stayed at the ranches. He helped Mother hold together the property Father had left. Mother kept clean clothes in his closet and never asked him where he'd been. For a while it seemed he would remain a bachelor, the youngest child, the son petted by the one who needed him most. No matter what time he came in, she cooked his supper. Yet she would say, "I won't be here forever, Kenyon. You'd better find a wife to keep you warm at night." They had a running battle over the thermostat at the house in Leon. Mother's arthritis demanded constant warmth, while Kenyon threw open every window in his room before going to bed. He wanted fresh cold air and lots of cover.

"Edward, I wonder where that stove is?"

"What stove?" He watches her in a speckled mirror on the wall by the door.

"The Franklin stove that used to be in this room. It was the only heat he had besides the kitchen oven." She speaks to his reflection, to a ghost of himself already present, an idea so unbearable, she whirls around to face him.

"I guess he moved it to a house on one of his other leases."

They walk into the only other room, where a long cedar chest, an old one of her mother's, sits in the middle of the floor taking up most of the space.

"Do you want to—?"

"Yes." She wants the chest opened though she fears what may be inside. All her life women have kept what they couldn't bear to part with in chests like this. What would a man keep?

Dirt daubers' nests cling to the inside lid. Is there anyplace they can't get in? Quilts, old ones made by a grandmother she never knew. Roughly sewn, first attempts, not the fine ones she made later. The batting, after years of washing, is lumpy and the large cotton squares faded. Ugly, yet serviceable, they must have been given to Kenyon to use out here. Mother's mother. Poor in the beginning, yet hardy. She and her husband were small ranchers. They had five children, and each one went to college. Only one finished. Kenyon was expelled from two high schools and wouldn't stay in college past the first semester. Two generations later he also refused to live within the boundaries of his grandparents' or his parents' dreams.

"I'd rather chop cedar."

"Why?"

"I can't stand sitting still inside all that time. What good will it do me?"

Celia, four years older and a college senior, didn't try to answer him. He joined the paratrooper corps for three years. Afterward he worked as a day laborer—cowboying—on other people's ranches, got a job as an assistant to a vet, got his father to co-sign his note at the bank, and began ranching. It took him six years to complete this cycle, about as long as it took her to finish a B.A. and an M.A. By the time she had two children, he'd leased three ranches and was buying one of his own in Colorado. He showed up in San Antonio sporadically. Mainly he came to see Edward, to talk with him about the cattle market, mohair prices, taxes, to tell stories about wetbacks, honky-tonks, sharp traders. He seldom spoke of women.

Celia pulls out another quilt.

"Whose books?" Edward picks up an old copy of Montaigne's essays.

Celia takes it from him and reads, "No one makes a definite plan of his life, and we think about it only piecemeal." It is heavily underlined. Had she marked it, or had Kenyon? Books . . . her only gifts to him. He'd asked for them as they both grew older. There was one he'd bought himself, *The Stockman's Handbook*, and another, *Farm and Ranch Spanish*. "Yd. puede vivir en esta casa. You can live in this house." Kenyon's hoard . . . collections of stories, *The Sheep Book*, *Immortal Poems of the English Language*. Pragmatists and poets lie down together in his cedar chest.

"I loaned him the Montaigne. I'd forgotten it." She leans forward to scoop up the books, and as she does, her tears splotch the covers.

"Here. Here." Edward takes the books from her and holds her against him with both arms. The ache she has been stifling in her throat rises. She cries quietly and is soon silent. Almost a year ago when Edward had to tell her, her grief was defiant.

"No!" She screams again and again. Kneeling on the floor while Edward talks to someone on the phone, she denies. "It isn't Kenyon. They just think it's him."

"Honey, it is. Sally's brother called from the funeral home. She couldn't speak."

Edward bends to lift her up. She resists. It's 2:00 A.M. Both of them have been in a deep sleep after coming in from a party an hour ago. Isn't she still asleep? It must be a terrible dream. Terrible. Edward, wake me up. Edward? She slides her hands away from her eyes. In the selfishness of new grief, she has almost forgotten the strong friendship between her husband and her brother. She rises to hold on to him.

"How?"

"He had a wreck in his pickup. He was at an auction,

the cattle auction in Georgetown. It goes on till pretty late. Then . . . they think he stopped for a beer. He was driving home. The truck ran off the road. There was a ditch, a deep one. He smashed into a metal culvert."

"How?" She can't visualize any of it; the road, the ditch, the culvert. A month later, staring at the splinters of Kenyon's windshield twinkling in the fresh spring grass, she will trace the route of his death backward from the gaping culvert's dented steel circle to the tire marks still impressed in roadside weeds where he veered into the ditch, but neither she nor anyone else will ever know exactly how it happened.

"They think maybe he went to sleep at the wheel. Celia, they want to know when to tell your mother."

He was thirty-six years old. Thirty-six, married seven months. Poor Sally.

"I've got to call him back."

"Who?"

"Sally's brother. I didn't even know his name. I wrote it down."

She had written on her desk calendar next to September 10: Kenyon's wedding day. For years he gave laconic answers to Mother's tentative questions: "Wouldn't you like to bring someone to dinner?" "No." "Don't you want to ask somebody over for a drink?" "I don't." Now he began talking about marriage.

"He even talks to me about children," Mother says during one of her weekly phone calls.

"Who is the girl?"

"I don't know her name. You know how it is around Leon. Everybody knows everything, but nobody here

knows Kenyon's girl. She must be from somewhere else."
Amused by him as usual, yet annoyed at his reticence,
she sighs. "We'll just have to wait till he's ready to tell
us."

A month later Celia and Edward go to Leon for Sunday dinner. Afterward Kenyon announces, "I've got
some new steers that need doctoring. You come with
me." He takes her to the ranch thirty miles away.

Never before has he asked her to help do anything out
there. For fifteen years all she's been asked to do is buy
Christmas gifts. Dressed in city clothes, a pants suit and
a long cloak, she rides a cow pony through a pasture.
Dried eryngo thistles, purple in October, are gray by November. The fuzzy mullein leaves remain pale green.
Celia frees her cloak hem from a low-growing cedar.

"That's some outfit you've got on."

"I feel like a character in a nineteenth-century novel."

Wind flips the cloak's red lining back over the saddle's
cantle. How did women ride side-saddle with all those
clothes on?

"You get that one." Kenyon nods toward a steer. If she
hadn't been there, if he'd been working with a man, he
would have only nodded.

"How do you know he's sick?"

"Look at the rims of his eyes. Too pink. Shipping
fever."

They cut out four steers from the herd and drive them
to the corral.

"You can still ride."

"Reflex I guess. The horse is doing all the work.
What's his name?"

"Celia, you know I never get around to naming horses."

He calls all horses "Horse" and all dogs, even the ones he works sheep with, "Dog." He'd had a series of pets when they were growing up; an Irish setter called Rufus, a colt named Whiskey, a crow with a broken wing called Poe, a tomcat named Killer who brought the crow home. When he began using animals on the ranch, he quit naming them.

She watches him give shots. He handles needles and syringes deftly.

"I'm cheaper than the vet." Kenyon grins, turns the steers loose, unsaddles the horses. All the way home, a long roundabout way over country roads, he asks questions.

"You and Edward. You're happy?"

"Reasonably."

"How did you know you would be?"

"We didn't."

Realizing she's playing the laconic role now, Celia tries to help. "Tell me her name."

"Sally . . . Sally Morgan . . . from Lampasas. She has three children. Her first husband was a bum, a drunk. She finally took the girls and ran. Do you think I can be a father to three little girls? I don't know anything about children."

"At least you like them. You could learn. Sometimes step-parents are better than real ones. Certainly they're better than none at all." She waits a bit then asks, "Kenyon, why this particular woman?"

He's driven to Leon's airport—a hangar, a wind sock, a graded pasture—where he lands after trips to the Colorado ranch. Both of them lean against the warm grille of the car. In the dusk Celia can barely see a short concrete runway; she hears the wind sock flap.

Without looking at her, Kenyon answers, "She's the only one I ever wanted to go back to."

"Well," she shrugs, "you're the one who has to decide whether to stay."

"I know."

Once they're back in Leon, he leaves her at their mother's, picks up Edward, and wanders all over town with him asking the same questions.

On the way back to San Antonio the following day Edward says, "Do you think he'll marry?"

"Yes. I don't know when, though. Right now he's going through the confirmation stage. He's made his choice. He only wants us to approve."

"Do you?"

"Oh, Edward! I don't know the woman. Kenyon's thirty-five. He's old enough to take his chances with the rest of us."

His wedding, like all the other decisive moments in his life, seemed accidental, something he found his way to by chance. He and Sally quarreled, then parted, apparently forever, Celia learned through her mother, the only person who had the slightest idea of his goings and comings. In a few months, she delivered a different message.

"He came home this afternoon early. You know he never does that. 'Mother, you want to go to a wedding?' he said. What was I to say? There wasn't even time to call you. I spent thirty minutes looking for his suit. Never did find it."

"Where was the wedding?"

"Sally's living room. She looked lovely. All the girls were dressed up, even had nosegays. There was Kenyon in an old sports coat and a pair of slacks. He didn't have a tie on. I tried to get him to wear one of your daddy's. It was a new one he'd never worn. But would he do it? No!"

"Who else was there?"

"Sally's brother and sister-in-law."

"And that's all?"

"Except for the preacher."

"Why didn't he let me know?"

"Celia, he hates any kind of fuss, any kind of cere-mony. Sally's brother and his wife were probably just convenient when they needed witnesses."

A week later Edward and Celia were on their way to Sally's house carrying a bottle of champagne, which Celia threatened to crack over Kenyon's head.

"Did he go through the windshield?"

"I don't know."

"Why do I have to know? After someone's dead, what does it matter?"

"The details." Edward spreads his hands before him palms up as if he had already gathered the facts and was presenting them to her. "Maybe we deal with death this way."

"Let's not tell Mother till in the morning. She might as well sleep tonight. And I don't want anybody calling her on the phone. Someone must go to the house. Tell Sally's brother." For an instant she puts grief aside while she ponders how to tell her mother. Leon is four hours from San Antonio. The nearest kin is a cousin. Yes, she's close enough and loving. Celia gives Edward the cousin's name. "She'll stay with Mother till we come."

All the way to Leon, Cynthia cries sporadically. William, thirteen, two years older, pats her on the head. They were too young to go to their grandfather's funeral, too young for this one, really. But when is anybody old enough?

Her mother meets them at the door, all her suffering caught in her eyes. "How could . . . how could this happen?" she asks, knowing, surely, the futility of the question. She has lost so many already, a husband, her parents, a sister, a brother, and all of them before they were old. But Kenyon is the youngest, and she has seen him through everything, the escapades, the expulsions, the derelictions, and has hoped always he would become a man with a man's sense of responsibility. His life was a promise finally delivered and almost immediately destroyed.

They cannot escape by busying themselves with details. It is a duty belonging solely to his wife, though she asks, at various times, for their agreement. Kenyon is buried with his boots on. Sally, knowing he habitually went without, requests no tie, no belt. His hands lay folded under his best gray Stetson, which Celia doubts that he ever wore.

An old friend of the family's, a lady in her seventies, says, "Doesn't he look handsome?"

Celia, utterly sick of conventional pieties, forgets herself. "No," she replies in a dry, cold voice, "he just looks dead."

Edward closes the top of the chest. For a moment
Celia sees a closed coffin. Through the thin walls she
hears the windmill's painful creak. The same breeze that
moves its blades scratches oak limbs against the house's
unpainted boards. She walks across the small rooms,
pacing the enormous wilderness of the past. Longing to
be outside, she starts toward the door. On the opposite
wall of the front room she notices, for the first time, a
crude drawing of a woman in blue chalk, the kind used
to mark sheep and goats. Wavy lines represent hair, two
dots form nipples, a dark triangle indicates pubic hair.
Two open, unfinished angles become legs—an image
made to summon up woman, to ease loneliness, to give
shape to sexual fantasies. Which one of the wetbacks
had drawn it? Juan? Luis? Who else did Kenyon stake out
here? Kenyon himself? The unknown male figure retreats,
a shadow on horseback as mysterious as her brother's daily
life, as inexplicable as his death.

She carries the Montaigne, the *Farm and Ranch Span-*
*ish*, and two kerosene lamps. Edward brings the speckled
mirror, then the cedar chest. A truck arrives to move the
house and all remaining contents away. Within a year a
new ranch house is finished. Sheltered by a grove of live
oaks, it has long double porches, high white ceilings, a
fieldstone fireplace, and many windows. Celia, gazing
out these windows, still sees her brother's shabby old
house whenever she looks over at the cleared site.

# The Circuit Rider

 EXCEPT FOR THE FACT he'd been called for, he hardly knew what he was doing at Edna Sommers's bedside. Sure he'd been by to see her, dropped in from time to time, but never as a minister. He'd come as a neighbor only. This morning the oldest Natham boy, who should have been in school yet never seemed to be, had banged on his door, shouting, "Mister Hardeman! Mister Hardeman!" The wind blew his wail back and forth across the porch, through the door to his bed in the front room, and into his early morning dreams, where it became a faintly accusing voice demanding something.

No one but Edna knew he used to preach. If he had known, the Natham boy would have shouted for Brother Hardeman. Country people didn't bother to discriminate between a Methodist, a Baptist, or an Episcopalian; as far as they were concerned, he would simply be Brother, and he was Brother to no one anymore. He made that plain to Edna two years ago when he first came back.

"I have retired from preaching and I don't want anybody calling on me to—"

"There isn't anybody to call on you here but me and the Nathams, John. That's everybody in Pinto unless you count Walter, and I wouldn't."

"Walter?"

"Walter Ammons. He lives five miles or so out by the creek in a shack he built himself. Martha, his niece, brings him groceries from Leon. The only way I know he's still there is she waylays me at the store sometimes and gets me to haul his stuff out when she can't make it. That's not often. When I take his sacks by, I may see him and I may not. More often not. He's a regular hermit, always has been. Writes poetry. Used to. I don't know if he still does. I'm glad you came back. Pinto is a god-forsaken ghost town."

"I noticed. The general store, the hotel." Everything was boarded up. No vacant-eyed windows stared at him, each one was blinded by weathered gray boards.

"You haven't said anything about the P.O."

"I thought maybe you were still—"

"You forgot. The P.O. was in the general store. They closed it—the government did. At least they waited till I retired. I don't mourn for it. If you look the public in the face for forty years, you can get sick of the public's face. Get a box in Leon if you want one. That's the nearest P.O. now."

"The depot's still here." Though he spoke casually as if ruminating about the weather, he was pleased the depot survived.

"I bought it when the train stopped coming. The Nathams live down there. They're cedar choppers, but they pay the rent most of the time. They won't bother you. I don't think they've got any religion."

She didn't ask him why he'd come back to a ghost town, what brought him or pushed him, and he was grateful for her easy acceptance. He could not have explained it anyway; he hadn't enough words to propel her forward in time as he'd known it, to folk-rock at the eleven o'clock service and day-glo paint sprayed on walls.

God Is Dead in garish pink—adolescent malice spewed
on the walls of his church, and he could do nothing
about it except retreat. Edna lived in a fuzzy extension of
the nineteenth century, and it was just as well. Because
that was what he wanted, to live there, too.

Go away, she told the Natham boy when she saw them
together. He left without questioning her, obedient and
dull as he would be the rest of his life.

"Don't you need a doctor, Edna?" A heap of pillows
propped her up. Over her legs a gaudy star-patterned
quilt rippled. Her hair, usually worn in braids wrapped
about her head, was a long coil of gray white reaching
down to a white shawl thrown around her shoulders.
The ties of an old-fashioned drawstring nightgown, the
kind his mother used to wear, showed above a fold of the
shawl. Without powder or lipstick, her face had become
another more complex mask. Illness made her seem
weaker and at the same time had drawn the strong lines
in her face deeper. In one instant her expression was
helpless, and in the next she became imperious.

"I don't want a doctor. I'm eighty. I've lived long
enough. My mind is clear. Thank God for that."

He drew a chair up to her bedside in a room he'd never
seen before. Beneath a window he noticed someone had
recently lit the gas space heater. Its small red and blue
fire would soon cut the cold of the November norther
which had blown in that morning. A table, covered with
stacks of books nudging a tall lamp, stood next to her
bed. Behind him he was aware of a closet door slightly
ajar; he had suppressed an instinct to close it when he
came in. Over her head on the wall above the bed's high

carved knobs were two men's pictures in gold-painted oval frames. One he recognized as her father, a sepia-toned patriarch, his authority faded to ineffectual pleasantness. The other man, a young dandy wearing a derby hat, he thought he knew but couldn't be sure.

"That's Billy Burrell, the drummer who boarded with us. He used to travel all over this part of the country in a buggy with a valise full of samples, squares of cotton, velvet, wool, silk. Once he told me he'd give me whatever I wanted. I took nothing but the samples. This quilt is pieced from them. He had to go all the way back to Dallas to get some more." "Yes, I remember him now." He was a small man, always wore a suit and the same black derby he had on in the picture. Only man in that part of the country who owned a derby hat. Mostly he remembered the buggy wheels—yellow, all the spokes and rims painted sulphur yellow. Impractical for dusty roads, but eye-catching. Standing on the wooden walkway in front of the general store, he'd watched those wheels whirl away like dizzying earthbound suns. He'd thought, long before he ever saw one, circus wagons must have painted wheels like that. Billy Burrell in his buggy was the world full of possibilities.

Edna's eyes flickered. She stared so intently he did not know whether she was really looking at him or was about to focus on a distant memory.

"How would you remember? You were only a child."

"I must have been around ten years old when he was through here last. Nineteen-sixteen. In the fifth grade. You were my teacher." Not once since he'd returned had he mentioned she was fifteen years older than he was; he had put those years tactfully aside. Until today the difference in their ages had been compressed, squeezed until it vanished. Now she drew it out, playing time's concertina in her mind.

"I had forgotten," she said without remorse. "There were so many. We had to teach all ages then, but I should have remembered you. That was my last class. I was an old maid by country standards, twenty-five. I detested being an old maid and a school teacher, one reason I quit. . . . I liked the children though. Some of my students were bigger than I was. Great hulks of boys standing in the doorway watching me ride up on horseback, the only way I could get there in the snow. They would take the horse behind the school to the corral while I went inside to change from trousers to skirt. White, everything snow-covered. Beautiful. Did it used to snow more then or do I only think so? I gave you Shakespeare's lines from *Love's Labour's Lost* to memorize because that was the only time of year you could feel them. 'When icicles hang by the wall. And Dick the shepherd, blows his nail, And Tom bears logs into the hall, And milk comes frozen home in pail.' . . . That they understood. In their bones, they understood—"

She stopped to catch her breath and in the wheeze of her lungs he thought he heard pneumonia.

"Let me get you a doctor, Miss Edna." He hadn't called her Miss until now. Talking about school did it.

"Too late and I don't want one anyway. I intend to die a natural death, not to be taken to one of those old people's homes to be kept alive, an old mummy dottering." Then as the wind hurried around the corner, she said, "I have something to confess."

He reared back so heavily the straight wooden chair creaked with the weight of his recoil.

"I'm not a priest. I was an Episcopal minister."

"Doesn't matter. I'm not a Catholic."

"Then there's no reason for confession."

"I don't mean it that way exactly. Long ago I asked God's forgiveness, but I could not repent. I could not say I was sorry."

"Are you now?" He was shocked to hear himself falling into a pattern he wanted to forget, the rote of guilt, repentence, judgment. "I had no right to ask. It doesn't matter."

"No. I wasn't sorry then. I'm not now. But I've never told anyone. Now I must. I've lived longer than I should have. Nobody here to talk to till you came but the Nathams. Might as well be shouting down a well. Walter . . . never could rely on him. If you weren't here I'd be talking to myself. I've done plenty of that in my day. Here, take this." Raising her head slowly, she lifted her arm then let it fall. "You'll have to do it. The key. Around my neck. It's to a box. Top right-hand drawer of my dresser."

Clumsily he pulled at the thin silver chain around her neck, unhooked it, felt the key warm with her body's heat. Smelled of talcum powder, too sweet. The odor always made him want to sneeze. Opening the drawer of her dresser, he saw himself wavering in the mirror. Contortions of the glass or the mind? He couldn't be sure. Reflected behind him was Edna, a harridan queen waiting for her minister to do her bidding. The drawer was a tangled mass. Ribbons, hairpins, cards—old birthday cards—artificial flowers. From a hat? Spilled face powder, a cameo brooch with a bent clasp, broken pencils. She'd made them keep their desks so neat, books to one side, pencils and pens in a cigar box on the other. In the back on the right. Did left-handed people keep their treasures on the left? A narrow, gray metal box, light, not heavy with hidden misery.

"Open it. Go on, open it. You bring to mind people I used to want to scream at in the post office while they held onto a letter they had been waiting for too long. I must have known every lovesick boy and girl in town."

Some terror possessed him, made his hands unwilling to turn the key in the lock. He cursed his timidity—it had held him back for years, kept him at a distance from the people he most needed to be near. His left hand clutched the side of the box as he used to clutch the wooden ridge on top of the pulpit when he preached, something obdurate to cling to, to hold him up before the closed, unchanging faces of his congregation.

"Go on, John, there's nothing in there to bite you."

Her persistence moved his hand. He turned the key, lifted the lid. One long envelope and a piece of folded paper lay inside. On the envelope was the printed address of a lawyer's office in Leon and in Edna's handwriting, her name. He studied it as he had studied her brief corrective notes on his papers more than fifty years ago.

"My will. Not important. I've nothing to leave but the depot, this rattletrap of a house and two hundred acres, all that's left of Papa's ranch. Nothing on top of it and nothing under." She grimaced and he knew she was thinking of oil. That had been the rumor for years in Pinto. Everything had been built on it: the hotel, the general store, even wary bankers had committed themselves. But there had been nothing. Drillers came and left wells capped. For a while everyone based their dreams on cement well-tops, thinking, conjecturing there must be oil under those mild gray circles. In their minds they painted dollar signs on them, and beneath every handshake with a newcomer a portent of greed scratched. Weeds grew up around the cement, and farmers eventually came to hate them for obstructing straight rows. Ranchers used them for salt licks for cattle, a safe place to leave a block of salt, no sense in killing another patch of grass. Oil fever died and Pinto became one more country town to be obliterated.

"They'll sell it to somebody who never wanted anything except the land adjoining his."

"They?"

"My nephews and nieces . . . scattered all over the state. Some of them don't even know each other. Never mind. Land takes its own revenge."

Eroded, overgrazed, covered with horehound and clumps of mesquite, useless now. Was that what she meant? Her father had been a rancher.

Her legs moved restlessly under the quilt she'd pieced from samples Billy Burrell had given her, a Texas star pattern, one giant star of diamond shapes.

"The other paper. That's the one I want you to see."

When the paper crackled open she said, as if to prepare him, "I had a child."

A photostatic copy of a birth certificate, crisp, like new, not often looked at. The blanks were filled in by the same precise hand that had corrected his papers. County of Williamson, Franklin, Tennessee. Full Name of Child: Eleanor Sommers (Taylor). Female. Legitimate? Blank, the question unanswered. Date of Birth: July 28, 1917, the year after Edna quit teaching. Father's Full Name: William T. Burrell. Mother's Full Name: Edna Sommers. The lines of handwriting, photographed white on black, streaked across the page.

"Why, Edna?" Meaning, why must he know this?

"I couldn't get to it and I couldn't pull myself out of bed to that drawer. It must be destroyed. I haven't the strength. You're the one who'll have to do it. I felt you ought to know what I was asking of you. Will you burn it, John?"

"When's the last time you ate?"

"I don't want anything to eat."

"When did you eat last?"

"Yesterday. Mrs. Natham brought me some soup."

"I'll fix you something." He stood up and started to the door.

"No! That's not what I want. Promise you'll burn it. It was my secret all my life, the only one I had. My parents knew, of course, and the Taylors, my aunt and uncle I stayed with in Franklin, but there's no reason for anybody else to come prying around in my things after I'm gone and find out. Aunt Eleanor and Uncle Todd raised her as one of their own. Eleanor even gave her own first name to my child. They never told her and neither did I. It would be a shame for some busybody to go through my papers and tell her she was my illegitimate daughter."

"Edna—" He stopped himself before he could say, anybody can go to the courthouse any time and get their birth certificate. Instead he asked, "She used to visit here, didn't she?" Summer afternoons late when he was home on vacation from seminary he used to see her riding out of town on horseback with a young girl beside her, a cousin or niece, everyone thought. Later, still before the sun went down in those long days, they would return, riding more slowly, both of them with wet hair, and he'd wondered then how a woman the age of Edna could still enjoy swimming in a creek.

"Yes, in the summer when she was a child. Aunt Eleanor came to visit Mama and Papa—she was his only sister—and she couldn't leave the children at home. People didn't then. I watched my daughter grow up in snatches, saw moments of her life. Hard not to show how partial I was to her, but there were so many children around, first and second cousins visiting. No one noticed but Aunt Eleanor, and she watched us all the time. Later she came by herself. Those were the years I thought I should have let her be adopted by strangers. Todd made Eleanor let her come after Papa died. It was even harder then, to keep from telling her when she was alone. I gave my word to Todd, though, and he never doubted it. A generous man. Last time I saw her was in thirty-eight. She was graduating from college. I went back to Tennessee for it, to Nashville. She was in school there—Peabody College. After that I didn't see her again."

"Why not?"

She sighed and looked at him like an adult trying to be patient with a child. "It was time for her to have her own life. I was afraid I might get in the way. Afraid I couldn't keep my mouth shut any longer. I was terribly proud of her. Peabody was a teachers' college and I had been a teacher. I wanted to turn to all those parents at that graduation and say, "That's my daughter." Even then, after so many years, I wanted to claim her. Aunt Eleanor was good to write to me about her though. But Eleanor died thirty years ago, and so did Todd." She turned her head away from him and looked toward the fire as if she were considering the limitations of her life, then calmly looked directly at him again.

John cleared his throat. "What about?" He nodded toward Burrell's picture behind her head.

"He left that here one time. I didn't put it up till a year or two ago. He had it with him on one of his trips. Meant to take it home and forgot, I guess. I thought he'd come back to get it, and when he didn't, I didn't want to know what he intended. I didn't tell him I was pregnant . . . probably he guessed it. Billy was married. Had a wife and two boys. I knew it when I took up with him. It's an old story, the traveling salesman and the farmer's daughter." Her lips turned up slightly at the corners, a half-smile acknowledging the vulnerability of a woman who loves a worthless man. A rasping cough shook her. As soon as she could get her breath, she whispered, "Burn that certificate, John. Get the skillet off the stove in the kitchen and burn it. Here. So I can see."

He glanced at the two gold ovals above the bed, framing her life like a pair of parentheses, yet she had eluded them both. She bent the harsh morality of her father's generation to include her child in her family and pushed aside her lover's callousness to attend to her own needs. Starting out again, he sensed the direction of the kitchen, though he'd never been in it. On all his visits they had either sat on the front porch or in the living room.

When Edna came to see him, they sat in his kitchen.

The hall, closed doors, sallow daylight at the end. He hurried toward the light. Yes, the kitchen. Cold, an empty can of tomato soup and a pan with some left in it on the stove. Mrs. Natham hadn't bothered to clean up. He searched cabinets until he found another pan and another can of soup. Tomato was all she had, must be all she liked. Wasn't there anything else to eat in the house? When had she gone to Leon last? She had no regular schedule. He saw her drive by his house or heard her car. Once a week, on Saturdays usually, she'd stop to give him his few necessities. He'd planned to live off the land. For the most part he had. Raised chickens, kept a garden. Taught himself how to by remembering what he'd learned as a boy, by reading *The Whole Earth Catalogue*, and by sending off for free government bulletins. Hadn't been easy, learning how to subsist. Caught up in instructions about organic gardening, reading cookbooks on canning and preserving, making repairs on what was left of his parents' house, busying himself playing Crusoe, he'd not had time to notice all of Edna's comings and goings. Matches? Some in his pocket. He struck one to light the stove, put the soup on, and went back to Edna, carrying a black cast-iron skillet in one hand. In the other hand he carried a glass of water.

"Here." He held it to her lips. "Drink some of this. I've put some soup on." He had to tilt the glass to her mouth. She drank a little; the rest trickled down the sides of her chin.

"It would be easier if we had a straw." He pulled out his handkerchief, folded it over till he found a clean corner, and wiped her mouth.

She shook her head slowly. "Don't worry with me, John. Did you get the skillet?"

"Yes." He showed it to her.

"Burn this then." She pushed the paper away from her side toward him.

He crumpled it in his fist, placed it in the frying pan on his knees and struck a match. For an instant it flared up. Looking over at Edna, he saw she was smiling, and for a moment he was happy watching her. Her hands moved lightly over the violent colors of the quilt. Red, purple, pink, yellow, light green, all made to catch a woman's eye. In the wisps of smoke from the burning paper he saw dust spun by yellow buggy wheels. The fire wouldn't burn long enough to heat the skillet through. Flaky black ashes covered the bottom.

"There. It's done, Edna. Edna?" He placed the skillet carefully on the floor, leaned over, touched her hand, took it in his own, and tried to find her pulse, but there was none. He put his head to her chest and heard nothing. Easing her body flat, he closed her eyes with his thumbs and drew the star-patterned quilt over her.

What must he do next? His grief, so new, was contained within like a splinter that had pierced his skin but couldn't yet be felt. There was no one nearby but the Nathams living in the old M.K.T. depot Edna owned—had owned. Walter? Five miles away.

Practical in small matters if not in large ones, he turned off the gas space heater and picked up the skillet. She'd died believing she was keeping her secret from the curious eyes of survivors. All those kin. Where were they? Scattered, uninterested in an old aunt who insisted on living by herself in the country. Carrying the charred skillet, he went back to Edna's kitchen, where he saw the soup he'd been warming for her boiling over the top of the pan. He dropped the skillet on a cold burner and saved the soup.

He'd gone without breakfast. Only mildly surprised at the demands of his body, he picked up the spoon he'd stirred the soup with and began eating out of the pan. Never liked tomato. Could make better himself. In his own house, using food he raised, he prepared his meals carefully and read while he ate.

He finished half the soup, washed the pan and spoon, then went out the back door, catching the screen so it wouldn't slam. Habit. No need now. Edna was past caring. For a moment he stood on her back steps staring at the sky, waiting as though held by the quiet cold. The sky was overcast. He guessed it was around noon. He'd freed himself from counting hours by giving away his watch when he came back to Pinto, back to sun time he'd learned as a farm boy.

Hurrying now, he walked toward the depot, a frame railroad mustard-colored building standing by the tracks behind town, what was left of town. Two limestone buildings remained: the general store with the P.O. in one corner, where Edna had been postmistress for forty years, and next to it the hotel, its second story crumbling. Across the street the bank's red brick vault looked peculiarly solid even though the building around it had long since been removed. Down the road toward Leon was a similar reminder of the schoolhouse, two broad stone steps dented in the middle by hundreds of hurrying feet. On the north side at a short distance from everything else an abandoned Baptist church sagged as though all the long-winded revivalists had finally weakened the walls with their fervor.

He was relieved to see Natham's pickup in front of the depot. He hoped he could get Natham—he didn't know the man's name, had no reason to as they'd never done more than nod at each other—to drive to Leon twenty miles away for an undertaker.

Since he'd returned to Pinto, almost two years ago, retired early from the ministry, Hardeman had avoided the county seat. He had no car or telephone, no radio or television set. The one luxury he'd allowed himself was an old Victrola that had to be hand-cranked and records he'd collected on long bachelor afternoons in secondhand shops. Edna had brought him what he needed from town: coffee, salt, flour, sugar, dried milk, matches, razor blades. Everything else, books and catalogs mostly, came by mail, and she'd brought that too. By astute planning he'd succeeded in removing himself from a world he no longer liked or wanted to understand.

"Mister Natham." He walked to the pickup and shouted, not wanting to go to the door of the depot, not wanting to see the inevitable squalor on the other side of it. They had six children, usually without enough clothes, certainly without sufficient wits. Cedar choppers tended to pass on their defects to their children; whether by intermarrying or not marrying at all, they remained a tribe to themselves.

A little girl's head popped up at one of the truck windows.

"Where's your daddy?"

She ducked out of sight.

Hardeman went to the window and looked in. The

child was crouched down in the seat. On the driver's side he could see Natham's head upside down on the floorboard. His daughter pulled at one trouser leg.

"Goddamn, Carrie Lou, you go inside and leave me be!"

The little girl stuck one finger in her mouth and giggled.

"Mister Natham."

The face, dirty, dry brown, moved up toward him.

"Goddamn, can't get nothing done. Kids! Get in if you want to talk."

Hardeman stood by the window. "I don't like to bother you, but Miss Edna Sommers has died."

"Did she? When?"

"Just now—about thirty minutes ago."

"She musta been three years older than God."

"She was eighty. Could you go into town and get an undertaker? I'll pay for your gasoline."

"I wouldn't mind helping you, Mister Hardeman. Miss Edna . . . she was good to me and mine, but this here truck is broke down. I been working on it all morning. Usually I can get her to going, but today—"

"What am I going to do?" His voice clogged with desperation.

"Well, that's easier than you think. Miss Edna's car's still running."

"Could you—?"

"I could, but I got this here truck to work on. Don't you know how to drive?"

Hardeman nodded, wondering if Natham's truck really

was broken or if he simply didn't want to go to the undertaker's.

"You ain't wanted for nothing, are you?"

"Wanted?"

"By the po-lice?"

A picture of himself in clerical collar: Wanted! John Hardeman, 65, ex-minister. Escaped— "No. I'm not wanted."

He walked back toward Edna's to the barn she used for a garage. The humped back of her car, a bloated turtle-shaped coupe of indeterminate age, stuck out of the open doors. Where were the keys? Where would she, a maiden lady—? No, not a maiden, a woman with a se-cret lover and a child she'd hugged to herself, lived with in pride and female silence. Where would she have kept the keys? In the car? Yes. There they were waiting for him in the ignition. Country carelessness. Trustfulness. She'd probably never had anything stolen from her in her entire life. No breaking and entering, no robbing, certainly no trashing . . . only the inevitable words on the school outhouse wall dutifully covered up by a coat of whitewash every spring, painted over by the same boys who had penciled the words earlier in the year. That couldn't be called trashing. The senior boys joking, laughing among themselves, writing the familiar dirty words on the back wall in huge white letters, drunk up by wood, obliterated by more whitewash from their brushes. No envy or hatred goaded them to destroy, to rip, to slash with jack knives. The altar cushions— Some of the women of his church had laboriously designed symbols of the twelve apostles on narrow bands, then had embroidered cushions to go in front of the altar rail. Each one had been slashed down the middle in a long methodical tear. After that he'd had to ask the janitor to lock the church every night. He sighed over the memory, an old one. He'd prayed with all his congregation to forgive, and he'd preached forgiveness, but had he forgiven? Yes, for that, but that was only the beginning of the malice.

Sitting in the car in barn-darkness, he looked up through seasons of cobwebs to cracks of light in the roof's inner triangle. Sanctuary. He had believed in a medieval concept of the church, a place open to all, to criminals even, an inviolable shelter. It was no longer so; he'd clung to his belief only to thrust it from him at last, to lock church doors and to caution women about their own safety. It was an old Episcopal Church in the downtown part of the city. Why must he think of it now? Perhaps it was Edna's death, her body covered by her bright-colored quilt, a star pieced out of diamond shapes on a white background. Looking at the work reminded him of women sewing.

On the road to Leon he was glad to find his reflexes were still working. He hadn't driven for two years. Now he must hurry. Bearing down on the gas pedal produced such alarming clanks, he reasoned Edna must never have driven over thirty miles an hour. She'd probably bought the car sometime in the late forties after the war. By now it had acquired its owner's temperament—independent, somewhat careless, amiable, but stubborn. The blacktop road to town was in better condition than such a sparse

country population deserved. A whole system of farm-
to-market roads had been strung out over the land,
finished just a few years before the real need for them had
disappeared. Now they waited like Roman roads had
waited in the farthest stretches of the empire to amaze
coming barbarians. Except the barbarians lived in cities
and would not return. Their sons or grandsons might
come back as real estate developers, to sell small chunks
of nostalgia, ranchettes, countryaire. Not back to Pinto
though. It was too far from a city for weekend hide-outs,
sixty miles south of Waco, a hundred northwest of Austin. This was the country of new empire builders, men
who put together small farms and ranches in an ever-
widening expanse they called their own even if they
never lived on it.

Why should he consider the empire builders? Something to do, anything so he would not have to think of
what he was doing. Yet his trouble was urgent. The dead
must be buried. Edna. He'd seen her at least once a week
these past two years, sometimes at her house, mostly at
his. When she dropped his mail and groceries off, she'd
stay and eat supper with him. Cooking was the one thing
she would let him do for her.

After attending to the problems of the soul for most of
his life, he discovered he was happier attending to the
needs of the body. Planting, watering, weeding, then
cooking vegetables from his own garden; doing anything
with his hands gave him pleasure. Every week Edna
stayed for supper and they would feast on chicken he'd
raised and had to pay the Natham boy to kill, watercress
salad from the creek, plum jam from the wild plum trees

that grew in Edna's far pasture, potatoes and green beans from his garden, bread he'd learned to bake, and butter Edna brought from town. He could do without butter, but Edna wouldn't.

"Why eat bread without butter? You could make it yourself if you don't want to buy it from the store. I know you won't countenance electricity. A mixer would make life too easy for you! If you want, though, Mama's old churn is in my attic."

"I'm not that much of a purist, Edna. For butter I'd need a cow and I don't want one."

"I can understand. Who wants to milk every day! I could bring you milk from the grocery—fresh milk instead of that dry skim stuff you use."

"No."

"You're more of a purist than you want to admit, John. You want things, people too, I guess, to be better than they can be."

She passed judgment on him, had no self-consciousness about doing so, having never learned the new form of morality which counseled silence and admitted of no judgment save what the individual passed on himself. From his old school teacher he'd learned more about himself than he'd wanted to know. Of her, he realized, he'd known too little.

Worrying about his self-centered blindness, paying no attention to the bends in the road, he swerved to miss a jackrabbit jumping out of the brush and found himself in a ditch by the roadside. He sat there trembling, his head resting on the steering wheel, trying to reconstruct the impulse that had taken him there. He placed his hands on his sides to feel his body, to be sure it was present. For a second he felt he had flashed past consciousness and reeled away from the earth. Waiting to quit shaking, he sat with one hand on the gear shift, thinking, I'll never get out, never be able to get this car out of here. The door opposite leaned toward a wall of earth. Mashed dried grass pressed against the closed window. A glass coffin, oh dear, a glass coffin. Pulling his hand off the gear shift, he leaned all his weight against the door beside him. It swung open so easily he fell out to the ground carried by his own panicky momentum.

Walking. Someone was bound to stop and pick him up. He could make it till then. He'd done plenty of walking in the past two years, strolling aimlessly, looking for nothing in particular at first. Gradually his city-tired eyes had learned to see quails' nests on the ground, a snake sleeping in the sun, rabbits' burrows, coyote tracks. The busy cycle of hidden life and imminent death, taken for granted when he was a boy, became miraculous to him as an old man. Leaving his house with no goal in mind, he'd go whatever direction his feet took him. Now they had to get him to Leon unless someone came by. There were others living out in the country. Someone would stop for him eventually, wouldn't they? Or did he look too—? He rubbed a hand over his face. Stubble above his beard. No time to shave. The beard. How long had it gotten? And his hair, white, fanning out behind him. Oh Lord! No! No one was going to stop for a wild man. An old pair of khaki pants, the nearest thing to hand that morning, bagged around him. His shirt, khaki too, and not even clean since he'd fallen out of the car.

His jacket, brown once, was mottled with the season's usage—stain of tree bark, stain of dewberries, of wild grapes, of chaparral, of the fruits of the earth, of the earth itself and faded by the sun's blessing. He was a sight. He threw back his head and laughed as freely as a madman, laughed at the spectacle of his sixty-five-year-old bones creaking down the road.

Riding. Loping back toward Pinto the next day on a horse Walter Ammons had loaned him, he laughed again, this time less hysterically, because by then he'd seen the town's reaction, found himself confirmed in his own mind, but not in theirs. That was what he'd not counted on. He'd come down a long dipping hill into Leon at sunset, the sky apocalyptic red behind him, riding a mottled gray horse called Blue. Walter, with perverse simplicity, had said it was named after its color. How old the horse was he didn't know, old enough to be tired after carrying him fifteen miles to town, old enough to have bad memories about bridges. He balked at the Leon River bridge; Hardeman had to get off and lead him across. He mounted again to ride to the funeral home on the other side of the square, the part of this journey he had feared most, for that was where he'd expected to be stared at. Somebody, a boy maybe, would shout derisively. "Hey, look at the old coot on horseback!" It didn't happen. He was seen by only a few people sitting in cars around the courthouse. No one remarked on him. No one apparently noticed him. He'd forgotten that riders on horseback were a common sight in Leon. In these people's lives man and horse were still linked.

Some rode for pleasure only; others, ranchers with cattle, still needed good cow ponies as much as they needed antibiotics for sick animals. He had fancied himself an anachronism, and truly he was, but the undertaker was the only one who confirmed his belief.

"You mean to tell me you rode horseback all the way from Pinto to get me?"

Hardeman, sore from his spine down to his heels, nodded.

"Doesn't anybody out there have a telephone?"

"No one I know."

"You could have stopped at a gas station. I guess they were all closed though. Thanksgiving."

"Is it Thanksgiving?" Standing in front of the under-taker's door, Blue on the sidewalk behind him, Harde-man did not wonder so much at the date as he wondered why he hadn't stopped to telephone. Had any place been open? Once he'd climbed on the horse, he'd only thought about getting to town. He'd ridden to Leon, slowing down to a walk only to let the horse rest now and then. He needed an undertaker for Edna, but there was an-other reason he'd ridden in. Waiting in a yellow pool of light falling from a single bulb above the door, he tried to understand. While he followed Otis Parker through the dark to his house next door to unsaddle Blue in Otis' backyard, he decided he'd come to town to declare him-self, to tell people he was an eccentric, and to take his place by Walter Ammons. No. There was no room by Walter. He was a true hermit. He'd acknowledged that when he had walked in on him at his shack. A spiral of smoke from Walter's chimney could be seen from the road. If he hadn't noticed the smoke he would not have known the house was there. Walter, older than he, or perhaps only aged by solitude, was asleep in front of a fire. Hating to wake him, Hardeman stood staring at the gray wisp of a man. His face, relaxed in sleep, still bore slight lines of the forehead. The room was littered with books, stacks of them on a work table, more on the floor. Everywhere, on the mantel, window ledges, shelves, were things he'd picked up—cows' and goats' skulls, weathered pieces of wood, odd shaped stones, empty brown, lavender, green, blue bottles, bits of harness, frayed rope, rusty handmade nails, hinges—scraps and bits he'd taken as a bird chooses odd bits of string to weave into his nest. Between the books on the table were papers covered with script, marked through, crossed out lines and many more running furiously down the pages. Edna had said he was a poet. Hardeman wished he could read the lines.

Cold wind blowing in the open door woke the sleeping man.

"What do you want?" His eyes, dark brown, were deepset.

"Edna Sommers has died. I'm trying to get to town to an undertaker. I was driving her car. It broke down . . . in a ditch. I had an accident and drove it into a ditch. A rabbit jumped in front of me and I was trying to miss him. I haven't driven in so long. I misjudged the distance I guess." Every word he said sounded superfluous in the silence surrounding Walter, a silence unaltered by the scratch of human voices where one man could sit listening to a fire crackle, a squirrel scrambling over the roof, a pencil whispering on a page.

"You want me to help you dig a grave?" There was no

indication of surprise in his voice, certainly no grief. Here was a man, Hardeman saw, so lost in time he didn't even know it was illegal to bury people at home now.

"No. Her family's all buried in Leon. I guess she would want to be taken there."

"I have a horse." He rose from the chair which contained an imprint of his body in deep hollows and went out the door with an astonishing economy of motion. No long unbending, no uncertainty or tottering; he was up and gone, a gray fox intent on escape.

Hardeman ran after him, helped him saddle, and without another word passing between them, mounted the horse.

"What's his name?" Surely by this time he'll ask me mine.

"Blue, his color." Walter Ammons disappeared in his house without waiting to see him leave, without asking who he was. It was not a matter of trust; that was implied in the offer of his horse. Walter didn't care, didn't want to know, couldn't be bothered. All his life was given to written language, to the words and voices in his head. Obsessed, protecting himself, perhaps a little mad, but gently so, Walter could not allow anyone in his life. I need someone in mine. At least one other. Edna. I cannot wean myself from people. What will I do now that she's gone? He put the question in the back of his mind while he went in to make arrangements with Otis Parker who had already refused to go to Pinto that night.

"You can sleep here, then first thing in the morning we'll drive out to get her. She'll be all right. Nobody to disturb the dead in Pinto."

"Her people—?"

"She's got none in Leon." Otis, corpulent, middle-age rolling around his waist, sat in his living room with his shoes off.

"Three deaths today. I'm worn out. First funeral at ten tomorrow morning. That's the earliest you can get any-body up to go to a funeral in Leon. One of my staff can take care of that." He spoke with the satisfaction of one able to command others.

"You want somebody to say a service, a preacher?"

"I hadn't thought—" John looked at Otis spraddled in a lounge chair, his feet propped up on a sagging hassock. He probably had some service, a nondenominational burial rite for anybody. Most of them did. I don't have to— Yes, I do. For Edna. She ministered to me. "I'll do it myself. I'm an ordained minister. Episcopalian," he added.

Though she wasn't a church-goer, he thought Edna's family had been Methodists. There was little difference in the denominations. Episcopals had a more formal rit-ual and were less evangelical. Yet here I am after riding all day, bent on getting to town like a pioneering Metho-dist circuit rider carrying the true religion.

At six the next morning he saddled Blue, rode through the dark streets of the town and back out to Walter's. Otis would pick him up at the gate at ten. He'd offered to borrow a horse trailer for the return trip, but Hardeman said no. He would not give anyone else the opportunity to pry open that perfectly contained space Walter lived within. Let there be hermitages for those that need them.

He took Blue to his corral, pulled the saddle and

bridle off, and watched him chomp oats that had been left in the trough. Otis's grass had suffered from Blue's hunger the night before. At Walter's door he stooped and slid a note through, one he'd already written, saying: "Thank you, John Hardeman." If Walter ever needed him, which he doubted, he would at least know his name.

"Let's go to Miss Edna's first. Then I need to stop by my house and pick up some clothes."

Otis, waiting in his hearse, was listening to a transistor radio. When Hardeman opened the door, he turned it off, his face suffused with guilt as though he'd been caught acting in an undignified manner. Last night he'd been the weary businessman. Today he meant to show his professional side.

Looking out the window, hurrying through country walked the day before, it seemed to Hardeman he'd moved a thousand miles out of all his past. The preceding day was a jolting memory and all the years prior to it were only remotely connected. Physically exhausted, he felt himself drifting in a landscape that was both well known and peculiarly foreign. As they drove through Pinto's main street, he glanced toward the depot. Natham's truck was gone. He must be at work clearing brush or chopping wood into fencepost lengths on someone's place.

"Turn here. We'll go in the back way." The back door was open. Perhaps the wind—

"Oh Lordy! I should have come out here last night."

Otis, groaning, climbed out of the hearse.

"Why?" The screen he'd shut so carefully the day before flapped against the wall, springs stretched to the breaking point.

"Why, man, can't you see? Somebody's been in here. Burglars."

The word jarred him. Burglars. It was the first comment the policeman made when he'd come to the church. Until that moment it had been a slightly comic term to him. "Breaking and entering. Willful destruction of property." Faint legalistic words for profanation—the chalice stolen, a stained glass window broken, God Is Dead smeared on one wall, pews gouged by knives, an ugly doll tied on the altar's cross. "Maniacs." He was a young policeman, but his eyes were already lined by cynicism. Madness, thought Hardeman, and put the idea aside, thinking madness was too easy an excuse. So were ignorance, poverty and adolescent rage. Many lived in worse ghettos without desecrating their churches. No, it was malice, evil in its purest form. And they had caught them, boys from his own church. He'd had to testify. They had been sent to a reformatory, a place where they would only harden. He, sure of his failure, his inability to move his own parishioners, had resigned and fled.

Lifting his head, Hardeman led Otis into the kitchen. Cabinets open and empty. They'd taken even the saucepan he'd left on the drainboard. A smudge on the floor was all that was left of the refrigerator. The stove remained, too old to be of any value.

Otis swore. "Some sorry sons of bitches!"

Hardeman, running down the hall to Edna's room, felt tears wetting his face. Her body, covered with the quilt, lay on the bed still. Over it the oval pictures of her father and Billy Burrell gazed, her father with stern indifference, her lover with bemused arrogance, at the room utterly stripped.

"She's here."

"Well, thank God! Thank God they didn't—"

"Who would—?"

"Steal a body? Perverts." Otis' voice shook with loathing. "These, whoever they were, were just ordinary robbers. Looks like they took nearly everything she had. I wonder who—Who else lives out here now?"

"There are some cedar choppers living in the depot. Edna rented it to them." Through a window he could see its mustard-colored smudge on the horizon. "It must have been— They must have—"

"Who were they?"

"I— I don't remember. Edna never called them anything but the cedar choppers."

"You don't know their names?"

Hardeman shook his head. The Nathams stole from need. Edna was in need no longer. If her heirs wanted to pursue, let them. Since none of them had visited her for at least two years, he doubted they would be bothered by the loss of household goods.

"Probably it wouldn't matter if you did. Trash like that gets lost in a hurry. Here. Give me a hand."

Together they secured the quilt around Edna's body, lifted her onto a stretcher Otis had carried in, and carried the body out to the hearse.

"I wonder if they took anything from you?"

"I don't think so. I've got nothing of value except a record player, and it's an old one."

"They don't seem too particular to me. Anybody that'd steal pots and pans—"

"Otis, my record player is so old you have to hand crank it. But we'll see. I've got to stop and get my clothes anyway."

They turned down the main street again, this time to his house, a shabby box he'd refused to paint even though he'd had both time and money to do it. He'd decided he liked its worn appearance; it fitted in with everything else in Pinto slowly mouldering back to earth. Returning to the house with Otis, he came back as a stranger who recognized his hermitage was not a nest like Walter's but an austere monkish cell. The living room held a metal cot, covers flung back hastily the morning before, a faded green easy chair he'd bought from Edna, a Coleman lantern sitting on top of shelves he'd made from old boards, and a big low table he'd built to hold the record player. It was still there, and so were all the records, a shelf of bulky 78's.

He gestured toward the records, "I guess they didn't fancy Bach or Handel."

Otis grinned. "No. I don't reckon they would. Nothing's missing?"

"The other rooms are empty." Hardeman walked past him to the kitchen and looked out to the back porch where his gardening tools hung in a neat row on the wall. "Everything seems to be here. There's nothing much to take." The Nathams had stolen Edna's pots and pans but left his on the shelves. Why? Were they sure he would return to stay? Did they think he was as poor as they were? That couldn't be it. Poor steal from poor. No. He could not grant the Nathams any charitable notions. Goodness, he conceded, was often as accidental as evil.

"A wood-burning stove. I haven't seen one of those in years." Otis was running his hands over the bright blue enamel as though he was admiring a delicate piece of carving.

"My parents left it here when they moved into Leon. I never got around to selling it after they died. Keeps the place warm."

It was the only cheerful object in the house. Looking at it, he knew he'd been living in lumpish discontent. Oh, he'd been happy enough at times, working in his garden, walking through the country, reading, cooking for Edna, listening to music . . . listening for Edna's car, looking forward to seeing her, but there were long hours, days in-between when music was no comfort, books could not bear re-reading, the weather confined him in his cell and Edna did not come. He'd slept or sat alone sunken in misanthropy. Where would he live now? He did not know, but he couldn't stay in Pinto. He would not be the last survivor dying in the ruins. There must be something in the world he could do. A sixty-five-year-old man who could ride thirty miles on horseback could do something.

"I'll get my clothes, Otis." He fumbled through the closet in his parents' empty bedroom until he found his dark gray suit. Hanging under the coat was a black shirt with a narrow white band around the neck.

"You'll look different in that outfit. I thought you were a real wild man when I saw you last night. Collar turned backward changes a man." Otis sounded a little disappointed, but years of professional circumspection held his tongue.

"Just remember how I looked last night." Hardeman flung the clothes over his shoulder and went out to the hearse waiting in the sunlight.

# Running Around America

 EVERY MORNING BETWEEN seven-thirty and eight Martha Adams pushes her front door open, hits the button on top of the stop watch, and begins running a circular mile. Her husband's bird dog whimpers and strains against his chain, begs either to run with her or investigate the neighbors' garbage cans. She can't put up with his uncertainties or the dog fights he'll get into along the way, so she leaves him there barking now at Jacques, the toy poodle across the street. Jacques is intelligent enough to remain on his own lawn, free of chains, insouciantly defending his territory. Even in this suburb so close to town the ancient wolf within every dog growls, bares its fangs, and chases anyone crossing those invisible lines marking her patch of ground. Martha's sympathetic postman has given her a tiny spray can of mace, but the stop watch is enough to carry. She leaves the mace can by the doorway much as pioneers dumped household objects by the roadside on their way west.

The dog problem could be avoided altogether if she'd drive to the local high school stadium and run on the track, something she tried once, and found she despised. Running in circles while expressway traffic screamed by on two sides made her feel like a robot on a treadmill. She prefers the quiet anarchy of her own neighborhood.

Two houses down the block she sees Luis Angel, Mrs. Payne's Mexican yardman on Mondays, hers on Wednesdays. A stout man with habitually a sad face, he's divorced, lives with his mother, and has rheumatism so bad he cannot work on damp days. Bending over a can of gasoline he's pouring into his lawn mower, Luis looks up and waves. To help Martha's fourteen-year-old daughter with Spanish, he once brought her two magazines printed in Mexico. Both were designed like comic books only photographs were used instead of drawings, and both were soft porn tales of adultery. The whole family, two children, Martha, and her husband, worked on the translations. Because of Luis Angel's immense dignity, Martha decided he hadn't looked at anything except the covers.

Mrs. Payne has lived in the neighborhood longer than anyone. She came to Texas from Virginia; Martha hears her birthplace in her voice when she calls to share news of friends who lived next door before moving further west to Denver. "Ah do miss them. Such ah-dor-able little girls." Mrs. Payne misses everyone; her husband who died years ago, many of her friends, most of her family, the "little girls" who've grown to teenage now. Luis Angel drives her everywhere she needs to go since her cataract operation. Every spring for the last two years he has planted her yard with a new kind of grass. The St. Augustine withered, victim of a strange malaise, SAD— St. Augustine decline—oddly reminiscent of what ladies of Mrs. Payne's age might have called "a sinking spell." Mrs. Payne herself has no intention of sinking or of letting a single standard fade. She was immensely angry when she discovered someone had stolen her parents' tombstone.

Three days ago she phoned to report, "The police tell

me people use them for coffee tables or to practice their horrid rites."

Vague, macabre ideas about witch trials and Black Masses swirled in Martha's head. She switched them off to see unknown hands clanking saucers and cups on two-foot-thick marble and began to wonder, inappropriately, how anyone could carry a tombstone into a living room without breaking his back. This was not a question she and Mrs. Payne would pursue. Desecration is a severe term in her language, and when she used it, Martha understood its full meaning. People's monuments should not be stolen for they are the survivors' signs of love; stones declare respect. To be buried in an unmarked grave is the fate of a victim or a criminal.

Martha took her to the police warehouse where among the stolen bicycles slumping on flat tires, rusting lawn furniture, and TV sets with their antennae all criss-crossed, Mrs. Payne searched for her parents' stone. It was not there. She ordered another.

Once past her house and across the street, Martha is on the outskirts of foreign territory dotted by houses of people she knows. There's Will backing out of his drive-way. Where is he going to work? He has a daughter the same age as her youngest. They have been in school to-gether for six years, but Martha still doesn't know what Will does for a living. She's been told and has forgotten. On his house, nailed to the wall of the second-story porch, there's a wooden eagle with wings widespread enough to hold gold letters spelling TEMPERANCE. Will's wife Nancy put the eagle there. Martha's sure she's not, nor has ever been a member of the WCTU. The eagle is a whimsical reminder of prohibition, that pecu-

liar era which attracted and held adherents in the Bible
Belt.

Martha's mother, whose home is ninety miles northwest of Austin, lives in a dry county. Not even beer is
sold there. For her, and for some of her friends, Martha
acts as a modern-day rum-runner carrying scotch, gin,
and wine of all sorts in her car trunk. Deliveries are made
at her mother's properly isolated ranch. There is no real
necessity for secrecy—"Drink, and vote dry!" is the un-
spoken slogan during all local option elections; mock
furtiveness has become custom. They sit out on the
porch at the ranch, ice rattling in glasses, watch the sunset, and as the whiskey goes down, Martha sees a buz-
zard, his wings spread as he rides the air currents.
Remembering Nancy and Will's eagle splayed against
the wall proclaiming TEMPERANCE, she has a second,
lighter drink. The gold letters fuse and part until they
read MODERATION. Together Martha, her mother,
and a friend silently consign Carry Nation and her axe to
the historical twilight.

Across the street from Will's and Nancy's, Miss Bryce
pulls out of her driveway. She's off to the university to
rescue Shakespeare from that twilight. Miss Bryce, once
Martha's teacher, is the kind she hopes her children will
have—an enthusiast. Every semester she invites her students over for an Elizabethan dinner. Martha sees her at
the grocery store when she's collecting ingredients for
syllabub, meat pies, and rolypoly pudding.

"You remember the Elizabethans didn't have plates,"
she says. With her back to the frozen food counter, a
pragmatic frown appears on her good-humored face. Six-

teen seminar students are coming to supper, and her oven burned out yesterday.

"Do you have a fireplace? No, I guess it would be impossible to get a spit built by tonight," says Martha who's a bit of a pragmatist herself. Still, she's enough of a dreamer to imagine a roasted carcass turning on the spit while Miss Bryce, dressed in the ample skirt and low-cut blouse of a kitchen wench, bastes it.

"Use my oven. I've got two."

"Oh no, thank you. We'll make it. I've got a roaster, and an electric frying pan, and some other things you plug in."

Wry regret edges their smiles as they part. Both Miss Bryce, the scholar who perches on the edge of her desk talking about Shakespeare as if he were her best friend, and Martha, the romanticist, would like for everything to be exactly as it was in Elizabethan days for at least an evening. But they both work; neither of them will give the time necessary to exact reproduction. Thanksgiving, Christmas, Easter, the nation's feast days, keep them in the kitchen longer. Even so, Martha cannot imagine herself spending a holiday basting a turkey on a spit over an open fire.

What sort of fire burned the house next to Miss Bryce's? Was it a frayed cord, a hot wire loose somewhere, a smoldering menace you wouldn't think to look for until it flamed? That was the day that seven fire engines moaned down the street followed by a pack of children suddenly freed from rainy Saturday boredom. Both of hers had gone only to return quickly.

"Did the firemen tell you to get out of the way?"

"No," said Anne. At twelve, she's given to short answers.

Beth, the oldest, filled in. "A woman came out and hollered at us, 'What are you standing there staring at?' She had a lamp in her hand, and she . . . she was crying. Then she started shouting. 'Go home!' So, we came home."

The angry woman sold what was left of her house. When the new owners remodeled, they painted the smoked brick a soothing shade of gray and hung dark green shutters.

Martha lopes past the limestone house of The Man With the Red Robe, his character fixed forever in her mind by his appearance at 7:30 the morning after Agnew resigned. Hair brushed, spectacles gleaming, feet neatly encased in black calf slippers, a proper middle-aged figure wrapped in glowing crimson, he bent to get the paper, opened it, and snarled aloud at the headlines. Where was he yesterday afternoon when the news broke, and what was he doing last night when most everybody in the country was gaping at their TV sets? He turned away to walk back up the immaculate sidewalk winding through his lawn. Twisted live-oak branches shaded his back. Against a white front door he shone bright red once more, then vanished, a gnome returning to his rocky cave. She has not seen him since. Will he appear only at irregular intervals like those unreliable ghosts who sometimes walk after upheavals are over?

Right here on this corner behind a tall clump of pittosporum, Mr. Winkler was mugged. An engineer, sixty-seven, with cotton white hair, he walked home from his office in the early December dusk. Two adolescent boys rolled him behind the bushes. They beat him, grabbed five dollars from his billfold, snatched his father's gold pocket-watch, and drove off. Too dazed to see the license plates, Mr. Winkler stumbled to the nearest door for help. They wouldn't let him in. They would call the police. Exactly which house did he go to? The newspaper didn't say. "An isolated incident," the police commented: people are seldom robbed and beaten in that part of town. Martha knows they are correct, yet the phrase sticks in her mind. Mistrust and self-protection isolated Mr. Winkler, left him alone outside the door. What would she have done with a stranger bleeding on her steps? Vaguely ashamed, she admits to herself she isn't sure. Mr. Winkler strides by her place late each evening now. He's changed his route but not his habit.

Jogging in place, feeling a bit foolish, Martha waits for a break in the stream of traffic on Pecos, one of the suburb's busiest streets. Oh, will it never end! Why are people in such a hurry to get to work? A more useless question she's never asked for she runs against time herself—one way or another she runs against a clock all day—and is absurdly eager to go on. Across Pecos is the house somebody new is always renting, faced by the house somebody else new is always buying. Does a FOR SALE sign come with the property? The renters deposit their hopes on the small porch in empty cardboard boxes. The latest buyers have built a new fence and covered depressing brown siding with a coat of orange paint. In their front yard a new tree is planted. Perhaps they'll stay. Only optimists would select orange. Perhaps the fence will help dull traffic noises—a glib hope she immediately cancels. How can a few wooden boards seal out hundreds of rumbling tires and throbbing engines?

On down the street she runs past the place so hidden in woods it resembles a Mafia hideout. There are usually four cars parked in front; often a man is asleep in one of them. Does he work the night shift, does he fight with his wife and sleep in his car, has he gone to sleep on guard duty? She wonders, but would not consider waking him up to ask. Here one rule prevails: you can ask for help, you cannot pry. Martha believes it is a civilized rule.

Next door to the hideout a huge two-story house is being built on a tiny lot. Thirty-five years ago when this area was first opened, a city council anxious for growth and governed by real-estate developers' greed, decided lots could be as narrow as fifty feet across. In the middle of Texas where land is abundant, houses are as jammed together as they are in the over-populated East. Yet every summer Martha says, as her friends also say, "I wouldn't want a bigger yard to water."

Carpenters stop hammering as she goes by. This intimidating silence is broken by a pair of small hairy dogs who yip at her heels for a block. If she stops, they'll back off. She longs for one of them to get close enough to kick. Their delight over having somebody to chase is echoed by a frustrated dog in his pen. Until she's past, he's on his hind legs yelping to get at her. His owner beats on the window to quiet him every morning when she comes by. Why isn't the window broken yet?

Around the next corner is a group of small houses. Shopkeepers, university professors, students, lawyers, retired couples, grocers, store managers, and painters live there. There are also many old ladies, salesmen, at least one artist; there are no blacks, no chicanos.

Set in the dead center of one lot is the square stone house of The Man With the Hat. Martha sees him walking often on her own street. He always carries a radio on a shoulder strap and wears a hat, straw in summer, felt in winter. His hats have a classic shape, one you'd find in a child's ABC with HAT written in block letters beneath it, a type of hat many men wore before World War II. She associates it with memories of the hats her father wore then, and is startled to realize that she still sees vestiges of her father in the world though he's been dead for seven years. Except for his hat, this man bears no resemblance to anyone she knows. He has an Eisenhower smile which reminds her of the fifties, yet The Man With the Hat is himself, entirely another being. He stops to speak only to Luis Angel; he nods to her. After many months of seeing him daily, she found an excuse to speak.

"You have a visitor."

"Yes. My grandson." He smiled.

Martha waved to the little boy who wagged a lollipop in her direction. In two days he was gone. Now The Man With the Hat and His Wife are in their yard stationed just behind their garbage cans—eight of them.

"Why so many garbage cans?" Martha calls. They have a system of communications established now, telegraphic lines they exchange.

"Dirtiest people in town," says His Wife.

"Been cleaning leaves off the roof," says The Man With the Hat.

Their house stands behind them, metal exterior blinds

shut, looking like a guardhouse or a small prison. Not one shrub grows against the stone wall. A few trees edge the lot's boundaries. By the front wall a single spindly rose bush crooks a branch. It's the emptiest yard she passes, and in this emptiness Martha sees the dreadful isolation of the old.

Lately she's noticed The Man With the Hat standing on a ladder painting his gutter, and has repressed the desire to call, "Be careful!" Be careful, neighbor, for if you fall and can't be mended, it means a nursing home for you. We put old people out of sight in this country when they can't walk. I know. Ask me what happened to my grandmother, to my great-aunt. All the love in the world cannot prevent it. Take care! Stay on your feet.

The house next door is for sale, and has been for eight months. Martha watched a group of young men paint it, add a room, set up a picket fence. A quick face-lifting job. House prices are wildly inflated in this section of town. Decorate and speculate is the formula. This time it failed.

From a garage on a side street, she sees Princess emerge dragging herself on crutches. She also carries a full backpack. What is in it? Old poems, old newspapers, old rags? No one is sure. Nor does anyone know where she lives. Her home could be that garage, or a shed, or a back room—somehow she's sheltered. Princess wanders the city's streets all day; sometimes she takes the bus, a substitute for the bicycle she used to ride. Always moving, out in all seasons, covered from head to foot— kerchief, shirt, sweater, pack, skirt, stockings covered with gray knee socks—her long face is weathered brown. Bright red lipstick, carefully applied, outlines a mouth which mutters to itself; however, she will carry on a type of conversation with people she recognizes.

"What do you think we should do about the world situation?" Princess stopped Martha outside a shop after one of the Arab-Israeli flare-ups.

"I don't know. I worry a lot."

"I pray." Princess dragged herself away toward the shop's door.

Martha, knowing she'd curse anyone who tried to help her, stood by while Princess bumbled through the door. Through the window she saw the owner composing her face in a resigned, tolerant mask. Princess would ask her for money; for years she's depended on the charity of shopkeepers though she has invented an elaborate fiction which keeps her from calling herself a beggar. As owner of an imaginary newspaper, she solicits advertisements and subscriptions. When she was younger—in her bicycle riding days—she would write down subscribers' names. Now she no longer bothers to keep records. Each year she grows more querulous; in her mind her enemies multiply. Everyone still donates. Though she gave herself the title, the whole town is her kingdom.

Martha rounds another corner. On the curb a boy has spelled his name, glued it there with bits of broken Coke and beer bottles. Harley glints in the early morning sun; the H has come unglued leaving only a dark outline of the letter. She knew a boy with the same name twenty years ago. What has become of him? He was poor, and joined the Air Force to escape his poverty. The last time she saw him he was angry because she was engaged to her husband.

He pointed to her ring, "That's too small a diamond."

"I'm not marrying him for the size of the diamond."

"You never loved me."

Had she said she did? She let it go. He'd been out in the world for almost a year. She was still in college when he marched back into her sorority house. (Her father, filled with egalitarian scorn, called it "that luxury hotel" and paid the bills anyway.) Young—oh, Harley was such a young man, lean and proud of his Air Force uniform. Silver bars gleamed on his shoulders, his cap was folded on one knee. Sitting beside him, she remembered a lavish party where they both got so happily drunk on sparkling Burgundy they had to prop themselves up against the curve of a grand piano. Laughing, they insisted to each other that they could not walk to the door. He was wearing a charcoal gray suit, and she had on an iridescent blue-green dress, a shade called peacock-blue that year . . . 1952. And they had walked to the door— glided, it seemed exuberantly.

"You could have waited."

His vehemence disturbed her; she hadn't known he included her in his future. While he was gone he didn't write often, and when he returned she thought of him as an old friend who would share in her joy. Was his the jealousy of someone who'd had half an idea about marrying her on some distant day when he was rich and powerful at last, or was she only the spark provoking instant male rivalry? There is no knowing.

Seeing his name on the cement, she longs to know if Harley is still alive after Korea, after Vietnam. The memory of his anger, though it satisfies her vanity, hurts still. Believing, at twenty, she loved more often than she was loved, Martha, at forty-one, remains appalled at the rawness of others' passions.

"I ought to wish you luck, but I won't." He shoved the heavy front door open and was gone. His bitterness flowed like a current through the air around her. She stood in the red tiled foyer mutely understanding why lovers murder each other.

Martha runs away from this moment in her life wondering if all women, when they reach their middle years, mull over lost lovers, singing swan songs to themselves. "Grow old along with me. . . ." There's but one man who can do that, her husband, and she's not at all sure he will. On the shaky seesaw of marriage, they are at present, balanced. Nothing impends—no lovers for either of them, no great conflict of personalities. There's a tension, a strained complacency, at times. And crises don't necessarily impend; they often explode. She could get home and find thieves wheeling the girls' bicycles out of the garage. Dan drives too fast, has to fly too often. One of the children might—Oh no, don't count the might-be miseries. There are enough to cope with as it is. Dan's radio stations give him his share. All have to be shored up, developed, managed. Internecine warfare breaks out daily among the staffs in Austin, San Antonio, Mobile, Orlando.

He must soothe, confront, hire, and fire people all year. They call him for everything. A disc jockey who smokes pot "breaks up"—giggles slyly in the Orlando air while listeners phone to ask if he's gone mad. An engineer falls off a transmission tower in San Antonio, cracks three ribs, and fractures a hip. The station manager in

Mobile juggles time slots so his favorite racist politician gets favored minutes. "Never mind the FCC. They ain't listening to Mobile, Dan." One more manager to fire. Some days Dan swears he will sell all the stations and go live someplace where people never listen to radios. Where might that be? And wouldn't he soon be bored? She likes the job as script-writer for a local PBS-TV station. For the most part, she enjoys writing the news or finding the right spot for the lion to roar on the children's show. Some days though the lion is cranky, and the news is nothing more than a familiar recital of horrors. Some days she and Dan hardly see each other.

The smell of honeysuckle in September's second bloom blows across the street to her. All the long summers of her childhood are captured in that fragrance—front porches where people waited for the house to cool off enough to sleep in those nights before they had air-conditioning, moonlight, the sound of voices telling stories. They wove together intricate strands of relationship, mused over Uncle Jim's boy, Tom, who was so tight he'd walk to work rather than spend a nickel on a streetcar, or laughed over Aunt Julia's daughter, Edith, who demanded, "Don't forget to make arrangements for me!" an exclamation endlessly repeated in the family. When honeysuckle time was over they listened to F.D.R.'s "Fireside Chats," the "Bob Hope Show," the "Red Skelton" show, the "Hit Parade." Walter Winchell's staccato delivery of the news frightened them, but they were compelled to hear him. Somewhere in the house a radio was always on. While the men in Martha's family were off to war, the women waited, listened to reports of battles, and told family stories like so many Penelopes weaving as the war unraveled. The men came home restless. Old people died, the family dispersed, moved in every direction. Martha's children have cousins two thousand miles away they do not know. She'd known every one of hers.

"Ours is the last generation that'll care about families," Dan said once.

"I don't know. There must still be some people who stay in one place long enough to raise a generation to care." She dislikes being the last of anything.

What's that up there dangling from the chinaberry tree? It's a tiny toy Superman, his fist aggressively thrust out ready to make his lightning bolt declaration: Behold! Superman! Behold! He is stuck fast in the midst of wrinkled, yellow chinaberries, caught by a handkerchief parachute some child has made. Ridiculously, impotently, he sways in the wind, a small sign of egoism, personal and national. We thought we could save the world, we thought we were supposed to. We could barely fly over the Great Wall of China, we couldn't retreat with dignity or honor from Vietnam. Our comic book heroes capture our imaginations: Supermen and Captains Marvel, we marched out to find not even Tarzan could save us from Indochinese jungles. We had to save ourselves from our own president.

"Watergate." She mumbles the seventies' curse to herself.

Here come the old ladies, one with a cane holding the other's arm. She sees them walking most mornings. Young people leave in cars to go to work or school abandoning the neighborhood to the old or very young all day. Sometimes Martha passes a middle-aged couple walking. By the man's pale face, she judges he's had a heart attack, or is just recovering from an operation. His doctor has probably told him he must exercise, and his wife, who is learning to be a practical nurse, is there to be sure he walks briskly.

"You're making us look bad in comparison," called the wife one day as Martha went by.

"I only run downhill."

They both, Martha feels, enjoy the social lie. Raillery and self-deprecation are forms of address between strangers here. Sometimes there's praise. "You sure are ambitious," an older woman comments rising from the weeds in her flowerbed. Martha doesn't equate exercise and ambition. To her, the remark is peculiarly Texan. She has lived in Georgia, California, and Pennsylvania before settling in the Southwest. Regional speech survives, she's sure, or else why must she always translate, "You sure are ambitious," to "You sure are working hard."

Down the street of the early workers or late risers— she doesn't know which—she jogs past four or five houses where she never sees anyone but the yardmen. Their names are unknown to her, and they wait for her to speak first.

"Good morning!" she calls. Runners can speak to anyone.

"Do you know what time it is?" one man asks.

"I've only got a stop watch," Martha huffs. She smokes too much and is getting winded.

Here's Pecos again. Two dogs sit in the middle of the street; Martha runs toward them. The minute she crosses they'll be snarling at her heels. Sherlock, a beagle, and his buddy, an aggressive black and white mutt Martha has privately named Bully, are her familiar enemies. She picks up a stick to wave at them.

Last summer on the cross street just ahead she saw a dark-skinned young man running. He carried a long stick in his hands. In the early morning sunlight shining through trees, the stick became a spear, the man a forest hunter, a descendant of the Tonkawas who used to roam this ground.

"Go home, Sherlock!" Martha shouts and raises her stick. "Go home!"

He and Bully fall back, both of them barking still. They will growl until she passes the driveway to Bully's house, or their owners come out to call them off.

She's within a block of home now at The House of the Shouters, a man and woman she seldom sees and often hears. A long, agonized "God-damn-it!" breaks through brick walls. This morning there is no answer, only the single wail of his frustration. Other mornings Martha hears a woman crying, "Son-of-a-bitch!" over and over as though she is depending on the four words to express all her rage. Do they howl at each other or the world?

Back on her own block there are the Jays. He's an ear, nose, throat specialist. His wife works as a lobbyist at the state capitol. This year Mrs. Jay is pushing mental health. She often wears a wig slightly askew, which makes her look a little batty, and does her cause no good. She is a tremendously determined woman, though. Within five minutes, people listening to her admire her will and forget how she looks. Because of Mrs. Jay's insistence, Martha, who hates asking for donations, will collect for mental health in the neighborhood this year.

Mrs. Payne is out on her front porch talking to Luis Angel. Martha waves at them, runs down her walk, and punches the stop watch. Thirteen minutes, not fast enough yet. She wants to make the run in twelve.

The dog whines.

"Hush, Jake."

She lets him off his chain. Jake dashes madly around the house. Martha, having completed her own circle, goes inside to continue the quiet anarchy of her life.

# Amnesia's Child

 TOLLY WAS TELLING Lou about himself. Either
he was doing better than usual, or she was the
most attentive listener he'd ever found. Her
long straight blonde hair dripped forward over
her shoulders to the table, her face, propped on one fist,
was quite serious, and her blue eyes seemed to be stuck
open.

"We completely reconstructed the boat—white paint,
red velvet curtains, paddle wheel. When she was finished
we steamed down the Mississippi. I managed the saloon
and the stage. The only drinks served were beer and
mint juleps. We were always running out of mint. Everyday I went ashore for some. I know every backyard with a
mintbed in it from Memphis to New Orleans. Finally we
built boxes beneath the windows on either side of the bar
and grew mint in them. All you had to do when you
wanted a sprig was reach out the window."

"You said you had a stage. Did you act?"

"Madam!" Tolly rose and made a swashbuckling bow.
"Melodramas every Saturday night. Old ones like *Uncle
Tom* and new ones we all wrote, *The Good Girl Goosed*,
*The Rotten Sheriff of Ratty Ridge*." He flourished an invis-
ible cape and sat down. "For my art I suffered popcorn
bruises, buttered britches, salty hair!"

Lou threw her head back and laughed. Her eyes stayed
open. Did she sleep with them open? Careless of him not
to have noticed. He should have wakened in the middle

of the night and checked, but how could he without waking her? Tolly grinned. She was easy to amuse. The trip down the Mississippi on a paddle wheel steamer, the red velvet curtains, and the portable mintbeds had just occurred to him. The more elaborate his stories were, the more she believed them. If he'd simply said, "I took a trip down the Mississippi on a riverboat," she would have said, "When?" And he would have been caught, for he couldn't remember exactly what he'd done in the last couple of years, nor did he remember how he'd been filling in the lost time. To plot his tales out in advance would be cheating. The only way to make those years real was to recreate them on the spur of the moment so they sounded as spontaneous as memories. For memory he substituted invention, and he made his own rules; first, no planning; second, baroque elaboration on any theme. The melodramas were partly true. He had acted in them when he was in high school. Where did he get the steamboat? Perhaps from the family up the lake who owned one. Theirs was not a real steamboat, however, just a replica with an ordinary engine. His boat was better. The Mississippi was a better river for it than the dammed up lake of the Colorado he was living next to at the moment. The boat had existed sometime. He could so easily imagine he'd been on it riding down the Mississippi from Ohio to New Orleans watching the river turn brown and widen as he went south to the Delta with a boatload of tourists, an amiable partner or two, and a batch of mint juleps. The white boat on brown water was so clear to him he wanted to tell Lou more about it.

"Have you ever been on a white boat on a brown river?"

She blinked her eyes. Tolly relaxed. He was sure she'd done it before, but this was the first blink he'd caught. Wide-eyed innocence made him nervous.

"No. I have been on a gray ship on a blue sea."

"Ah." She was trying to play by his rules. Dorothy must have been talking to her. He would have to talk to Dorothy.

"I was in the Waves."

She was too smart. Dumb women gave him no trouble, only he never liked the dumb ones.

"You were on the waves."

"No. In."

"You are too young to have served in the Waves. They're gone, disbanded, obsolete."

"Oh, Tolly. You don't really know if they are or not. I'm the latest model. You can't disband me." With a jerk of her neck she swept her hair back.

Tolly reached out and pulled a piece forward over her left shoulder. "Venus rising from the sea. Lou-Lou lolling on the waves."

Lou pushed her chair away from the table and jumped up. "It's getting late. I have to go."

"Go then."

"What will you do when I'm gone?"

"Bless you. Bless all beautiful twenty-one-year-old women who can still ask ingenious questions. I don't know what I'll do. I may throw myself off the balcony."

"You're impossible."

Tolly smiled. He believed he was; still it was nice to be reassured. Lou left, her robe billowing behind her. She'd forgotten to tie it. Practical as she was, she often showed "a sweet disorder in her dress." Tolly muttered the line as he admired her drifting off his porch and down the steps to her own apartment. He'd probably made her late for class again. Walking to the stone balustrade of the balcony, he looked down at the lake. Richards was climbing out of the water onto the dock. Only an Englishman would punish himself so on an October morning. Since he'd learned British consular officers in Houston were given hardship pay for duty in the subtropics, Richards had decided Austin should also be classified as subtropical. "It's a jungle, a lovely jungle," he said, and insisted on his morning dip in the tropical waters of Lake Austin which wouldn't be warm enough for swimming till noon. Tolly resisted shouting a warning about octopuses. Richards was doing well enough with his own fantasies.

Wheeling away from the balcony, Tolly caught sight of the breakfast dishes, green glass variety store plates and cups chosen for their ugliness. "Mungies," he whispered softly. He stacked them in a neat pile and carried them to the far corner of the porch. Raising the dishes above his head, he threw them down. They fell crashing and splintering on a heap of green glass below.

"Shards. Every civilization leaves its own trash heap. This is the midden of Tolly Cull," he announced to an audience of future archeologists. "Northern Americans, by the early 1980's had reached such heights of affluence they stood on these heights and banished drudgery by throwing away their eating utensils instead of washing them. We find, by examination of certain sticky remains, that they subsisted entirely upon hen eggs, fruit juices, whole-grain breads, and coffee."

"Tolly, stop it!"

"It's a beautiful day."

"You woke me up again! Can't you wait till nine o'clock to do your dishes?"

"Good morning, Sister. You are growing more beautiful every day in every way. If you'll say that to yourself six times while facing the mirror and take those pieces of watermelon out of your hair, you can come up. I want to talk to you." He leaned precariously out over the stone balustrade.

Dorothy, her hair bunched in pink foam curlers and both eyes smudged with last night's·mascara, stared up at him. "What about?"

"About how you're not supposed to go around telling family secrets to my tenants, particularly women."

"I haven't told anybody anything."

"Are you sure?"

"Why should I tell? It's your problem." A faintly malicious light glowed in her eyes, "Don't you have to teach today?"

"Of course I do. It's Friday, isn't it? I teach Monday, Wednesday, and Friday, don't I? I haven't forgotten that. Thank you anyway."

Dorothy's window slammed shut. Tolly swung safely back to the terrace. He was slim enough to wrap his legs over the balustrade and hang by his knees. It would be fun to scare Dorothy with his long arms and doubled fists dangling in front of the window by her bed, but the stone was old and crumbling in some places.

The whole apartment house looked as if it might crumble and slide down the cliff into the lake. It had been built by his grandfather, Captain Cull, a retired navy man. Unhappily married, he used his work as an excuse to get away from his wife on weekends. All his frustrations, including the towering dreams of his youth, had gone into it. Odd-shaped and vari-colored stones formed the walls; the pillars were made of concrete mixed with small stones; the chimneys were solid and drew well though they were crooked; carved stone balustrades collected from older houses outlined balconies and terraces. The total effect was that of an immense Mediterranean villa imagined by a man who had only seen one from a distance. It looked like a ruin on the day it was finished, and when vines covered most of the walls and trees pressed against it, the place became a monument to a dream.

He had begun with the two L-shaped apartments on the ledge. By the time these were finished, building had become an obsession. He topped the L-shape with two more apartments moving each one back a little as he progressed up the narrow curve of the ledge toward the upper level to the street. When the fourth apartment was roofed he looked down to discover he'd created a courtyard. Pleased with having made a space where there was none before, he constructed winding stone steps down to it, an arched gallery on the bottom level to frame one side, and garages on the far side to make it useful. The courtyard remained an empty space. There was nothing to do but fill it with a small house. Once this cottage was finished, he ran out of room. Only the face of the cliff overlooking the lake remained. He pushed his way down to the water by scaling the steepest parts with old iron fire escapes, and at the lake's edge he finished his last and simplest form, a square wooden dock. Without any land left to him, he turned to the water and began making boats. While down at the dock one day he'd taken his billfold out of his pocket, removed his trousers, folded them neatly, and placed the billfold on top. Jumping in the small sailboat he'd been working on, he headed for the middle of the lake.

The Lake Patrol found the capsized boat that night. Though they dragged the lake for his body, it was never found. Everyone who knew him was convinced he was suicidal as well as mad. During the morbid week long search for the body and a flurry of rumors that she'd driven her husband to death with her dragon tongue, Mrs. Cull died. Eventually Tolly inherited Captain Cull's monument.

Living in the apartment on top of the whole pile, he adopted his grandfather's obsession as his own justification for not marrying. "Look what it makes a man do!" he'd say, standing on the only patch of grass left on the ledge. Or he'd point to the extremely narrow hearth of his fireplace and declare, "There's only room for one."

Lately, however, he thought he might be changing his mind. There seemed to be plenty of room when Lou was around and a great empty space when she was gone. Yet how could he know if he was actually ready to marry, or if Lou was either, or if she'd have him if he asked? He hadn't had enough experience with women to know. All he could recognize was the willing and the unwilling. That one aspect took an amazing amount of time. How long had it taken him to understand that no said a thousand times usually meant yes?

Tolly walked through his living room with its one-man hearth to the hall mirror. Streaked with two lines of black paint, it added when he stood up correctly, a dashing moustache. He put his hand to his upper lip and tweaked the end of the surrogate moustache. "Dirty old man!" He leered.

"Unhand the fair Ermmagrude!" He stepped to one side.

"Nevah!" said the villain.

"Now!" said the hero, and with a twist of his arm, ran the villain through.

Tolly stepped over the body and entered his study where he stuffed some papers into a briefcase. In his bedroom he picked a tie off the rack without checking on color or pattern. He started whistling while knotting it, then stopped abruptly.

"You have been told and told," he scolded, "whistling while you work is a sign of vacuity of mind. It is an insidious habit and must be overcome. One does not, particularly if one is a professor of literature, want to be thought of as a human organ grinder." It would be good to be an organ grinder—more fun than being a professor—to stand in the sun under people's windows with a monkey holding a tin cup, and turn the handle on a box while the monkey did all the work. When had he last seen an organ grinder? Was it one day in the park in San Antonio, in New York somewhere? He waited, but the memory would not come clear. He sat on the edge of his bed and waited a while longer. All he could see was the monkey dressed in a little bellboy cap, a vest, and trousers . . . red, and yes, room for his tail to curl out the back.

Tantalized by this fragment, he creased his fingers in his palms as if he might clutch the whole. Somewhere he'd lost a lot of his past and been reborn an idiot—

kicked in the head by an elephant. No, not true, nor had he had shock treatment though that was sometimes a useful story to tell women. They were so understanding about his mental problems. Nor was he a war veteran with a silver plate in his skull and a memory a minute long. He was not even the victim of a head jarring automobile accident. None of these dramatic fates had fallen to him. What had fallen was a large rust-colored stone from one of the arches of the gallery. On an afternoon early in September he had been standing within the arch when the stone jiggled loose and hit his head, a blow that knocked him unconscious and made him wonder if the ghost of his grandfather was angrily reminding him about all the repairs needed on the place. Dorothy was in the nearest apartment when it happened. He rang her bell.

"Sorry to intrude, but something fell on my head."

"Oh, Tolly!"

Luckily he'd staggered to her door or he wouldn't have had a name. He hoped she wasn't his wife.

She led him inside and made him sit down. "What's wrong?"

"I got hit on the head by my grandfather."

"Grandfather's dead."

"I know that. It was his ghost. Was he your grandfather too?"

She stared at him, her gray eyes getting rounder and rounder, closer and closer. "Do you know who I am?"

"Never saw you before in my life," said Tolly beginning to enjoy himself. His head began whirling again. This time when he woke he found himself in a bed he knew was his own. He knew the doctor, knew Dorothy was his sister, and Captain Cull was the name of his grandfather. Doctor Rogers scared him. He never made housecalls unless a patient was dying.

"I'm not dying, am I?"

"No, you've just had a blow on the head." Dr. Rogers' head was quite bald on top which did not in any way make him appear vulnerable. His glossy baldness was that of polished pink granite; any falling object would be split in two by that head. He never touched it or even stroked it thoughtfully. His head shone on top of his shoulders, a sacred object to be worshipped.

"You mean *my* head," Tolly insisted. "You make it sound like it doesn't belong to anybody."

"All right, your head. Evidently you know who I am."

"You look familiar except you're in the wrong clothes."

"Oh? What should I be wearing?"

"Your white jacket. You look funny without it." My God, didn't he know what he was supposed to have on? After all those years in med school he ought to at least know what the costume was.

"I only wear it at the office."

"Why are you here if I'm not dying?"

"Your sister," he inclined his head like a great beacon toward Dorothy clinging to the post at the foot of the bed, "was convinced you were out of your mind."

"I was. I'm in it again, but certain things seem to be missing."

"It'll all come back," said Dr. Rogers and faded quietly out the door.

"How do you feel?"

"Head hurts. Bring me a mirror."

Dorothy brought him the small mirror hanging on the opposite wall. "Have you forgotten how you look?"

"Shut up!" He stared at himself. "Why do I have a moustache?"

"No one knows. You brought it back from Europe."

"It has got to go."

"I've been telling you that."

"Dorothy, I've forgotten everything you've been telling me and a lot more besides, but I'm telling you, don't ever sic Dr. Horrid on me again."

"He's always been our doctor."

"Before this . . . this accident . . . did I like him?"

"You've never liked him. You were terribly rude to him. Getting hit on the head hasn't improved your character at all."

In two days a lot came back. He knew who he was, knew the people around him, but the past for at least two years back was only a collection of vivid fragments. Dorothy could corroborate some of these, but for the most part, they were years she didn't know much about. He had been away from home since he was twenty-one, had received a Ph.D. from Columbia, taught at Dartmouth for several years, been to England on a Fulbright, and had returned at thirty to teach at the University of Texas. He had not—Dorothy emphasized this—been estranged from his family; he had simply been away. His parents and grandparents were all dead. (He remembered these awful facts easily.) Several aunts and uncles were living though not in Texas. Since he had no memory of seeing them in the last two or three years and couldn't conceive of writing to ask if they'd seen him, Tolly began to construct his own past.

At first he'd thought to forget a few years was to be relieved of a burden, yet the glimpses he had, the clear pictures of events he'd had a part in, demanded explanation. Instead of using fantasy as an escape from reality, he imagined things in order to make himself more real. The various histories he invented were inaccurate, but he easily forgave himself the distortions by concluding that everyone mythologized their pasts, and no one could remember himself exactly as he had been. Certain documents and papers helped him as far as his personal geography was concerned.

Dorothy didn't always know exactly where he'd been. "After the year in England you were on the continent some of the time, Tolly. I know you were there last year. You sent me the most hideous cuckoo clock from Germany." And she couldn't be trusted about the facts she was supposed to know.

"If I was in England on a fellowship I must have been doing research. Where are my notes?"

"I can't help it if you hide things from yourself."

"Sister, you could try to help me find them."

Sister wouldn't. She protested the untidiness of his desk, the junk collected in his apartment, and revealed fears of mythical beasts hiding in closets or under the bed. Further, since she worked at a museum and spent most of her time looking after other people's possessions, it was his business to look after his own. "I am not the cataloguer for the world in general and you in particular!"

Shortly after he met her, Lou revealed she'd seen him locking a large cardboard box in the trunk of his car. So the notes were happily recovered. Though he thought it an oddity, he had no trouble with intellectual memory. Once he looked at his notes, he relearned everything he'd known about obscure seventeenth century manuscripts. Nor had he forgotten knowledge acquired in his university years. Finding himself was not so easy. After rifling through several drawers, Tolly dredged up his passport, some old letters, and a few postcards. Lacking any other clues, he'd come to rely on these. The postcards were the most intriguing as they all contained cryptic messages and were signed with initials, "Everything in Pompeii a ruin except me. L.L.G."

One from Brig, Switzerland, had arrived after his accident. "A town, not a jail. We are on the way from Adermatt to Zermatt." was written in L.L.G.'s hand. Below it a feminine hand had written, "The weather is behaving perfectly, 12 ft. banks of snow but sunny and warm."

Dorothy had gotten to the mailbox before he did the day it came. She met him at the door, held the card out, and asked, "Who's L.L.G.?"

"Lee L. Grant, fellow I knew when I was teaching at Dartmouth. He's in Italy on a Guggenheim."

"He's in town, not a jail, in Switzerland now. What's the middle L. for?"

"How should I know?" He didn't know what the other two initials were for either.

Tolly got up off the bed and yanked out the top drawer of his bureau where he kept his passport. Yes, he had been in Italy. Perhaps that was where he saw the organ grinder and the monkey. According to the dates on the stamped pages he'd gone from Austria down to Italy. What if the damned monkey hadn't been in Italy but in the zoo in San Antonio? What difference did it make anyway?

He shoved the passport into the back of the drawer. The sight of it was frustrating. He had no memory of visiting England, France, Germany, Austria, or Italy, and there were all those official purple stamps assuring him he'd been to all those countries. He might as well have gone to Houston for a year. The Grand Tour was lost on him.

His clock made the whirring, strangling sound it always made before striking. Ten-thirty. He'd have to leave now if he was going to get to his eleven o'clock class on time. Tuesdays and Thursdays he taught in the afternoons. Usually he spent MWF mornings on office hours. Now he spent them on Lou and himself. Much better. Academic life could desiccate a single man.

Dorothy called to him, "You're going to be late."

Tolly looked down at her over the railing of the narrow walk suspended around one side of his apartment. She was standing in the courtyard beside the small stone cottage where Peeler lived.

"Shh! Don't wake him up."

"He's already awake. I hear him tuning." She remained, her arms planted on her hips, a rather short girl who never could seem to get her lipstick on straight. This morning she wasn't wearing any. Peeler liked his women without lipstick, and Dorothy liked Peeler. Some women did all right without. When Lou didn't have lipstick on she assumed a look of intentional naivete, but when Dorothy didn't wear lipstick she just looked like she'd forgotten something. Today she'd forgotten her coat as well. All she wore was a sleeveless electric blue sweater with a gray skirt and electric blue stockings. Peeler evidently also had a preference for electric blue.

"You're going to freeze," he shouted down to her.

"No I'm not. I'll be inside most of the time until it warms up. Anyway, I've got a jacket out at the museum."

"You're going to freeze on the way out there. 'First chill, then stupor, then the letting go.'"

"What?"

"Emily Dickinson." He left her standing in the court-yard and strolled on down the walkway to the door of his private garage, the last room in the series that made up his apartment. The floor plan was only another example of his grandfather's lack of planning, an eccentricity Tolly had always enjoyed. On Sunday afternoons when the old man wasn't building he used to come by for him. Together they'd climb into his battered pickup to drive around town scavenging for pieces of houses that were being demolished. If he found a door he liked, he built his next doorway around it. This was also true for win-dows of all sizes and any sort of carved woodwork that caught his eye. The garage was made when his grand-father stepped back to admire his work and discovered he was standing by the road winding down the hillside. Tolly was glad to have his garage to himself. All the others faced the courtyard, so he was able to watch everyone else's comings and goings. His own were secret. The superi-ority of the overview helped his constant anxiety. Since he'd lost a part of himself, all his actions were in some way suspect. Amnesia had made him a spy in his own skin, an investigator of dreams, an eager collector of the trash of consciousness, and an expert at masquerade.

Some of his clothes looked like costumes to him, and

few of the labels carried the name of the country of origin. One jacket seemed to be Irish tweed though it could have been English. A ridiculous black corduroy cap was definitely from London. The label read: HILLHOUSE & CO., Hat & Cap Makers, II New Bond Street, LONDON. Staring at this thorough designation only aggravated him more. He might have bought it on an impulse, or picked it up in a flea market somewhere, or a forgotten friend might have given it to him as a joke. No wonder so many missing persons were never found.

He'd collected other equally mystifying objects; an unsmoked meerschaum pipe shaped like a Turk's head, a map of the U.S. dated 1728 (provenance also unknown), Roman coins he must have fancied in Italy. Even these were frustrating, for the empire had been so large coins could be found anywhere. Certainty evaded him. Yes, he agreed with Dorothy only last week, everyone dealt with uncertainty every day. Yes, accidents were common. Who knew that better than he did?

"But when you've been a victim, you get edgy."

"You don't seem nervous."

"I'm good at dissembling. So are most people who have something to hide. I don't know exactly what I'm doing because I'm not sure what my actions are based on."

"Who is?" Dorothy argued.

Grateful for her opposition, he finally admitted his worst fear, "Maybe I've done something wrong."

"My brother, the criminal. Interesting, but excessive."

Peering over the rail again he saw his willing adversary getting into her VW parked next to Peeler's Jaguar, which he'd bought when he came back from his last performance in New York.

"Had to wait," he told Tolly. "Can you see a singer driving through the Appalachians in a Jag? The image, man. The image! Had to take the bus."

"Why don't you ride a horse here, Peeler? How can a man who sings country rock own a Jag in Texas?"

"Here it doesn't matter. The folk here get off their horses and into their Mercedes-Benzes as quick as they can sell their steers. Here I'm part of a tradition. There's two ways to go at it: git rich quick and buy you a fancy car, or git rich quick and drive your same old car to show you are so rich you could buy any kind, but you're too damn smart to spend yore money on gee-gaws and gim-cracks. I don't have not even one old red wagon. So, I got to git me a new, fancy-cat car. You unnerstand?"

"Have you ever thought of teaching, Peeler? A course in logic maybe?"

"What you doing? Trying to corrupt a good old country boy?"

Tolly shook his head. Someday he would have to bring one of the linguistics men, an expert in dialect geography, out to tape Peeler. Shuttling to and fro, up and down the country, he'd collected a weird mixture of vernaculars—Ozark mountain, western redneck, southern Negro, New Yorkese. A dialect geography man would have a wonderful time unscrambling Peeler's wanderings.

Tolly ran to the garage, got in his Volvo, and backed it out. The streets leading to the university were mostly downhill; he left the gear in second which acted as a convenient brake, and left him free to admire the scenery. For several blocks he coasted, then a horn honked furiously behind him. He stuck his arm out the window to wave the car on and caught sight of Richards's grin showing between a long flap of hair over his forehead and a long flap of beard below.

"Road hog!" Richards shook his fist out the window.

"Bloody foreigner!" Tolly shouted and slowed down until he was barely moving, a maneuver sure to annoy Richards, as he'd learned to drive only a few months before and still did not like passing. He drove a white Ford Mustang with red leather seats. "The West, you know," was all the explanation he offered when asked why he, the only foreigner among them, had an American car.

Tolly kept going downhill and up in second gear all the way to the parking lot. Richards pulled in next to him.

"Should have dented your fender for you. Next time I will."

"Richards, why are you wearing a white tie?"

"It's the Queen's birthday."

"No!"

"It's my birthday."

"I don't believe that either."

"It's someone's birthday. Why are you wearing a black tie?"

"Oh God! Is it black?" Tolly stopped in the middle of the walk.

Richards examined the tie. "A bit purplish around the edges. I'd say it is black. Even if you were color blind you'd know it's black."

"I'm not color blind. Ties are cards I shuffle through every morning. There's one black one, the Queen of Spades, and when she turns up—"

"Ominous thing to drape around your neck. What about that green paisley you had on yesterday?"

"Jack of Clubs, another bad one."

"And you wear the bad ones whenever they come up? What do you do, close your eyes and choose?"

"That's my rule."

"Do you read your horoscope in the paper every morning too?"

"No. This is just as accurate. I'm Cancer. Evidently someone decided readers couldn't stand seeing Cancer in big black type every morning, so they changed it. We are now called Moon Children. I refuse to read my horoscope now that I'm a Moon Child. I keep remembering my sign is really Cancer, and before I put the paper down I'm worrying about dying of cancer."

Richards bent his head. "I'm a Capricorn. Horoscope reading is a dreadful habit. We don't have them in the better papers in England. I don't believe in the stars, of course. Ridiculous actually, particularly your American horoscopes. They're all written for the struggling businessman. Today mine said, 'You can begin riding on the crest of the wave of success.' I had a vision of an enormous tidal wave sweeping across the country with me riding on top singing 'Rule Britannia.' Perhaps I ought to brush up on the words." He started briskly down the sidewalk singing, "Rule Britannia. Britannia rule the waves."

Tolly caught up with him. "You're making a scene," he hissed.

"Freedom of the Englishman on foreign soil. Some of us come unglued in hot climates."

"Rule Britannia," sang Tolly. They marched together over to Parlin Hall, both of them running upstairs to their mailboxes. Tolly discarded the usual pile of text-

book advertisements, a heap of purple-printed depart-
mental notices, and began opening a letter postmarked
Vienna on the way to his classroom. He didn't know
anyone in Vienna, but that wasn't unusual. Since the
rock had fallen on his head there were lots of people on
campus he didn't know who obviously knew him. He'd
come to dread the look of friendly expectancy on faces
he didn't recognize. The standard traveler's excuse, "I
haven't seen you in so long," satisfied most. Fortunately
his accident happened a week before the semester started.
By telling others they'd lost weight since he'd seen them,
or by claiming he was getting near-sighted or just had his
eyes dilated, he managed to get by. The only troublesome
people were women who called him "Tolly, dear." Something was implied, yet he could never gauge how much.
As he and Richards reached the hallway, he pulled the
letter out of its envelope.

> *Tolly, dear,*
>
> *It's raining and terribly dreary, so I think I'll come on
> home now instead of waiting till June. Will arrive in
> New York the 10th, fly to Dallas the 18th and on to
> Austin that afternoon. Don't try to meet me at the air-
> port. I'll take a cab to your place. Am terribly excited. I
> expect Mother will fuss, but we should be able to ar-
> range an October wedding without too much trouble.*
>
> *Love,*
> *Eleanor*

"Richards," Tolly clutched the sleeve of his friend's
coat. "Do me a favor, will you. Go to my class in 310 and
give them a walk."
"A what?"
"Tell them to go away for a day. I'll be well Monday."

"What's up?"

"I'll tell you later." He ran down the hall to the telephone.

"Dorothy?" His voice cracked.

"Has anyone else ever answered the phone out here?"

"You've got to tell me something. Who's Eleanor?"

"You don't know her last name?"

"I only learned her first name this morning. Come on. Who is she?"

"I don't know."

"Well, we're both going to have the pleasure Monday afternoon. I got a letter from her this morning. She's flying here from Vienna to marry me. And if you tell Lou, I promise I'll come out to the museum in the dark of night and unhang all your pictures, and I'll paint 'DOROTHY LOVES PEELER' on his door with red paint, and—"

"You don't remember asking her to marry you?"

He heard a strange noise like a swallowed laugh. "I don't even remember her! My God, Dorothy! How can I remember asking her to—"

"Perhaps that's why you have amnesia. You're trying to forget you asked her."

"I called you for aid, not analysis."

"I'm sorry. I'm truly sorry your bride-to-be is someone you don't know. Maybe you'll get to like her."

"You are a comfort."

"Tolly, I've told you. You're being ridiculously secretive about losing your memory."

"It's supposed to come back, and while I'm waiting I don't want to be treated like a crazy."

"Nobody's going to think you're crazy. You haven't changed in the least."

She'd told him that before, too, but she couldn't

imagine his fears. She had never stared at the dark while hoping sleep would bring a dream to fish something from the river of forgetfulness. "Ok. Suppose I do tell Eleanor I don't know who she is. Why should she believe me?"

"I could call Dr. Rogers for you . . . get a written excuse."

"Maybe she won't show."

"Tolly, that's absurd."

"I know."

"*Song*," Tolly announced as he entered his class. They were waiting for him, twenty-two growling stomachs, martyrs to a one o'clock lunch hour.

"'Go and catch a falling star,'" said Tom Crewe. The oldest senior in the class, he was a ski bum who left for the slopes in December right after finals. He usually got the first line.

"'Get with child a mandrake root.'" Cathy Donaldson smiled. She was obviously pregnant. Would she make it to the December finals?

"'Tell me where all past years are,'" chanted Ed Sommers who looked like he knew more than he did.

"'Or who cleft the devil's foot.'" Albert Rollins, naturally. He was interested in the demonic.

"'Teach me to hear mermaids singing.'" Ellie Stevens sighed. A music major, she lived in a world peopled only by other musicians. Just as Cathy Donaldson could be depended upon for lines about childbirth and reproduction, Ellie could be relied on for all things musical.

The recitation continued until Donne's *Song* was finished. Tolly began every class this way, assigning a new poem at the end of each lecture. "You will forget most everything else you learn in this course," he told them, "but you may remember a few lines of a poem you've memorized. They will be useful to you if you're ever cast away on a desert island, in jail, or in love."

His vehemence about memorization was well known. The day after he first made them recite something in chorus his students began calling him, "the Chinese professor." He did not care. They were learning the poems.

Richards waved at Tolly as he entered the faculty lounge. He could not simply come into a room; he made an entrance, walking briskly through a doorway like a foreign prince who'd left his retinue outside. Tolly wasn't sure how he managed this effect. Perhaps his beard gave him an appearance of mysterious significance, or perhaps it was because he walked as if propelled by matters of national importance that would have to be discussed immediately.

"I dismissed your class for you. Told them you had the pox and you'd be back Monday."

"Did they ask what the pox was?"

"I assumed they knew."

"Never assume anything with American sophomores."

Richards frowned and chewed his lower lip. His beard bobbed up and down. "What's up with you? The black tie brought bad luck already?"

Tolly took him by one arm. "Richards, have you had much experience with women?"

"Enough to make me wish I'd had more."

"You mean some?"

"I don't know the American standard of measurement."

"My God. I thought it was international!"

"If you mean 'it' to be sex, you can safely—"

"Have you ever been married?"

"Do I look as though I have been?"

"I can't tell by looking."

"I haven't, but I wish I had. It gives a man an air of expertise. Women usually believe a divorced man knows more. They trust him more readily, a lovely paradox, don't you think? Usually the fellow has already proved he's unreliable, got divorced for running around with other women or beating his wife. A man could be an absolute sadist, and women fall at his feet once he's divorced."

Tolly shook his head to clear away the buzz of confusion. "It's not divorce I'm worried about—it's marriage."

"To Lou?"

"Someone else."

"Been a bit busy lately, haven't you?"

"Come on. Let's go eat, and I'll tell you about it."

With Richards leading they walked over to a cafeteria in the Union. Once in line he had his usual difficulty making a decision. Five people behind Tolly coughed and clanked their trays while Richards wavered between potatoes and macaroni with cheese. Finally he took both.

"How about a little rice on the side?" Tolly asked.

"Too much freedom of choice," Richards sighed, "leads to self-indulgence." He picked up two rolls and moved serenely on.

When they reached a table, unloaded their trays, and sat down, he turned to Tolly, "Now, tell me about your . . . hmm, your marriage."

"First you've got to understand something else. I got hit on the head with a rock and—"

"Love," said Richards wisely, "always seems like that."

Late that afternoon they were still discussing the problem while sitting on the dock below the apartments.

"We've got to have a plan," said Richards. He was dangling his legs in the water.

Tolly frowned. "What do you mean *we?*"

"Exactly what do you mean to do when your intended turns up at five Monday afternoon at your apartment and Lou happens to drop by then as she usually does?"

"You know when she comes and goes?"

"Not only when, but usually where. Who wouldn't watch her if he could? It's not my fault if the darling girl lives next door to me. Have you a plan, Tolly?"

"I thought I'd disguise myself as an old man and tell them both I'm out. Or I could fake a suicide, leave my wallet and a pair of pants on the dock, swim across the lake, and disappear for awhile. That's what my grandfather did except he vanished forever. It's a deep lake, you know."

"You're quite sure he's—"

"Everyone was sure of it then. He had reasons. Grandmother drove him wild, and he was running out of something to do when he finished building this place. It gave him a thousand excuses for staying away. On rainy days he'd say he wanted to test the roof for leaks, or if the roof wasn't up yet he'd sleep here to protect the property from robbers. When I was a child I was more scared of robbers than ghosts. He had me convinced that someone was always after his two by fours!"

"Wouldn't it have been simpler to get a divorce?"

"My father always thought Grandfather didn't try divorce because he was too used to Grandmother. It was, to him, a sort of familiarity breeds calluses marriage. I think divorce was too simple a solution. Grandfather loved intrigue. He really liked inventing excuses for spending the night away from home."

But how can you be sure he died?"

"My parents were so sure they erected a tombstone for him next to my grandmother's. There's something awfully convincing about a tombstone, especially when a memorial service has been said over it."

"Well, I don't think the wallet and trousers on the dock bit will work for you. I know something that will though."

"Such as?" Tolly stared at Richards. In a bathing suit with his legs concealed in the water, his hair sticking up in tufts from his head, and his beard dripping to a point from his chin, he did look like the goat god. "Nevermind. I know what you're planning. Since your bed is empty, you think Lou can be lured into it, and I'll be left alone with Eleanor What's-her-name."

A crackling noise on the bank silenced him. He turned to see Lou climbing down the iron fire escape.

"Don't forget the sixth step is broken."

"I won't, Tolly. I know every broken step all the way down here. You ought to do something about them. Someone's going to break a leg and sue you. The third step on the first ladder has an awful crack. I put a rock under it, but I don't think it'll hold. You need a welder." She jumped from the last step to the dock. "Hello, Richards."

"Hello, love."

Tolly shoved him into the water. He came up snorting. "It's only a manner of speech."

"He says it every morning. Isn't he sweet," said Lou settling herself in the sun next to Tolly.

"He's a large, bearded old goat," said Tolly. He took a can Lou handed him. "What's this for?"

"Suntan lotion. You spray it on."

"At last they've invented a way to banish the sense of touch. What's it called, 'Hands Off'? Don't you enjoy having someone rub suntan oil on your back?"

Richards crawled back on the dock. "Turn it on, Tolly."

"Here, turn it on yourself since you're dying to play with a new toy. Innocent European! You lost the industrial revolution, you lost the empire, now you'll lose your soul following after false gods—the 400 horsepower engine and the spray can."

"There's a place for you near Marble Arch any Sunday," said Richards aiming the spray at him. Tolly dived into the lake.

"Are you going in, Lou?"

"It's too cold."

"How can you say it's cold?" Richards shook drops of water from his beard. "It's like Tahiti. All you need is a frangipani blossom behind one ear, Peeler for tropical background music, and I'd think we were there."

"I don't think he knows any South Seas songs," said Tolly climbing up beside them. He began drying himself with Lou's towel.

"You could ask him," she murmured then stretched out on the wooden planks in what was left of the sun. "He came in a little while ago with Dorothy."

"He couldn't have been with her. He's never with anybody. He's a lonesome traveler. He's 'the cat who walks by himself'—"

"'In the wild wood by his wild lone,'" Richards finished.

"He was with Dorothy," Lou insisted. "They both drove in. Peeler got out of his car and opened Dorothy's car door for her, and she went into his place. He had his arm around her."

"Where's Peeler from?" Richards asked.

"From the grass roots, the high plains, the other side of the mountain, the back alley, Birmingham jail."

"Fort Worth," said Lou.

Tolly looked down at her. "Louise," he said pleasantly, "you have a literal mind."

"I know, but it's so useful."

He leaned over and kissed her shoulder. It tasted of suntan spray. "I'm going up to Richards's apartment. He's giving me a drink. Why don't you come up in a little while." Taking Richards's arm, he led him away from the dock.

"I didn't ask you—"

"I didn't ask you to stay down here whispering sweet Tahitian to Lou. It's time for a drink anyway, and you were going to tell me a way out of this."

"Thought you weren't interested." Richards stopped to investigate a spring trickling through the ferns on the cliff.

"I am."

"It's quite simple, actually. Marry Lou."

Tolly stood in the middle of the last fire escape as if he

were glued to it. Almost Nude Bachelor Ascending . . .
an awkward conglomeration of iron, trees, rocks, and
flesh. Artist unknown, obviously belongs to Impaired
Memory School. He shook his head. "I don't want to
marry."

"Why not? Go on, won't you!" Richards huffed.
"You're certainly old enough. She's a lovely girl. And
you already know her, which is more than you can say for
Eleanor Whosis."

"Maybe I've known Eleanor."

"Don't you think you'd remember that?"

"I remember only certain scenes. The worst part is I'm
not sure I haven't made those up. This morning for some
reason I kept thinking about an organ grinder and his
monkey, something I'd seen somewhere. He's familiar
though I can't see him really. I can't see the organ grinder's
face quite."

"All those fellows look alike. They have sad wrinkled
faces, bushy mustaches, and gleaming teeth. What about
the song he was playing? Perhaps that's it . . . a tune
you're trying to remember."

"Oh, that's too easy! To hear a tune and have it all
come back. The next thing you'll be talking about is
Blinding Flashes!"

"Perhaps you should arrange to get hit on the head
again. Isn't that the way it's usually done? You sit down
on the porch here, and I'll run in and get something to
bash you over the head with." Richards started into his
apartment.

"I don't want to be hit on the head again!" Tolly
shouted. He wished he'd never mentioned his amnesia

to Richards. For a supposedly detached observer, he had become much too helpful. "You haven't got anything heavy enough to knock me out anyway."

"No problem." Richards reappeared with a copy of *The Oxford Universal Dictionary*. "Wouldn't this do?"

"No!" Tolly jumped up and put both his hands over his head. "I won't let you. It's attempted assault."

Richards let the book thud on the porch. "I'm only trying to cure you."

"Get us a drink then. I don't like any of your other solutions. They all involve immediate physical danger or getting married, which is worse. I hate all this scheming."

Lou, her towel draped around her shoulders, waved and walked up to the porch. At the same time Peeler and Dorothy appeared holding hands and looking pleased with themselves.

"Hurrah!" cried Tolly. "It's International Tap Dance Week! Let us all join hands and tap dance!"

Lou gave him one hand and took Peeler by the other. He pulled Dorothy onto the porch with his free hand. They shuffled around, Tolly humming loudly and Peeler making up a song, "Tap dance. You got to do the tap dance, the in-ter-na-tion-al tap dance. Every-bud-dy tap dance."

Peeler, maybe because he traveled so much, could be depended on to take up anyone's fantasy, and if they needed music he would provide. Tall and bony, he flapped his elbows by his sides and snapped his fingers like a large bird trying out his own style in a new flock. Lou's towel fluttered from the straps of her bikini. Dorothy moved slowly while looking all the time at Peeler.

Richards hurried out carrying glasses of gin and tonic. "See the natives dancing."

"Explorer!" said Peeler dropping hands. "Explorer bearing large glasses of corruption." He helped pass drinks around.

"Americans dance in little circles to ward off evil," Tolly muttered over the rim of his glass.

All day Saturday Tolly worried. He looked after the necessities—did his laundry, went to the grocery store and the liquor store, graded a set of papers—but just behind every bit of ordinariness, Eleanor waited. If she was so determined to marry, why hadn't she written earlier? Of course he could have written to her in September before the rock fell, and she could have been away. Where was that letter? Friday's jacket pocket. Coming to New York the 10th. Nothing about traveling before that. "Raining and terribly dreary." Bad weather was no excuse to give up on a whole country. On the other hand, why not? Did she even live in Vienna? He riffled through his address book once more and found only an old American Express box number under his own name.

Though he tried, he couldn't envision her, couldn't envision Vienna, certainly couldn't combine the two. This failure bothered him more than any since his accident. If he'd absolutely forgotten her, how many other people had he cancelled out? Maybe he'd had a whole unknown life in Europe. In two years? Well some people lived a lot in one.

Saturday night Lou said, "I have something to tell you."

"Don't begin like that. It's too ominous."

"I'm going to France in January. I've gotten a scholarship to the Sorbonne."

"That's very good," said Tolly. "It's wonderful, only Paris is awfully cold in the winter." He started to tell her about the terrible winter he spent in France but was too depressed to make up a good story.

Later in the night he dreamed he was standing in one of the huge glass boxes suspended from the ferris wheel in the Prater, Vienna's amusement park. At first he was only acutely aware of getting more than the usual one-time-around ride on "the world's largest ferris wheel," a guidebook phrase circling in his head as the wheel circled without stopping. He didn't particularly mind the sensation until he saw the organ grinder with his monkey below and heard the familiar music . . . Mack the Knife's theme from the *Threepenny Opera*. He couldn't see the organ grinder's face although he caught brief glimpses of it everytime the wheel descended. Though he opened his mouth to shout, "Stop! Let me off!" he couldn't speak, and the machine continued going round and round. Searching for the operator he discovered there was none, and he was completely alone on the wheel; the other boxes which usually held ten or more people swayed emptily in space. Mack the Knife's insoucient tune was quickly charged with all the sinister implications of *The Third Man Theme*. The ferris wheel stopped soundlessly. He opened the door at the end of his box, walked over toward the organ grinder, and woke up. When he was fully awake he was convinced the man's face was his grandfather's and the monkey's face was Richards's.

This vision so annoyed him he got out of bed and started dressing.

"What's going on?" Lou mumbled.

"I'm putting my clothes on, can't you see?"

"No. My eyes are still closed."

"Well, open them."

"I don't want to. I have a feeling it's still dark." She sat up and frowned at the gleaming phosphorescent dials of her clock. Tolly didn't like the idea of a clock watching him all night and made her keep it on her side of the bed. "It's four A.M. Tomorrow's Sunday."

"Today's Sunday."

"All right, but why are you getting dressed?"

"I'm going fishing."

"With a tie on?"

"It's Sunday, isn't it?"

"Fish don't know what day it is."

"How do you know what fish know?" Tolly sat down on the edge of the bed next to her. "What color is this tie?"

"I can't see." She switched the bedside light on. "It's red. Did you have to wake me up to ask me what color tie you're wearing?" She let her head fall back on her pillow.

"Hearts," said Tolly.

"Diamonds are red also." Lou sighed.

"No, this one's hearts. I've got a brown tie with diamonds printed on it."

"Turn off the light, please."

He flicked the light off and started toward the door humming. Immediately he clapped one hand over his mouth, but Mack the Knife's song played on in his head. Slamming the door in an attempt to jar the sound loose, he went to the garage and fumbled among the cane fishing poles stacked in a corner until he got one free. Covered with dust and cobwebs, they had been standing in the same corner since his grandfather last used them. A line was wound around his pole, but there was no hook on it. All right. He didn't want to catch anything, he only wanted to be doing something, anything but sleeping. He could have gotten in his car and driven around till sun-up, but he rejected the idea as soon as he thought of it. Driving seemed dangerous in his state of mind. Brooding on the portentous atmosphere of the world at four A.M., he started down to the dock.

He was gazing up to see if any stars were still shining when the third step on the first ladder gave way beneath him. He was still dreaming, he was certain, dreaming he was falling out of the damned ferris wheel. Any moment he would wake up in bed with Lou beside him. In the instant of falling he willed himself to wake up. Instead his head knocked against the iron steps and he fell to sleep again, the deep sleep of the unconscious. The fishing pole slithered away through the underbrush below until it was stopped by a boulder.

He was lying on something hard as marble. Was he at an undertaker's? But the dead weren't supposed to know anything. He hurt all over. Ached. His head was split open . . . but he was thinking wasn't he? Yes. A light. Dark night again. Where are the stars at four A.M.? He was being tilted, the glass box on the ferris wheel was tilting. He would be flung into space. He'd shout. He wouldn't go into space silently. A harsh stuttering noise . . . the ferris wheel was stopping. It rocked violently.

He had to shout. He couldn't fall out again. "Help!" he called, "Help me!"

The X-ray technician, a man who had heard many strange unconscious ravings in the dark, made no reply.

Late Sunday afternoon Tolly regained complete consciousness. He had a number of things on his mind, and there were a number of people in his room. Dorothy and Peeler stood on one side of the bed, Lou on the other, and Richards watched him from one end. They all looked as though they were waiting for instructions.

He touched the bandage on his head carefully. "Hello, I'm in the hospital I guess."

Everyone started, nodded, but remained silent. It was a test. What was he supposed to do, name everyone? Yes, that was what they were waiting on, recognition, probably Dr. Horrid's idea. What if he refused to? He could give them all new names, then he would have to create characters for them, and pasts, and families— mothers, fathers, sisters, brothers, aunts, uncles, grandparents for five people—too much. Recreating his own past had been too much, and what a poor job he'd made of it, a few exaggerations, some thin lies. What a lot he'd left out! No, he wasn't up to it. They were perfectly all right as they were.

"Isn't anyone going to say anything to me, poor Tolly Cull who fell down the hill on October 17 in this year of our Lord? Dorothy, Peeler, Richards, Lou," he named them clockwise around the bed, "which one of you found me?"

In the babble of voices the one he heard clearest was Lou's.

"You didn't know me. I was holding your head in my lap, and you didn't know me."

He was once more in the beer garden in the Prater, and the old man was telling him, "You didn't know me." He was a kindly looking old man with a white moustache, such a shame not to know him.

Tolly moved his head from side to side on the pillow trying to negate the double accusation.

"I do now, Lou."

"You haven't any concussion," said Richards.

"When can I leave?"

"Tomorrow," Dorothy promised. "They want to keep you under observation for awhile."

"They might keep you longer," said Richards hopefully.

"No! I've got to be out by tomorrow." Should he tell them? No. Better to wait and have it verified, better to be sure. He wouldn't tell anyone he'd recovered most of what he'd forgotten when the rock fell on his head. His memories were improbable to anyone else, and now that he had them again he would hug them to himself until he was certain . . . until Eleanor showed up.

Dr. Rogers crept in. "How's the patient?"

"Fine," said Dorothy.

He walked over and beamed down at Tolly. "Head hurt?"

"My head doesn't hurt as much as it did."

"It shouldn't. We've given you a little something for the pain. You have to stay here overnight. I want to make sure you're all in one piece. You must rest and keep quiet. Don't try to read anything. It'll only make the headache worse, and no TV."

"I will lie quietly and stare at the ceiling," Tolly promised, "if you'll let me out in time to teach my class tomorrow."

"We'll see," said the doctor edging quickly out the door.

Everyone except Lou drifted away.

"Has everything come back?"

"Dorothy told you, didn't she?"

"About the amnesia? Not exactly. She just confirmed what I'd begun to notice. You told me so many different stories. One summer you were a forest ranger somewhere in the Appalachians, and you spent a year on Martha's Vineyard fishing and cycling mostly. Then there was an expedition to Machu Picchu—"

"The Mississippi river boat. Don't forget that one."

She smiled. "I knew you'd been in Europe, but you never talked about it except in your sleep."

"What did I say?" He tried to raise himself up on his elbows, but it made him so dizzy he settled back down.

"Nothing you said made much sense. You worried a lot about losing your passport."

"Yeah. I would. Lou . . . the stories. I was trying to provide myself with an interesting past. People who spend a lot of time in libraries are prone to daydreams. Do you mind?"

"No. But I went to Machu Picchu the summer before I began grad school, and I knew you had to take a train. Nobody rides a horse all the way up there. That's when I began to know."

"How'd I do on the scenery?"

"Marvelous." She leaned over and kissed him. "You're great on scenery."

o o o o

A rude bright light shone in his face. Someone was pulling on his arm. He shifted his head slightly and focused on a nurse.

"There's a beautiful girl waiting to see you."

"What kind of hospital is this? I don't want a girl! I need something to eat."

"She says she's your aunt, but I doubt it."

"Could you roll me up a little?"

As the bed lifted he saw Eleanor Benson standing at the window with her back to him. He knew, before she turned around, exactly what she would look like. She'd have a long face with high arched brows, dark brown eyes heavily made up, a long elegant nose which she wasn't self-conscious about unless she had a cold. He was acutely aware of these details as well as thankful for the memory of them. Except for the eyebrows, which she said she inherited from her father, she favored her mother. They were both tall, fashionably dressed, Europeanized Americans. After living abroad for many years they had acquired a knowledge of capitals, and languages, and the distinction of always appearing slightly foreign wherever they were. Once he had told the two women they looked like a renaissance queen and reigning princess touring their provinces. Eleanor's mother, a rich widow who had met and dismissed many royal fakes, did have a queenly air of independence. She had said but one word in reply, "Nonsense!"

"Do I have a good view?" said Tolly.

Eleanor turned around. "Yes, at night anyway. How is your poor head?"

"All right, I hope. How did you know I was here?"

"I called your sister."

"Your visitor mustn't stay long," squeaked the nurse. "You are supposed to rest and be quiet."

"My visitor is my aunt who has just flown all the way from Vienna, Austria, Europe. Speak some German for her, Aunt Eleanor."

"Guten abend."

"I still don't believe she's your aunt. She's too young."

"I don't suppose there's anything in your beloved hospital's rules that requires me to give my genealogy, or is there a chart somewhere someone neglected to fill in?"

"Ah . . . there's a chart for temperature and blood pressure, but we fill that in. I don't know about the genes. Not even the doctors know all about the genes. Now, don't stay too long, Auntie." The nurse sidled reluctantly out the door.

Tolly straightened himself against the pillows, and Eleanor sat down beside the bed.

"I didn't tell your sister who I was. I just asked for you."

"That's good. I guess we'd better tell her . . . eventually."

"You'll have to decide about that." Eleanor's eyebrows arched in silent exclamation.

"Aren't you a day early? I thought you were coming tomorrow."

"I was, but I got a job in New York almost as soon as I arrived. I need to get back to it. I'm going to be the first reader of all letters to the editor of the *Times*. Isn't that divine!"

Tolly nodded. "Did they get married?"

"Who? Oh! That's what I came all the way down here to tell you about. They married right before I left. Mother

had planned the wedding for June. You know what a tra-
ditionalist she is. I told you she would dither, but she
managed. I simply couldn't take Vienna any longer—all
the cold rain, the intrigue, spies spying on each other—
and I wanted to see them married before I left. Your
grandfather was wonderful, Tolly. He said the wedding
vows in Italian accented German! They both loved Italy.
I think they'll probably go and live in Florence. That was
the last plan."

"What kind of passport does my grandfather have
now?"

"English, I think, but it doesn't really matter now that
he and mother are married. She's kept her American
citizenship. They could come back anytime."

"Not here. You're forgetting, Eleanor. He can't come
back to Texas. He's supposed to be dead and buried."

"He could come incognito."

"Oh God! Grandfather and his disguises! Do you remember the day he turned up dressed as an organ grinder
leading the monkey on a chain? And the monkey had on
a little cap, and vest, and trousers. The next day, the
very next day, he undressed the monkey so he could go
free, but the monkey wouldn't go. He sat there shivering
between us. Grandfather tried to get me to climb a tree
to show the monkey how. He was sure the wretched
monkey had forgotten. Do you remember?"

"Of course. He had a marvelous vision of the poor
monkey swinging by its tail through the treetops, and
the monkey wouldn't swing. Mother was furious with
him. She told him he'd be better off impersonating somebody like a deposed grand duke or an English lord."

"Yes, and he refused. He said she'd better be glad he

wasn't that type, that they were only bad copies of better times. Funny how I remember so much of what he said." He moved his hands across the covers as if he was trying to find something to hold onto.

"Startling clarity. Is that it?" Eleanor shifted in her chair a bit.

He thought he'd nod and decided against it. "Almost too much so." It was like an old movie unwinding in his memory; when two or three scenes had played, he knew he'd seen it all before, still he had to run everything through before he could be certain of the end. Somewhat interesting, not totally, however. A little frightening. Surely this rush would soon subside, become more selective. To forget two years of his life had been scary; to remember too much would be much worse. Total recall, when he stopped to consider it, was a form of madness.

"Tolly?"

"Yes?" He was grateful Eleanor was still there.

"Why do you think your grandfather likes disguises so?"

"I'm not sure. Perhaps . . . well, perhaps they give him a holiday from one reality and a chance to discover another. Perhaps they're a holiday from himself. Or it could be childish delight in dressing up, assuming a role. I don't know really. It's one of those personal kinks that's impossible for me to understand."

He looked over her shoulder to a bad painting on the wall. Two or three faceless people sitting on a sunny terrace . . . Mexico or Italy. A little brass strip was attached to the bottom of the frame. Probably donated by the artist, probably tax deducted. A motel room picture, one with no real identity, no real personal style. He begged Eleanor to take it away.

She lifted it off its nail and put it in the closet.

By this time she must be tired. Flying here from New York right after getting back from Europe, finding him in the hospital. He should let her go.

"Eleanor, I've been having a strange long holiday myself. Then I had this accident, stumbled down the hill out at the apartment and hit my head. Now that you've arrived it's over."

"What have I done?"

"Like a real deus ex machina . . . no, that should be dea ex machina, you've descended from the sky to unravel the threads."

Eleanor pushed a strand of hair away from her forehead. "Tolly, I don't think a dea ex machina would have to change planes at the Dallas-Fort Worth airport. Go on though. Tell me about your holiday.

"I've had this peculiar amnesia. I forgot most of the past two years, the Fulbright I took in England, all that time in the British Museum, tons of research, and the year I spent wandering around Europe. I completely forgot Grandfather . . . L.L.G., Long Lost Grandfather. He signed a card to me with those initials, and I didn't know who L.L.G. was."

"How could you forget him? He was so proud that he'd recognized you, his grown-up grandson, in that beer garden. It only took a few minutes for you to know him. You seemed really happy to find him alive."

"This rock fell on my head, for one thing. That happened in September not long after I got back. And then I suppose there was the shock of seeing him again, a delayed reaction maybe. When you think someone's dead and you run into them alive— I hadn't even told Dorothy he was still alive. I thought he had a wonderful secret. He'd made his getaway. I was afraid of spoiling it." Was that true? Or had it been merely more convenient to let sleeping grandfathers lie? To give himself credit, it must have been a little of both. He loved the old man, had mourned his death, yet his reappearance was troublesome. It was too great a secret to keep forever. Dorothy had a right to know. Of course his grandfather had taken the chance, had trusted him. He would have to trust Dorothy too. There wasn't anyone else left in the family who really cared.

The door swung open, and the nurse appeared behind a tray of food. She glared at Eleanor and went out again saying, "I'll be back to pick up your tray."

"You want me to feed you?" Eleanor asked.

Tolly stared at the tray which seemed to contain varicolored spots of mush. "I think I can manage. There's nothing here that requires energy or dexterity." He spooned pureed carrots down before turning his attention to mashed potatoes. "Don't mind me. I'll just sit here and dribble. The trouble is I'm hungry."

Eleanor got up and buttered a piece of bread for him. "That's terrible stuff."

"I know. Flabby. American bread has gotten so much better in the last few years. You don't have to eat flabby white junk unless you're in the hospital."

"I'd better go check into a hotel."

"Don't be ridiculous. You can stay at my place, my magnificent wreck Grandfather built out by the lake. I'll call Dorothy and tell her you're coming."

"All right, but what should I tell her?"

"Nothing. You'll only confuse her. Well, maybe you wouldn't. Actually I want to do the telling. I'll be out of here tomorrow and I do need to talk to her. I'll make all the necessary explanations then." He reminded her of his address and, using the phone by his bed, called a taxi.

When she was gone Tolly lay quite still for a little while. Were the old movies still running? No, not so far. Maybe they didn't show anytime he wanted but flickered on and off provoked by people, or incidents, or some peculiar connection in his brain. Maybe they would vanish altogether. Then he'd have a subconscious like everyone else. That might be pedestrian; still, a little dullness was more comfortable than too much action. Was that what shell-shock was like, a rush of memory that wouldn't quit? He wondered about it for a moment and felt vaguely ashamed since he'd done nothing to merit such a diagnosis. Being hit on the head by a rock didn't qualify him as a war-wounded veteran. His was only one of life's smaller accidents. Wasn't it odd, the ideas that could seep through a person's mind while lying about in a hospital?

He reached for the phone and called Dorothy to tell her a relative of sorts was arriving. He would tell her who Eleanor was later.

"Isn't that the woman who was coming to marry you?"

"No. I was mistaken. She was referring to another wedding. I'll explain everything to you tomorrow."

"I don't think you could marry a relative anyway."

"I could, in this case, but I'm not going to."

"You're beginning to sound like your old snappish self."

"Good and good night, Sister."

The nurse pushed the door open and crossed the room to take the tray. "How are we?"

"*I* am better. I think the pap helped."

"The what?"

"Gruel, babyfood, mush, the mess of potage you brought me to eat. Strengthening stuff."

The nurse leaned toward him, her hair and glasses both gleaming silver, the lines on her forehead showing faintly. "Your doctor ordered your supper."

"Thoughtful of him. I must do something for him soon."

She picked up the tray and wheeled away following what appeared to be an absolutely straight line out the door.

Tolly sighed, picked up the phone again, and called Richards. "I'm sending you a lovely girl. Go upstairs to my place right away and make her a drink. And, Richards, take it easy. She's recently arrived here via transatlantic flight to New York and various planes from New York to Austin. She's quite sensible and she's also tired. Please give her a cozy welcome."

"What's her name?"

"Eleanor Whosis."

"But isn't that the—?"

He hung up quickly before Richards could finish his question.

His last call was to Lou. He told her that Paris was dreadfully cold in the winter.

She laughed. "You're supposed to be resting, not making up weather reports."

"I'm not making them up. I was there last winter before I went to Austria. Everything turns silver gray and the wind whooshes down the river. Whenever I went out

I bought roasted chestnuts just so I could warm my hands with them."

"All right. Now I know what to do when my hands get cold. Tolly, I've got to take that scholarship. I want to."

"Suppose I come over next summer?"

"Suppose you do."

"You want me to wait that long? All the way through January, February, March, April—" The names of the months to come sounded grand.

"Till June, yes."

"For you, love, I'll do it. I'll see you tomorrow when Dr. Horrid lets me loose."

Tolly leaned back on his pillow and switched off the light. With his face turned to the window, he looked out to a few lights still showing from windows at the university. If she would have him, he would marry Lou in Paris. For so long he'd been concentrating on his uncertain past; he'd neglected future uncertainties. How pleasant to dream of what was to come.

"Fellow historians," he said to the lighted windows, "let it be recorded that in the 1980's in the U.S.A. man finally learned how to best use the machine. He made his mating calls by telephone and was jet delivered to his marriage feast."

"Did you call?" The nurse tiptoed across the room.

"Yes. I wanted you to know I'm planning to get married and live—"

"Happily ever after?"

"Surely you've got more imagination than that!" Tolly turned over on his right side and went to sleep.

This book has been set in
Goudy Old Style
by
G&S TYPESETTERS
·
The dustjacket painting is by
GLENN WHITEHEAD
·
Printed by HART GRAPHICS
Bound by ELLIS BINDERY
Designed by
WHITEHEAD & WHITEHEAD